For all the fierce and furious girls,
especially Georgia Elizabeth

Like A Girl

My story starts with me running.

Heart racing.

Legs pumping.

Head empty.

Feet pounding on to the track.

Sweat trickling down my back.

Out here, the rules do not apply. I am wind, soaring above the ground as I push harder and harder. I am fire, wild and out of control as I race faster and faster.

I am girl.

My story starts with me running and I'm pretty sure that it ends that way too.

Wake Up Like A Girl

The gift is waiting on the end of my bed next to Midnight. Melissa must have put it there when she came in to plant a kiss on my head before she left for work early this morning. I lift my leg from under the covers to let my toes explore the shape and only when I have confirmed that it has the correct number of edges and corners do I open my eyes.

The flimsy curtains she's always promising to replace are failing to stop the sun from leaking into my room and I blink in the light, still sleep-fogged. But even half-asleep, I can feel the flutter of excitement in my stomach at the hope that she might have got it right; that this present might be the one thing I genuinely want.

Sitting up, I pull it towards me. The package is reassuringly heavy, but it's not a done deal yet. Last year

I asked for a sports watch and instead she gave me a set of biology books and a scientific calculator, both of which are still unopened. This wrapped box might look promising but there is always the possibility that it contains a blood pressure cuff and a poster of the inner workings of the human body.

"What do you think, Midnight?" I ask my cat. "Has Melissa actually paid attention to what I want for a change?"

Midnight gives me a disapproving look and shifts into a more comfortable position. She doesn't like it when I bad-mouth my mother — which is ironic, because I'm fairly sure that if she could speak then it would be in fluent snark.

It's not because my mother doesn't care, I know that. It's just that she still thinks that she knows what will make me happy better than I do. Her ultimate goal is to get me into medical school, and don't I know it.

Going along with it is what I do to make *her* happy.

I put the gift down on my legs and stare at it, savouring this moment before the inevitable disappointment. I'm warm here in my bed, with Midnight curled up by my feet and the sun filtering through the net, illuminating my beloved row of cacti on the window sill. I've still got forty minutes before I need to get up and face school. I push away the usual wave of dread at the thought. This time, right now, might be the best part of my day and I'm in no rush to spoil it.

And yet – maybe, just maybe, my fourteenth birthday *could* get better than sitting here alone with an unopened present?

Quickly, before I can talk myself out of it, I rip off the paper and reveal the promising-looking box underneath. The logo is right. When I give it a shake, it has a hefty thud that makes me want to believe. And when I open the lid, it takes me a couple of blinks to see that she's done it. I do a quick check to make sure she's remembered my size, laughter bubbling up in my throat. Someone once sang that diamonds are a girl's best friend but that someone had clearly never seen the beautiful pair of trainers that now belong to me and that I have been coveting for months.

I reach down and pull them out of the box. There's a small envelope tucked into the left shoe. Melissa doesn't normally bother with a card, but when I open it, that's exactly what I find. The words *Trust That You Are Amazing, Strong & Brave* are scrawled across the front in a colourful rainbow font and inside is my mother's carefully printed, neat handwriting.

To Eden,
Happy Birthday!
Love, Mum xxx
P.S. I have the receipt if they don't fit.
P.P.S. I'll see you tonight to
celebrate with pizza.

I smile, despite myself. A day of school at Woodford High, then homework, then oven pizzas when Melissa finally gets back from her shift at the hospital are not what anyone would consider the perfect ingredients for a fun-filled birthday, but the trainers have lifted my mood.

Right now, that's all that matters.

A quick glance at my phone tells me I still have a spare thirty-five minutes before I need to get ready.

I also spot a notification that there's a new post on *Woodford Whispers*, but I have better things to do than waste my precious time looking at that. No doubt it will be another post celebrating Mikki, reigning star of the school track team, posing with yet another medal or trophy under her profile name of @silverbullet. She reinvented herself with this moniker at the start of Year Nine when she arrived back at school with newly dyed, and very striking, silver hair. It's meant to emphasize that she is incredibly small yet incredibly fast. Mikki is all about the quick solutions, no matter what dirty shortcuts she has to take.

It takes seconds to change into my usual outfit of a tracksuit and T-shirt. I pull on a clean pair of socks and then ease first one foot and then the other into each trainer, wiggling my toes to check for comfort. The universe appears to be working in my favour today, which is a pleasant change, and the shoes fit like a dream. Standing up, I give Midnight a quick stroke and then send a *Thank you!!* text to my mother before heading for the door. At the last minute I go back for the card and shove it in my pocket, along with my phone.

For the record, I am not amazing, strong or brave. All I want is to be unseen, unremarkable and left alone.

And at Woodford High, that means keeping one step ahead of the spotlight of attention that is constantly sweeping, searching for new victims to thrust on to centre stage and humiliate in front of the entire audience.

Fortunately, keeping one step ahead is what I'm good at. Mostly, anyway.

Invisible Like A Girl

The silence slaps me in the face the instant I walk through the doors of the canteen.

Only seconds ago I could hear the usual hubbub of chatter and the clinking of knives on plates, but now the entire room is still and staring in my direction. The absence of noise is more terrifying than the loudest war cry. My face reddens and I can feel my legs starting to tingle but before I can turn and run back through the doors, a voice rings out from across the room.

"Hey, girl! How're you doing?"

I blink. The voice belongs to Bea Miller, who is sitting at her usual table, and the likelihood of her enquiring about my well-being is exactly zilch. I quickly realize that this question is not, in fact, aimed at me.

"Come and sit with us and tell us *exactly* what you got up to at the weekend," calls Autumn Addiman from her seat beside Bea, her words dripping with such maple-syrupy sweetness that it makes my teeth wince. "You cheeky minx!"

Yep. *Definitely* not talking to me. I'm no expert but I'm pretty sure my thrilling weekend of cleaning the bathroom, doing my homework, going for a run, then eating beans on toast in front of the television does not qualify me for "minx" status, cheeky or otherwise.

A snigger ripples around the room and the air fizzes with tension. I turn and see Kacey from my maths class standing behind me. As in, right behind me, like she's hoping I'll shield her from the carnage that is about to ensue.

Over at Bea's table, Autumn is waving her hand enthusiastically, beckoning Kacey to join them. With her huge conker-brown eyes and her long auburn ringlets bouncing up and down, Autumn would look to an outsider like the loveliest, warmest girl you've ever met.

I learnt a while ago never to judge a book by its cover.

Kacey looks at me and opens her mouth, as if she's about to do something outrageous like ask to sit with me – even though the only words she ever throws in my direction are derogatory comments about my appearance – so I do what any sane person would do in these circumstances. I grab a tray and speed-walk towards the serving counter.

By the time I have accepted some dubious-looking cauliflower cheese and a plate of undercooked chips from Linda, the midday supervisor, and seated myself in my regular position in the corner (solo, back to the wall, facing the room, better to see the enemy), Kacey has given in. She's made her way across the canteen to Bea's table, unable to resist their instruction to join them.

I sigh and pierce a chip with my fork. She'd have been far better off just leaving, but some people can't seem to help themselves. Besides, not everyone is a runner like me. When I asked Melissa who my father was, she said that he was a student training to be a doctor on the same course as her who did a runner. Flight is in my DNA, along with the black hair and dark green eyes that I also inherited from him. It's who I am, and it's served me well up to this point.

"So, I hear you hooked up with Ethan on Saturday night." Autumn has a voice that, while sounding like honey dripping off a spoon, is also somehow able to ooze into the darkest depths of the cosmos and her statement is heard by everyone in the room. I glance over to see if there is the remotest chance of adult intervention, but Linda is safely on the other side of the serving counter with her headphones on and is clearly not the slightest bit interested in anything that might be occurring on the other side of the skirmish line.

"No!" Kacey's feet shuffle from side to side as she stands awkwardly in front of the girls. "That didn't happen. I don't even like him!"

Bea sighs and shakes her head, flicking her long, wavy blonde hair in her signature move, and fixes Kacey with a look of part-curiosity and part-sympathy.

I shovel some disgusting cauliflower into my mouth and try not to watch, but it's like driving past a car crash – the morbid curiosity wins.

"And yet you still hooked up with him," snorts Mikki Potts, AKA @silverbullet, who is sitting on the other side of Bea. "Classy."

She's a girl who prefers action to speech, which is maybe just as well considering the only words ever to come out of her mouth are as sharp as broken glass.

"That's not true!" Kacey stamps her foot, and it booms like a gunshot across the canteen. She's blown it now.

"Except it *is* true," Bea tells her. "It's even up on *Woodford Whispers*, so everyone knows."

I can see the blood drain from Kacey's face from all the way over here. I try to mentally urge her to walk away because this battle is lost, but the frantic, excitable mutterings that are spreading around the room drown out my silent message.

Woodford Whispers is the godawful online school gossip account. The administrator is anonymous (although I have my suspicions about who runs it) and anyone can spread spurious rumours or share humiliating photographs by sending them in for consideration. Not that there appears to be strict criteria for what makes it on to the page – basically, if the content is scandalous, back-stabbing, low-down dirty slander then it's all good to go.

Unless it's about one of the girls who run this school, that is. They're too clean to ever get any mud slung in their direction.

"Are you saying that Autumn has got it wrong?" Bea purrs softly. Unlike Autumn, Bea's voice is quiet, but that doesn't matter because when she talks, everyone listens. "And are you calling my good friend Kieran a liar?"

The queen has spoken.

Freeze frame.

Bea Miller, leaning back in her chair, an unreadable expression on her face. Her cool inscrutability is one of the many traits that allow her to maintain her reign. She is calm and collected, the glossy, flawless image of poise, with never a hair, a comment or a laugh out of place. She's like a magnet, pulling people towards her – and then, just when you think you've made a connection, she flips the poles and you're pushed away. And yet there's something about Bea that keeps people coming back for more. Maybe it's the way she makes a person feel in the glow of her undivided attention. Once you've experienced the high of being held in her orbit then it's hard not to chase that feeling.

I know something about that.

We knew each other once, what feels like a million aeons ago, when we were in primary school.

Actually, that's a lie. We didn't just know each other; we were friends. Best friends. The kind of friends who tell each other everything and promise that nothing will ever be more important than being there for each other.

We spent most of Year Six excitedly discussing our imminent move to Woodford High and any nerves I might have felt about entering secondary school were quelled by the knowledge that I would have her beside me.

Then it all went wrong. Bea found something that actually *was* more important than being there for me – popularity. When we rocked up to school on the first day of Year Seven, Bea acted like she didn't even know who I was.

Which is fair enough, I guess, because I certainly don't recognize her any more.

Perhaps the reason for her unending queue of fans is

not because of the thrill of her attention at all. Perhaps it's because she radiates danger. Everyone does whatever they can to mitigate the threat, stay out of her firing line. She has turned the entirety of Year Nine into Bea-pleasers. Nobody wants to be her victim.

Now, beside her, Mikki Potts is in her usual position of up-front and personal. Half-risen from her seat, ready to step in and defend her queen from any insult, both real and imagined. I would rather go up against Frankenstein's monster than Mikki. She's tiny, wears her silver hair in the cutest of choppy pixie cuts and has the face of an angel. She's officially the fastest runner at Woodford High and she is one hundred per cent the most terrifying person that I have ever met in my entire life. No mere mortal can outrun either Mikki's legs or her wrath, and she's as handy with her fists as she is her feet.

On the other side of Bea is giggly, sweet Autumn Addiman. With her pale skin and her impossibly long legs, she looks like a cross between the girl next door and some kind of mischievous, fun-loving fire sprite. You'd probably describe her as "beautiful". She's not in the same league of terror as Bea and Mikki and she knows it, but it doesn't matter because Autumn brings her own special set of talents to the group. While Bea sits on her throne and Mikki provides the protection, Autumn flits through the corridors, infiltrating every conversation, overhearing every rumour. She's the gossip collector. The banker who trades in secrets. The whispered voice in Bea's ear. Nothing happens at Woodford High without Autumn reporting on it, and quite a lot *doesn't* happen that she still reports on, which is what I strongly suspect is happening right now.

Bea, Autumn and Mikki. The judge, the jury and the executioner, all of them main characters in their own stories. I call them the Glossy Girls. The dictionary defines the word "gloss" as meaning *a deceptively attractive appearance* or *a bright, often superficial, attractiveness* or, my personal favourite, *to mask the true nature of something.* They are the most popular girls in school, loved and hated (the two are not mutually incompatible) by students and staff alike – and between them and their socials, which are their weapons of choice, they have the capacity to ruin a girl's life.

You might be thinking that three Year Nine girls can't possibly have the power to make or break another human.

You'd be wrong.

"I'm not calling anyone a liar," stutters Kacey, and the world speeds up, accompanied by howls of laughter from the table where the football lads are sitting and listening. Kieran gives Ethan a high-five, like he's won some kind of award, which I suppose he has – whether something happened between him and Kacey on Saturday night or not, the whole school now thinks that it did. Which brings *him* kudos and *her* shame.

"Why are you still here, loser?" Mikki asks Kacey. "Off you pop – go and sit with your boyfriend." She sinks back into her seat and raises one eyebrow at Bea as Kacey murmurs frantic words that I can't hear over the noise coming from the boys.

Bea rolls her eyes and then flicks her wrist. Kacey is dismissed.

I squish a bit of cauliflower into my plate, determined not to be yet another pair of eyes burning into her as she turns and moves between the tables towards the door, but it's impossible not to watch. She makes it halfway before the walk of shame gets too much – and only now, five minutes too late, does she run, too slow to outrun the tidal wave of laughter that surges around her and carries her out of the hall on its swell.

I focus my eyes back down at my food. I am just coating a chip in watery cheese sauce when a shadow falls across my plate, making me look up.

Standing in front of my table, making eye contact with me for perhaps the first time in over two years, is Bea.

"Happy birthday, Eden."

She stares down at me for a moment with that unreadable gaze behind her perfectly made-up eyes, and then the next moment she sweeps away, flanked by her courtiers.

I freeze, my fork halfway to my mouth, my eyes following as she glides out of the hall.

What was *that*?

Lie Like A Girl

Woodford Whispers is a hive of activity by the time I get home from school. I've thankfully never been the target of a post, though I get plenty of muttered comments in the corridors about being a loner and a loser and a weirdo with no fashion style. (For the record, we all have to wear school uniform, so the opportunities are limited – although to be fair that doesn't seem to hinder most of the other Year Nines.) *Woodford Whispers* is always fairly awful, but today it's worse than usual.

@trooth-hurts: A little bird told me that a certain girl got up close and personal with a certain boy at the weekend. Care to comment, **@kacey789**?

@alwaysautumn: Oh my gosh 🙈

@trooth-hurts: Yeah **@ethan-is-king** – really lowering yourself there.

@ethan-is-king: Don't have a go at me – who are you, anyway?

@trooth-hurts: Just your friendly neighbourhood speaker of the truth. Consider me the Woodford High lie detector.

@ethan-is-king: Anyway, it's not my fault the girls can't resist my charms…

@footballrules: My MAN!!!!!!!

@daisychain: Gross.

@alwaysautumn: Are you OK though, **@kacey789**? I'm worried about you, hon. People will like you without you degrading yourself.

@bonbon01: You're so sweet, Autumn. Everyone else piles on but you're thinking about why **@kacey789**

feels the need to seek attention like this. That's why we #loveautumn.

@footballrules: Urggh – get a room. But do you know who else piles on? **@kacey789** right on top of **@ethan-is-king**!!!!

@daisychain: LOL.

@kacey789: For the last time, nothing happened between me and Ethan.

@alwaysautumn: It's OK. We won't judge you.

@silverbullet: Much.

@ethan-is-king: I'd give you three out of ten, Kacey.

@bonbon01: 🤣

@footballrules: Maybe she needs lessons!! I'm available any time.

@kacey789: Shut the hell up, Kieran.

@silverbullet: You might want to think about who you're threatening on here, Kacey. You're online now but tomorrow we're all in school and you can't hide behind a screen.

@virtuallyviolet: Exactly. Don't say things on here that you wouldn't say to someone's face.

@kacey789: You're the ones having a go at me! What did I do?????

@footballrules: What won't you do????!!!!

@ethan-is-king: Not a lot. Lolololololol.

I swipe out of the chat, not wanting to read any more. I never comment on *Woodford Whispers*, but it pays to know what is being discussed. That way I can make sure to keep my distance from whoever is currently in the limelight.

There is someone else who never comments on *Woodford Whispers* – or not publicly. She's too clever to get her hands dirty – she has her minions for that. And I wouldn't be surprised if she's the one using the @trooth-hurts profile to comment anonymously.

Swiping the screen, I navigate to @BeaKind. (Are you kidding me?)

@BeaKind: Just slouching around, feeling chill.

Apparently, leisurewear is now in. The post is accompanied by a photo of her in a baby-blue cropped tracksuit top and the baggiest pair of tracksuit bottoms that I have ever seen. Her waist looks tiny, and the large expanse of exposed skin is tanned and flat. She posted it at four o'clock and already has three hundred and seventy-two likes.

I glance up at my own reflection in the mirror. The rushed ponytail that I shoved up this morning is drooped and tired, and the ill-thought-out fringe that I hacked into the front of my black hair a few weeks ago is choppy, but not in a good way. God – I hate the way everyone fakes their lives online and nobody ever calls them out on it. There's no way they're all having a perfect, wonderful time and effortlessly looking like Roman gods and goddesses every freaking minute of the day. I ignore the tiny voice in the back of my head asking if maybe they really are and it's me who is getting it wrong, and throw my phone on to my bed.

Walking across to the window, I check out the row of cactus pots that line the sill. People think that cacti don't demand much attention – and it's true, compared to lots of plants they're pretty low maintenance, but that doesn't mean that they like being ignored any more than anyone else does.

"Hey, Cosmo," I whisper to my feather cactus. It looks soft and gentle with its white fluffy exterior, but anyone who dares to touch it will soon discover the short, sharp spines lurking out of sight. "How's it going?"

Next, I turn my attention to Clarissa, my cute bunny-ear cactus. "What's up?" I ask her, feeling the soil in her pot. It's a little dry so I pick up the tiny watering can that Melissa got me for Christmas last year and water first Clarissa and then Caspian, my zebra cactus, before taking a look at Colin.

Ah, Colin. The most problematic of my collection. Not that it's his fault he's associated with such a complicated memory.

I can still hear her voice, as if she's standing right next to me.

"Look what I found at the weekend!" Her ten-year-old face was split with the biggest smile I'd ever seen. "You can add it to your collection!"

I hadn't been friends with Bea for long, but the week before she'd come over to my house after school and seen the three plants on my window sill.

"Thanks," I muttered, thrown. "I haven't got any money to pay you for it though."

Bea laughed and thrust it towards me in its fancy painted ceramic pot. "Don't be silly. It's a gift!"

"Why?" I held it up, examining the cactus from all sides. I recognized the red, yellow and green rainbow colours and star-shaped body as a moon cactus, a plant that I hadn't even bothered asking my mother to buy me due to the hefty price.

"Why not?" Bea had shrugged, like it wasn't a big deal. "We're best friends, aren't we? You can call him Colin and he can be friends with Clarissa, Cosmo and Caspian. He's a symbol of our undying bond with each other!"

"Thank you." I smiled at her, worried about how to break it to her that moon cacti usually only live for two to three years.

Here we are though, just over three years later, and Colin is alive and kicking.

Unlike our supposed never-ending friendship.

It's hard for me to think that there was actually a time I liked Bea, back when life was simpler, and our days were filled with laughing and running and playing and swapping Pokémon cards. That was before. Now, Bea is more interested in collecting people than Pikachu, trading them for information and status and whatever the hell else she wants.

"Pizza's ready!" My mother's voice floats up the stairs,

accompanied by the delicious smell of melted cheese. I put down the tiny watering can and rotate Colin and Caspian so that each plant has a new side exposed to the sun. Midnight makes a huffing sound from her usual place on my bed, and I grin.

"There's no need to get jealous," I tell her, moving across to ruffle her head. "You're still the most important being in my life."

I give Midnight one last pat and head downstairs, my stomach suddenly rumbling.

"Happy birthday to you!" she sings, as I enter the kitchen. A banner is hanging haphazardly from the kitchen cupboards, and she's blown up a couple of balloons and tied them to my chair.

"Happy birthday to you!" She walks across to where I'm standing, carrying a plate of pizza with a single candle stuck in the middle.

"Happy birthday, dear Eden." She smiles at me and takes a breath, ready for the grand finale. I smile back reluctantly – she's a terrible singer.

"Happy birthday to you!" Her voice is triumphant, and she nods towards the candle. "Go on – blow it out and make a wish!"

I groan, but I still blow out the candle and close my eyes. I could do with a bit of good luck in my life.

"Now let's eat," she says.

The pizza is good. She's bought my favourite flavour and the moment that I take my first bite and taste the spicy pepperoni on my tongue, everything feels better.

"So, how was school?"

"Fine." I reach across and pick up the carton of orange juice, pouring myself a drink.

"Just fine?" She leans across the table and fixes me with a look. "Come on, Eden. Tell me about your day."

I shrug. "There's not a lot to tell." I take another bite of pizza and then pause, mid-chew. "Though, Bea Miller wished me a happy birthday." It slips out before I've quite decided it's something I want to share.

"Don't talk with your mouth full," she says automatically. "And that's nice."

I shake my head. "It's not nice. She wasn't saying it to be nice."

My mother frowns in confusion. "Why would she wish you a happy birthday if she wasn't trying to be nice?"

That's the million-dollar question, isn't it? All I know is it could only have been a bad omen, a code, a secret threat.

I brought this on myself. I've become complacent in my invisibility; expected people's eyes to glance over me and move on. And now, thanks to my poorly timed entrance into the canteen ahead of that Kacey girl, I've been seen.

"It sounds to me as if Bea wants to reconnect," says my mother, snapping me out of my internal panic. "That'd be good, wouldn't it?"

"No, Melissa," I tell her. "It wouldn't be good."

She sighs, and I can't tell if it's with disappointment or because she's tired. She hates me calling her by her name and I know that she thinks I'm doing it to be antagonistic, but that's not the truth. Not entirely, anyway.

Maybe it started out that way, after the awful argument we had. That was because of Bea too. Most bad things that have happened in the last few years are because of her.

Not that my mother can understand that. She thinks we just had a silly bust-up, and I overreacted. She wouldn't think that if she knew the truth about how Bea treated me, but there was no way I could tell her – not when she was already so stressed out about work and money and everything. So, I downplayed the whole thing and hoped she'd move on.

But she wouldn't stop hassling me to have friends over. And then, on the day she told me she'd spent money we didn't have to hire the local swimming pool for my twelfth birthday, and that I could invite six friends for a party, I lost it at her.

Because how do you tell your exhausted, under pressure, constantly worried mother that you don't have even one friend to invite, let alone six? You don't. It's far easier to tell her that she doesn't understand you and that the last thing you ever wanted was a swimming party and that you hate her.

And when she finally snaps, and yells back that she didn't ever ask to be a parent and that she has given up all her hopes and dreams for you? Well, then things get really bad.

She apologized the moment that the words came out of her mouth, but she couldn't take them back.

So, yeah, back then, when everything got messed up with Bea, and Year Seven was awful, and my mother started doing longer nursing shifts at the hospital, I wanted her to know that I was angry. But then "Melissa" just sort of stuck. I started feeling like I should be old enough to figure stuff out on my own, and I decided "Mum" belonged to the old days, along with primary school and friendship and belonging.

"How was your maths test?" she asks, clearly looking to change the subject. "Weren't you getting the results today?"

Now it's my turn to sigh. "I got a D," I tell her. "Happy birthday to me."

Her face falls. "Oh, Eden. What went wrong?"

"I don't know." I knock back the rest of my juice. "I guess I'm just bad at maths."

"That's not true." She picks up another slice of pizza. "But you're clearly going to have to put some more work in, especially if you're going to get into the top set for GCSE.

"Maybe we can look into getting you some extra help?" She pulls out her phone. "Or I can email your teacher and find out if they run any additional study sessions. And there are bound to be some websites that can help you with anything tricky. You're going to need a decent grade if you're going to get into medical school."

I resist the urge to roll my eyes. It's the sentence that has come out of my mother's mouth more than any other since I was six years old.

Back then, I spent all my time dressing up in a white coat and a plastic stethoscope, proclaiming that I was going to be a doctor, just like my absentee father. It was only when I started in Year Seven that I realized it wasn't my dream after all. I'm not remotely interested in saving other people – it's hard enough trying to save myself.

I probably should have told Melissa, but instead I keep letting her think she understands what I want. Paving the way for me to be a doctor seems to be about the only thing that gives her any positivity these days. A generous person might say that's because she's aspirational for me. I would say she's keen to live out her own failed experiences through me, since she had me instead of finishing her medical degree.

"I'll go and see my maths teacher tomorrow," I lie. "Can we talk about something else now?"

She puts her phone down and smiles at me apologetically. "Of course. Sorry, honey – that wasn't very birthday-ish, was it? What would you like to talk about?"

It's the opportunity that I've been waiting for.

"Well." I rest my chin on my hands and try to look as appealing as possible. "Have you given any more thought to me getting a Saturday job, now that I'm fourteen?"

She brightens. "Oh, you've beaten me to it! I have, actually. And the answer is yes."

"Brilliant!" I grin at her, surprised, as butterflies of excitement flutter in my stomach. "So, I'm thinking that I'll put in an application form at—"

Melissa puts her hand in the air, stopping me mid-flow. "There's no need to worry about all that. I've already got you a position all sorted." She beams at me. "Surprise!"

The butterflies thud against my ribs. I should have known this was too good to be true.

"It's a good surprise," she says, clocking my face. "I've got you a job working with Jimmy – how about that!"

I stare at her. "Jimmy who?"

She laughs, like I'm trying to be cute. "*Jimmy* Jimmy! You know – Joyce's son."

"Who is Joyce?" I'm utterly confused now.

She frowns at me. "Joyce. My best friend at work? I talk about her all the time."

"Oh right – *Joyce*. Yeah, sure." I nod, even though I don't know who she's talking about.

"Right. So, I've got you a job working for a few hours every Saturday with Jimmy." She smiles excitedly. "You're going to love it, Eden!"

"OK." I take a deep breath. "And Jimmy works where?"

"I've told you all about him and his job." Melissa looks at me, slightly deflated. "Do you not listen to a word I say? He helps run the Delicious Doughnuts stand in the shopping mall. You'll get an employee discount too!"

I shake my head. "No way. I'm not working on a doughnut stand. And I'm definitely not working in the mall. I don't want to be around all those people."

She stands up and starts gathering up the plates. "Eden, Joyce had to pull a lot of strings to get you the position so you're going to have to give it a go. You have a trial shift this weekend, so let's see how you get on, OK?"

I pause. She's been adamant that I can't get a job yet because she thinks that I should be focusing on my studies, so this is a massive opportunity. And while a ridiculous doughnut stand was not my preferred employment, I do need to start making some money. She thinks that I don't know about the increased cost of electricity and petrol and food, but I've seen how more and more of the items in the fridge come from the nearly out-of-date, discounted part of the supermarket and I know that she sometimes walks to work instead of taking the car, despite the fact that it's a mostly uphill forty-five-minute journey. She does her best to give me an allowance now and then, but it doesn't feel right to spend her hard-earned income on stuff that I want.

"Fine." I push my chair back and take our glasses to the sink. "I'll think about it." I start to run hot water into the sink, but my mother shoos me away.

"Go!" she says, rolling up her sleeves. "You don't need to wash up on your birthday." Then she pauses. "Do you maybe want to watch a film together, or something?"

I take in her tired eyes and the way her back is hunched, as if keeping herself standing upright is an effort. I know that the shifts she does at the hospital can be brutal and I can't remember a time when she wasn't exhausted. And I think about the trainers and the birthday card and the balloons and the banner and I wonder what she had to go without to give me a birthday.

"I'm too tired for a film," I lie, picking up a tea towel. "Let's clear up together and then I think I'll get an early night, if that's OK with you?"

Her shoulders sag in relief. "I think I'll be joining you before long," she says. "It's been quite a day."

For a few minutes we clean up in companionable silence and then, once we're done, she gives me a quick hug.

"Happy birthday, Eden," she says, stifling a yawn.

I nod and then walk across the kitchen, stopping at the doorway.

"I'll do the trial shift at the doughnut stand," I tell her. "Thanks for organizing it."

She smiles and I head upstairs.

Flinging myself on my bed, I open my phone.

There's only one group of people who I can properly talk to. They are my only friends, if you could call them that – although we've never met in real life. That's partly because we all live on different continents and partly because none of us have any real desire to see each other face to face. We would prefer never to have to see *anyone* face to face.

I navigate to the Cactus Club chat and type in a new message.

18:54 **@just-eden**: Hey. Anyone there?

18:54 **@aussiekid**: I'm here. What's up?

18:55 **@just-eden**: Oh, I'm living the dream. Spent my day trying to fly under the radar and have somehow managed to get noticed by the one person who I would happily never speak to again. How about you? What's your day been like?

18:56 **@aussiekid**: Not bad. Not great. I guess I'd call it bland with a side serving of tedium.

18:58 **@TKOcactus**: Sounds like a riot. You all need to get out more.

18:59 **@aussiekid**: You're hilarious. The reason I come on here to talk to you losers is cos I hate having to talk to people IRL. Getting out more is the last thing I want.

18:59 **@just-eden**: Amen to that. Although who are you calling a loser?

19:01 **@aussiekid**: Answer me one question **@just-eden** – are you more likely to have a meaningful conversation with a) your cat, b) a real living, breathing person or c) your cactus 🌵 ?

19:02 **@just-eden**: Fair enough...

19:02 **@TKOcactus**: That's a trick question – we all know that cacti are the best listeners.

19:03 **@aussiekid**: True that. Although mine can sometimes be a little sharp in their replies…

19:04 **@just-eden**: Ouch.

19:05 **@TKOcactus**: You're both pricks. This is why you have no real friends, you know that?

19:06 **@aussiekid**: We're a prickly pear, for sure…

19:06 **@just-eden**: 🤣

19:07 **@TKOcactus**: Anyway, happy birthday **@just-eden**. Did you have a good one?

19:08 **@just-eden**: Yes. And also no. I'm glad it's over, anyway. Do either of you have any advice about how to avoid unwanted attention?

19:10 **@TKOcactus**: Find a cold, dank cave and make it your new home?

19:11 **@aussiekid**: Learn magic and cast yourself an invisibility cloak?

19:12 **@TKOcactus**: Fashion yourself a spaceship out of Lego and empty toilet roll tubes and rocket off to the moon.

19:13 **@aussiekid**: Valid.

19:14 **@just-eden**: Thanks, you guys. I knew I could count on you.

19:15 **@aussiekid**: You're welcome.

19:16 **@TKOcactus**: Speak tomorrow?

19:17 **@just-eden**: Absolutely.

19:17 **@aussiekid**: I need advice on my Frailea castanea so come armed with top tips, OK? It's got weird orange marks on it.

19:18 **@TKOcactus**: Dude – I've got you covered. Gotta go cos it's like 4am here, lol – chat tomorrow.

I turn off my phone. Discovering that there are other kids out there who feel like me and are into the same things I'm into was like finding a golden ticket to a chocolate factory. We started off just talking about our mutual love of the not-so-humble cactus but it's kind of drifted into chats about school and home and life and the universe – and it feels good.

Standing up, I walk over to my window sill and assess my own plants.

"I would quite like things to be not so hard," I tell them. "Got any hints for me?"

But it's like @TKOcactus said. They're excellent listeners but not so great with the life advice.

Alone Like A Girl

I'm scrolling social media, and just as I swipe to check out why Mikki's photograph of a single cherry tomato has got so much attention, I hear the unmistakable broken-glass sound of Mikki's brittle laughter. I turn off my phone and ram it in my pocket, unable to shake the feeling that by stalking her account I have somehow unwittingly conjured the Glossies out of thin air and lured them to my location.

The laughter increases in volume as they walk along the corridor, getting closer. I'm trapped. I found this place at the start of term and it's the perfect spot for thinking. Or hiding. It used to be the PE cupboard but since Woodford High was given a makeover a few years ago, the whole of B Block has been abandoned. Apparently, there isn't any money left to fix it up – or to rip it down. So, it's just here, attached but forgotten.

That's what I thought, anyway.

I listen to them approach, my eyes instinctively darting around the tiny room, searching for an escape – but it's futile. There's nowhere to go and nowhere to hide, so I make myself as small and silent and still as possible, curled up on the crash mats, trying to stop my pulse from racing. The Glossies have no reason to come in here, but they can smell fear from a mile away.

"Did you see what Ethan said on *Woodford Whispers* about scoring Kacey as a three out of ten?" Autumn's voice is filled with delight as their footsteps stop, right outside.

"Hmmmm." Bea sounds thoughtful; she's critical or calculating – it's hard to tell. "Kind of makes you wonder what score all the other Year Nine girls would be given, doesn't it?"

"Yes!" I can picture Autumn jumping up and down in excitement, her auburn ringlets floating in the air. "That's brilliant! We can set up a load of girls with some fake hook-ups and get the boys to give them a score. Kieran and Ethan will definitely be up for it!"

"How would you feel about Kieran kissing other girls, Bea?" Mikki's voice is trying to sound concerned but I can hear the undercurrent of slyness.

"I don't fancy Kieran," Bea snaps back icily. "And we're not going to set up some dodgy hook-ups. That's just weird."

"But you said—" starts Autumn.

Suddenly, as I shift nervously in the cupboard, I knock my water bottle. It crashes to the floor, where it spins around, making a lovely metallic ringing noise.

I cringe.

The door flies open, revealing the three people I least want to see.

"What are *you* doing in here?" barks Mikki.

"If it was anyone else I'd think she was planning a hook-up," says Autumn. Today's accessories include a hedgehog hair clip and the cutesy brown and orange folder imprinted with acorns and squirrels that she always carries, just in case people forget about her autumnal *brand*.

Mikki makes a snorting noise in the back of her throat, and I shoot her a silent death-glare.

"What *are* you doing?" asks Bea, flicking her blonde hair over her shoulder. She's staring at me with an expression I can't quite read, which is making me feel all kinds of uncomfortable. Being caught in the cross hairs of the Glossies for the second time in two days is bad news.

"It's Eden," states Mikki. "She's just being a weird loner. For a change."

I take that as my cue to do what I should've done the split second they opened that door.

Grabbing my rucksack, I push myself off the mats with force, aiming to sprint past them to safety – but my foot catches on a cricket bat and I end up pitching forward, my arms flailing as I steady myself. While my original plan was to dodge past the Glossies, sleek as a gazelle, the reality is more like a rampaging buffalo. My rucksack swings, making contact with something which, judging from the grunt, is possibly Mikki's chin. Autumn's eyes widen as I charge past her, my shoulder barging into hers. Bea has the good sense to sidestep out of my way, and as I regain my balance I hear her laugh. But then I'm flying out of the old gym and down the corridor, putting as much physical distance between me and the Glossies as I possibly can.

The rest of the day passes like every other. A combination of boredom and stress as I flit from lesson to lesson, trying to avoid anyone with a pulse.

Now, lessons are finally over and I'm here. The one remaining safe space in this dump of a school and the only place where I can genuinely relax. Even so, I must be smart about my timings. Get it wrong and this place could go from heaven to hell in thirty seconds flat.

I throw my rucksack on to one of the benches and sit

down. From up here in the stands I have a perfect view of the entire running track and if I'm careful to sit in the top far left corner, in the shadows, then it's almost impossible for anyone down below to see me while I'm checking the coast is clear. I should be safe though. It's Thursday. Nobody except me comes here on a Thursday.

I've already snuck into the changing rooms and put on my leggings and T-shirt, and now I take my new trainers out of my rucksack and lace them up. Walking in them feels like bouncing on marshmallows and I'm keen to see if they make a difference when I'm out on the track. I gave them a quick breaking-in yesterday, but this is different – pavement-pounding is fine but it's out here where there are no other distractions that I can really push myself to my limits.

I bound down the steps and on to the rubbery surface, stretching out my legs to loosen my muscles. I don't really know what I'm doing but I've checked out a few warm-up exercises on YouTube and, after once again checking that there's nobody around, I march on the spot and then do some calf stretches before starting to jog slowly towards the first corner.

And it feels so, so good. I pick up speed and let my legs take charge. My arms find their rhythm and keep time with my legs and my head stops thinking as I move faster and faster, away from everything that has happened in the day, the week, the month, the year. My mouth pulls in deep lungfuls of oxygen and it's like drinking from a cold tap, refreshing and refuelling and washing away every unpleasant thought.

If only I could keep running and never, ever stop.

I've done four laps of the track and am embarking on the fifth when it all goes wrong. As I round the top end of the track and start to head back towards the stands, I see them. I blink, hoping that maybe I've overdone it and am experiencing some sort of hallucination.

It's Thursday.

They should not be here.

I blink again, and as I start to slow the sound of their voices drifts across the track – and then there are more of them, flooding out of the doors to the changing rooms, easily identified even from all the way over here by their bright red running vests, declaring them to be the Woodford High Track Team.

And now I'm stuck, with only two options. The first is to keep running, which will take me right past where they are gathering around Coach. The second is to take a sharp right, push through the hedge that lines this side of the track, scale the three-metre-high security fence, clamber over the barbed wire at the top and run home to hide under my duvet. There is no doubt in my mind which is the easier and more appealing option but unfortunately for me, my rucksack, with my phone and house keys, is still up in the stands.

Taking a deep breath, I pick up the pace. If I have to do this, then I'm going to do it as fast as I possibly can and minimize the amount of time I will be exposed to them. My feet skim over the track and then I'm flying down the final straight – and in any other circumstance I would be loving every second of feeling this weightless, this free. The track team is focusing on their captain, Riley, as he leads them in a warm-up and their backs are towards me. Maybe there's a chance I can soar past without catching their attention...

But then pain-in-the-ass Coach steps out on to the track, shielding his eyes against the late afternoon sun as he stares towards me.

"Hey!"

I can keep running. I'm going so fast now that even Usain Bolt would struggle to catch me.

"Hey there!" He waves his arm in the air, giving the universal sign to slow down and I want to ignore him, I really do, but he's an adult and there are rules to be followed and I'm a runner, not a fighter.

Reluctantly, I let my legs slow until I'm standing in

front of him. I've never spoken to Coach before, but I've watched him motivating the team from the shadows on days when I'm waiting for them to finish up. He seems like he's maybe an OK guy if you're into the whole camaraderie kind of thing.

"You're fast." He pauses but it's not a question, so I don't reply. "We could use someone like you on the team. We're getting extra practice ahead of sports day tomorrow. Why don't you stay and train with us?"

And now I must give an answer. Maybe I could give him a multiple-choice quiz.

Why don't I stay and train with them?

a) Because I always run alone.
b) Because these kids make school look like a walk in the park instead of the safari-gone-wrong experience that I seem to be having.
c) Because running is my one good thing, and I can't let it be ruined by other people.
d) Because to be invisible is to be safe, and to run in the track team is to be seen.
e) Because all the above.

"You could just give it a go for today," he says, seeming to sense my reluctance. "We're about to do some training for the eight hundred metres and I've seen you out here before – you'd be a natural for that distance. You've got stamina, and with a bit of work on your form I think we could see some great times from you."

I open my mouth to tell him I can't, and then close it again. Nobody has ever said anything nice about my running before, not since I was a little kid anyway. It's a strange feeling and the thrill of it catches me by surprise. I let my eyes roam to where Riley is now getting the rest of the team to do some high-knee butt kicks, his floppy bleached-blond fringe swinging across his face and getting in the way. He sees me looking and gives me a quick grin, before yanking his hair back into a scruffy ponytail and yelling words of encouragement at a couple of kids as they start to slow down.

Maybe I could just stand at the back and watch? Maybe it would even be kind of fun to run with other people, just now and again – to see how far I can push myself?

And then – there is Mikki. She's finished her warm-up, which is a shame because if anyone ever needed a high-knee kick in the butt, it is her. She turns to look for the coach and sees me. Her face creases in confusion for a second but then her mouth breaks into a smile – the kind of smile that the wolf probably had, just before it gobbled up Little Red Riding Hood.

Mikki nudges the girl beside her and says something that I can't hear, her hand gesturing in my direction. It doesn't take a genius to figure out she's probably talking about finding me hiding in the PE cupboard earlier. The other girl starts to laugh, and I turn away, feeling my cheeks burn. Any brief hope that flickered to life at the idea of joining track is replaced by anger. I'm angry with Mikki for being such a cow, angry with this girl who I don't even know for joining in her mockery, angry with Coach for putting me in this situation, angry at Riley for his easy smile, but most of all, angry with myself for allowing even a moment of doubt to enter my head.

I'm better off alone.

"Shall we give it a go, then?" asks Coach, oblivious to the scene playing out in front of him.

I shake my head. "Uh – sorry. No, thanks," I manage. And then I do what I always do. I put one foot in front of the other with increasing speed until I'm hurtling back towards the safety of the shadows.

The only thing different this time is the tiny voice whispering into my ear, asking if running away is really going to solve all my problems.

Hide Like A Girl

"The weather forecast says it's going to brighten up later." Melissa hands me a piece of toast and then glances back at her phone. "So don't worry!"

"I try to keep my weather-related concerns to a minimum," I tell her, taking a big bite. "But thanks."

She puts down her phone and rolls her eyes at me. "I know how much you love sports day, Eden. Don't try and pretend you weren't up early, checking to make sure it isn't raining! I'll never forget the year you were nine, when it had to be cancelled because of the summer storm." She smiles at me and picks up her cup of tea. "You were inconsolable. We had to have our own sports day in the garden at the weekend, do you remember?"

I shake my head and cram the rest of the toast into my

mouth. I'm not in the mood to take a trip down memory lane this morning.

"You must remember!" She really isn't letting this go. "You won every race and I made you a medal out of cardboard and tinfoil. You wore it for days!"

I shrug. "That was then."

"Well, yes." She stares at me, her face a bit crumpled, and I feel instantly bad, but I really don't need reminding me about how rubbish life is now compared to when I was a kid. She doesn't get how painful it is — but there's no point in explaining. Not when I've kept it from her for all this time.

She isn't wrong. I used to love sports day more than any other day in the school year. The sun was (mostly) shining and we'd have a picnic on the school field. She'd always insist on us participating in the parent-child three-legged race, which would inevitably result in us lying in a heap on the grass, laughing like crazy. And it wouldn't matter whether we won or lost.

The last race of the day was always the "big run" — one lap around the field, with the finish line situated where the rest of the school and the parents were sitting. Two kids from each class would be chosen to race and the winner got twenty house points, which was ridiculously high stakes back then.

Our final sports day in primary school, it was Bea and me, jostling for top position, pushing each other to be faster and better. As we raced down the home straight, with me just a fraction in the lead, I glanced to the left and saw my mum. She was shouting my name and leaping up and down, with the biggest, proudest smile on her face. And I knew in that moment that I had already won. So, I held out my hand and Bea grabbed hold and we crossed the finish line together.

If I'd known that it was the last happy time I'd ever have in a school, I'd maybe have tried to hang on to it for a little longer.

"So – what events are you signed up for today?" Her voice is brisker now, as she spoons some cat food into Midnight's bowl and then starts to gather up her bag.

"None of them," I tell her.

She opens her mouth to say something then thinks better of it, slamming it closed again like a goldfish. Not that she needs to say a single word – I can see the disappointment etched across her face. It's killing her not to talk about how engaging in extracurricular events will make my letter of application *stand out from the crowd* when I eventually apply to universities.

I take a few gulps of orange juice and then, after the daily inquisition into whether I have my key and my lunch money, escape the kitchen. I hear the door slam a few minutes later and only now can I exhale properly.

It's not her fault that she makes me so tense, I know that. It's just hard when she brings up stuff I'd rather not think about. She makes me prickly.

The memories Melissa stirred are still floating around my head as I wander on to the running track after second period. They might have the same name, but this day bears very little resemblance to the sports day I remember from my younger years. The message then was to have some fun, cheer for everyone and to do your best.

The vibe now couldn't be more different. Kids at secondary school are basically divided into two camps when it comes to sports day. Those who love to prove they are better than everyone else, and those who would genuinely pay good money to never have to attend such a miserable, humiliating event ever again. It's not about doing your best – it's about being *the* best and if you aren't prepared to annihilate the competition then you'd be better off staying at home. Which is where I would be right now, if I didn't know that Melissa would never give me a second of peace if she found out that I was bunking off. Instead, I'm an unwilling spectator, clad in the compulsory PE kit.

I make my way over to the stands along with the rest of the school; all of us joyless observers of the elite few who are actually good at sport and the tragic others who were pressured into signing up and who, in a few short minutes, will be forced into displaying their lack of talent for all the world to see. I can only imagine that PE teachers are trained using the Roman gladiatorial combat approach, pitting the socially marginalized against the favoured warriors, while the spectators bray for blood.

A shout from across the track drags me out of Ancient Rome and back to reality. Woodford High is no Circus Maximus, but the survival rate of losers is probably comparable, and the girls' one-hundred-metre sprint, which is about to happen right in front of me, is prime for the production of failures. Much as I don't want to witness the carnage, it's impossible to ignore.

Miss Robinson, Head of PE, ushers the contenders towards the starting line before heading across to scrutinize her all-important clipboard. I stand and watch the kids getting ready to race. There are a couple of girls I recognize from the track team who start stretching and bouncing, eager to get going. There's Bonnie, a girl from my science class who takes every opportunity to barge me out of the way when she walks past me. And then there are the rest. The assorted odds and ends who have somehow been convinced to agree to this trial. The ones who probably thought the one hundred metres was an easy option, on account of it not being very far. If I were a different girl, living in another lifetime, I would be down there with them, showing what I can do. Another life, where being invisible wasn't my priority.

"Oi – Hairy!" The shout comes from just behind me and when I turn, I see the football team all leering at the girl standing closest to us, on the starting line. Her name is Mary, she's in my PE class and for almost two years she has only ever been referred to by this cruel, ridiculous nickname.

"Have you heard about this incredible new invention?" yells Kieran. "It's called a razor and get this – it takes all the hair off your body!"

They start laughing and Mary flushes a deep red. Back in Year Eight, when we were all getting changed for PE, one of the Glossies decided that Mary had hairy legs. By the end of the lesson, the entire class knew about it, and by the end of the school day there was an anonymous post on *Woodford Whispers*, declaring that Mary was hairy.

It's hair. It's natural. Most of us have it. And if it had been anyone else they'd have either laughed it off or told the offending party to go shove it, but Mary isn't anyone else. She's quiet and introverted and always on her own.

We've never spoken to each other, but I see her, just like I see all the others who live in the shadows. She's always appeared to be quite intelligent in class, so why on earth she has allowed herself to be coerced into running this race and being on such public display is beyond me, especially when ever since that day she has done everything in her power to get out of being forced to wear shorts and join in with PE. She clearly has no survival skills.

"Hey, Bonnie!" Ethan shouts. "How is Hairy looking today?"

Bonnie looks across, her face stretching into an unkind smile as she makes a big performance of peering at Mary's legs. "Pretty hairy," she announces. "I'm worried it's going to affect her speed — the air resistance is really going to slow her down!"

Everyone starts laughing, and out on the track Mary's shoulders hunch up to her ears as she tries in vain to shrink into herself.

"It's not her leg hair that worries me," shouts someone, gesturing rudely towards Mary's shorts. "Can you imagine what kind of a jungle she's got going on in there?"

The laughter notches up another level.

"Urggh, gross!" squeals Bonnie, squirming exaggeratedly and making a big deal of stepping away from Mary, as if body hair is contagious. "That's disgusting."

And then finally, Miss Robinson stops faffing with her clipboard and steps up to the starting line.

"Get into position!" she calls. "And on my mark—"

I get up and start to walk towards the side of the stands. Partly to get away from the mass of people and partly because I've seen enough. I can't help Mary, but I can be one less witness to the shame that is heading her way. The starting whistle blows and even though I'm not watching, I know exactly what is happening by the reaction of the people around me. The kids from the track team sprint clear of the others in the first two seconds, leaving the rest to stagger round the track with Mary, inevitably, right at the end. The loser. The ruined.

I guess it's difficult to run when you've spent the last year making excuses to sit fully clothed on the bench instead of joining in with the PE lesson. And it's probably impossible to run when you're dying inside.

I push through the hordes of jeering Year Nine kids and make my way behind the stands, just beyond where the teachers are all gathered in a gaggle, trying to look like they're here for the kids when really, they're just pleased not to have to teach period three science to feral Year Seven. My cunning idea is to find somewhere to wait out this misery until the bell rings for lunch, when I will casually rejoin my year group as if I have been with them the entire time. It's a foolproof plan and I say this with the conviction of someone who has used this tactic for the last two years.

Keeping an eye on the staff, I stroll around the edge of the stands and, when I'm sure that nobody is looking, dart behind to safety. There's a tree near the fence and I make my way towards it, settling down with my back to the trunk. I'm not completely hidden, but it's good enough to keep me from being spotted by any teacher that might glance in this direction. Pulling out my phone, I navigate to the *Woodford Whispers* page and look at the most recent entry, posted just moments ago. Whoever took the photo was obviously standing right next to the track and Mary's flushed, mortified face is broadcast in technicolour for all to see. I scroll down.

@trooth-hurts: I don't get it. Just buy a razor like everyone else, girl.

@footballrules: What's hairier – an orangutan or Hairy Mary?

@ethan-is-king: No contest, dude!

@alwaysautumn: Come on though, be fair. She

probably is shaving like the rest of us – she just has more hair to get through…

@silverbullet: Lol.

@kacey789: It's embarrassing. I wouldn't get my legs out if I looked like that.

@footballrules: Don't lie – you get your legs out at every opportunity.

@virtuallyviolet: Why is Mary having body hair a big deal?

@footballrules: Are you joking? Like I want to see a hairy girl??

@daisychain: Erm – you do realize that we have to look at your hairy legs?

@silverbullet: Ooh, Daisy – have you been checking out Kieran's legs?

@kacey789: OMG, Daisy! Do you fancy Kieran?!

@footballrules: It's biology. Hair on a boy shows that we're men. Hair on a girl is just grim…

@virtuallyviolet: Well, I think you're being ridiculous.

@silverbullet: So are you saying that you don't shave, **@virtuallyviolet**?

@virtuallyviolet: Of course not.

@alwaysautumn: Why not?

@virtuallyviolet: Idk. Cos I'm a girl?

@silverbullet: So if Hairy isn't a girl, then what is she…??? 😮

It's exactly as I predicted.

She's never living this down.

Public humiliation is alive and well at Woodford High, and sports day provides a wonderful opportunity to take down all those people who are already at the bottom of the pile.

I want absolutely nothing to do with any of it.

They're all welcome to each other.

Run Like A Girl

I ram my phone back in the pocket of my hoodie and rest my head against the gnarly bark of the tree. I hate this place. Everything is fake, like we're all just existing in a reality show where everything is done for the clout and the likes. Popularity is won and lost on everyone's socials – it doesn't matter what your world is really like or who you truly are, as long as your online life is sparkly and exciting and constantly updated. It makes me sick.

I sit for a while, running my fingers through the grass and contemplating whether anyone would notice if I just left for the day. It's unlikely a single person in this school would look around and ask themselves, "Where is Eden McCoy?" In fact, in the unlikely event of that question being posed, the typical response would probably be,

"Who is Eden McCoy?"

"We're just saying – maybe you want to think about it, yeah?"

Mikki's voice pierces the peace, approaching from behind me, and I press myself further against the tree trunk.

"What do you mean? What is there to think about?"

The voice that replies is small and a little bit shaky and I know immediately that the speaker is not one of the Glossies. Quietly, I peek around the side of the tree and then whip my head back in before they can spot me.

The Glossies are all there, huddled around Hope, a girl I have never spoken to but recognize as a member of the track team. She's got long, brown hair which she always wears in two pigtails, and seems like one of those shy kids who smile more with their eyes than their mouth. She's not like Mary or me, she isn't a full-time shadow dweller – but she's one of the many at our school who flit between their known safe places and the relative protection that anonymity provides.

"Are you serious?" Autumn's voice is incredulous. "Did you not just see what happened to Hairy out there?"

There's a slight pause and I hold my breath, desperate for them not to look in my direction.

"But I've been working really hard." Hope's voice has

an edge that wasn't there a second ago. "I was the fastest in the eight hundred metres at track last week, wasn't I, Mikki?"

"That was in training though." Mikki's voice is jagged, like gravel. "Come on, Hope. You know you can't cope when everyone is looking at you. And you know I'm better than you when it comes to the actual race."

"I don't think that's—" starts Hope, but she's no match for the Glossies.

"What do you think, Bea?" interrupts Mikki.

"It's awful," agrees Bea, her voice sad. "Being humiliated in front of people. So I've been told, anyway."

Autumn laughs, as if this is all one lovely joke. "Hope doesn't want to be humiliated! Which is why she's going to listen to us when we're giving her a friendly heads-up to sit this race out."

"She should totally listen to us," agrees Mikki.

"Thanks." Hope's voice is trembling now. "But I've been working really hard for this, and I want to at least try. If I lose, I lose, but—"

"Honestly, Hope," snaps Mikki, clearly out of patience. "If you run the eight hundred metres and lose, then your life isn't going to be worth living."

There's a pause as Hope considers what is being said – not a warning, but a threat.

"I think I can win." It's almost a whisper, a last-ditch, valiant effort to stay strong.

"OK, clearly you're not catching on, Hope. Let me make this a bit clearer for you." Autumn speaks slowly and with false niceness, like she's talking to a three-year-old. "If you run in the eight hundred metres and *win*, then your life isn't going to be worth living."

I blink, processing what I'm hearing. This is low, even for the Glossies.

"I mean if you *insist* then we aren't going to stop you," says Mikki. "You do you, yeah? I just hope you're ready for that photo of you kissing Ethan to go viral on *Woodford Whispers*."

"What!" The shock in Hope's voice is audible. "What photo? I didn't kiss Ethan! I've never kissed anyone in my entire life!"

There's a brief pause and then Autumn giggles.

"Did you get that, Mikki?" she asks. "Tell me you got it?"

Mikki's harsh laughter is answer enough.

A tinny version of Hope's own voice then rings out on loop from Mikki's phone:

"*I've never kissed anyone in my entire life. I've never kissed anyone in my entire life. I've never kissed anyone—*"

And suddenly, before I can ask myself what the hell I

think I'm doing, I'm getting up and stepping out from the safety of the tree. Autumn spots me first, and then Mikki. But it's Bea I keep my eyes on – she might not get her hands as dirty as the others but she's the puppeteer; she's the one in charge.

"Eden." If she's surprised to see me then she's hiding it well.

I glance at Hope, who is clearly struggling not to cry. If I were that different girl, living in that alternative lifetime, I would grab the phone that Mikki is waving triumphantly in the air and smash it to pieces. I would tell them exactly what I think of their dirty scare tactics, and I would demand that they apologize to Hope – and all the other kids whose lives they make miserable on a daily basis.

But I am only me, living right now and I am frozen.

The first tears have started to escape from Hope's eyes.

"How could you?" she murmurs.

Bea shrugs, and when she speaks it's with a voice of pure diplomacy, as if the situation is entirely reasonable. "Well, we won't do anything with this material, Hope – so long as you uphold your side of the bargain and step down from the race. There's no need for any drama – but it's up to you."

"Like we warned you," says Autumn, smiling like a

kindly crocodile. "Being humiliated in front of everyone is tough."

I catch Hope's eye. "Just go," I mutter. "Leave." And then I step in between her and the Glossies, breaking the weird spell that they've cast on her.

It works. With a final, subdued moan of anguish, Hope turns and runs. And as I watch her go, I know without a shadow of a doubt that she'd have beaten Mikki in the eight hundred metres.

And now it's only me, with Bea, Mikki and Autumn all scowling like I've taken away their favourite toy.

"That was just getting fun," complains Mikki, narrowing her eyes.

"Was there something that you wanted to say, Eden?" asks Bea, raising one exquisitely sculpted eyebrow. "It seems like you might have a bit of a problem?"

I open my mouth to tell her exactly what my problem is, but before I can say a single word Miss Robinson comes stalking around the side of the stands. Which is probably just as well, as I'd be more likely to emit some random squeaking noises than a well put-together argument on why I think the Glossies are horrendous human beings.

"Ladies!" Miss Robinson is clearly on the warpath. "The girls' eight hundred metres is about to start and yet you're all here having a gossip session." She claps her hands.

"Move yourselves immediately – we've got a race to run and if I'm not wrong then you, Mikki, should be warming up right about now."

The effect is instantaneous. I watch, slightly freaked out, as the Glossies' faces morph from angry, vengeful demons to compliant, cheerful angels.

"Sorry, Miss Robinson," simpers Mikki. "I was just getting myself into the zone."

Miss Robinson smiles at her and I resist the temptation to throw up.

"Come on, then." She starts to head back towards the track, and I have no choice but to follow along with the others. "Everyone else is already in position."

"Not quite everyone," snorts Autumn, and Bea elbows her in the side.

We walk past the group of teachers clutching their travel mugs and up to the start line. I peel off to the side, ready to blend back in with the rest of Year Nine, when Miss Robinson screeches to a halt.

"Where is Hope Fisher?" she demands. "I saw her a few minutes ago so I know she's in school today."

"I think she was feeling ill, Miss," lies Autumn, the words oozing effortlessly off her tongue. "Eden – didn't you tell her to go and see the school nurse?"

I tense. What I want to do is to pretend I haven't heard,

to keep walking, past the track team who are all standing together ready to cheer each other on, and into the crowd.

Miss Robinson has other ideas. "Eden? Is this true? Is Hope unwell?"

I pause and then turn slowly to face her, keeping my gaze away from the Glossies.

I can either go along with whatever game Autumn is playing or tell Miss Robinson the truth about what they've done to Hope.

I need this to be over.

"Yes, Miss. She's got cramps or something, I think."

"Oh, for goodness' sake." Miss Robinson throws her hands up in the air, as if this is the worst thing that she's heard all day. "Well, I need a replacement immediately." Her eyes roam over the Glossies. "Who would like to volunteer? Bea?"

"I would, Miss," says Bea, her voice earnest. "But I hurt my knee in bench ball last week. My mum wrote a note excusing me from sports – do you want me to get it?"

Miss Robinson shakes her head. "No need, Bea. How about you, Autumn?"

While the teacher's attention is diverted, I take the opportunity to back away slowly, focusing on becoming invisible again. If I can just make it to the stands, I can disappear in plain sight.

Three more steps and I'll be camouflaged in the mass of kids in PE kits.

Two more steps and this whole drama will be over.

One more step and—

"Eden should run in the race!" A voice rings out like a siren. "She's really fast – I've seen her."

I freeze. This cannot be happening.

"Eden McCoy!" Miss Robinson gives me a stern look. "Is this true? Can you run?"

I unfreeze and shake my head frantically as Riley steps forward to stand beside me.

"She's good," he tells the teacher. "Seriously. You should put her in to run instead of Hope."

"Stop talking," I mutter quietly. "Please, stop."

But Riley just turns to me and shoots me a big, reassuring smile. "You've got this," he says, nodding enthusiastically, like this is a wonderful opportunity for me. "Just give it a go, yeah? What have you got to lose?"

I blink at him, unable to form any words. And then Miss Robinson is in my face.

"You can run?" she barks, eyebrow raised in suspicion. "I wouldn't know this based on your lacklustre performance in PE lessons."

"Eden's a great runner," Bea chimes in – and when I look over at her I see that she's staring at me, head tilted slightly to one side. "She used to be, anyway."

"Well, then, this is your time to shine!" Miss Robinson ushers me forward and even though launching myself into the view of the whole school is the last thing that I want to do, I am unable to disobey her. "Pace yourself – it's two whole laps, remember, so don't go too fast too soon. I don't want the additional paperwork if you keel over."

I can barely process what's happening as she propels me on to the start line. Autumn and Bea scamper off towards the stands and Mikki takes her place beside me. While the other runners start stretching and warming up, I stand as still as a statue, trying to make my brain come up with a solution to this horrendous situation because there is absolutely, definitely no way that I can run in front of the entire school.

"So – this is going to be fun." Mikki shoots me a rare grin, which is way more terrifying than her scowl could ever be. "I always win the eight hundred metres, Eden – but I'm guessing you know that. Try to keep up, yeah?"

I close my eyes and try to breathe. If I have the slightest bit of interest in my own survival, then I will turn and run as fast as possible in the opposite direction.

"On my mark!" Miss Robinson appears at the side of the track.

Think, brain. Think.

"Get set!"

You can't do this. Not in front of all these people.

"Go!" The starting whistle sounds, and everyone launches forward. Everyone except me, whose feet appear to have melted into the ground, making me stumble, my arms flailing as I try not to fall.

"What's she doing?" yells a kid. "She runs like a girl!"

I hear laughter start to sweep through the crowd and I blink like a rabbit in the headlights, my heart thundering, looking over at the stands. And suddenly, there is Hope. One face among all the others, her eyes red from crying.

"Run," she mouths – and even though I can't hear her over the noise, it's enough. Somehow my feet unliquify and my legs start to move, slowly at first and then faster and faster until I'm charging down the track, the adrenaline in my bloodstream propelling me forward. It doesn't take me long to pass the first girl and then the second, and after that my body relaxes, settling into a familiar rhythm as I stop thinking and start doing the only thing that I'm any good at.

And the faster I run, and the more people I pass, the less I hear the scoffs and scorn so that by the time I've finished the first lap, there is only one person ahead of me and the world has become a blissful silence.

Now it's just me and Mikki. There are two hundred

metres to go, and I know this is the time to pick up the pace. I pump harder until I'm right behind her and then I settle my breathing, ready for the final push. A cry from the stands infiltrates through the sound of my blood rushing through my ears.

"She's right behind you, Mikki!"

Mikki glances back and the look on her face when she sees me, hot on her heels, would be laughable if it wasn't filled with utter threat. I slow slightly, reminding myself that I'm not here to compete; this is not about me beating Mikki. All I have to do is get to the end and walk away, without drawing any more attention to myself than I already have. The last thing I need is to bring the wrath of the Glossies down upon my shoulders. *Let Mikki win. It's a stupid race on stupid sports day.*

"Come on, Eden!" Another shout floats down on to the track. "Run, girl!"

I don't know a single person who would risk their reputation by supporting me, so I have to assume that it's some kind of joke.

And something snaps inside me. I'm sick of people like me always being the target for snide remarks and sniggering whispers. I'm sick of the Glossies always winning, always conniving to get their way, trampling everyone else in their path. I think of how powerless I have felt since that first day of Year Seven when Bea wrote me out of existence. I think of Hope's tearful eyes in the crowd, the way they bullied her into giving up before she'd even started. I remember the way I numbly allowed myself to bend to Autumn's power move, pretending Hope was unwell – as if the Glossies' dominance could never be questioned, as if going along with them was safer than standing up for what is right. I think about all the times it felt as if I had no choice.

But right now, I do have a choice.

My legs take over and I stop thinking, retreating deep inside myself to the place where nobody else exists; where it's just me and the track. The wind whistles past my face and my feet pound as I kick it up a notch – and then I'm gliding over the surface like a pebble skimming across a lake, oblivious to everything except how good it feels to be moving.

To take off.

To run like a girl.

Before I know it, it's all over and I'm doubled up on the other side of the finish line, dragging deep gulps of air into my lungs and revelling in the burn.

And it's only now, as sight and sound start to return, that I start to come to my senses. It's only now, as I wipe the sweat away from my eyes and see Mikki staggering over the finish line that I realize just how badly I have messed up.

In one reckless moment of reclaiming power, I've also reclaimed the one thing I have spent years avoiding: the spotlight.

"Eden McCoy!" shouts Miss Robinson in thrilled surprise, walking towards me with a plastic gold medal in her hands. "You won!"

As the kids in the stands start to roar, their laughter filling my ears, Mikki shoots me a look that makes my insides shrivel up.

"You won!" repeats Miss Robinson, hooking the medal around my neck.

She couldn't be more wrong.

Scared Like A Girl

It's ten o'clock in the morning and the shopping centre is starting to bustle with people. None of them are bothering me though – even the hardiest of shoppers clearly don't tend to crave a doughnut this early.

I perch on my tall stool behind the stand and attempt to look warm and welcoming, as dictated by Jimmy, my so-called line manager. Apparently, people are unlikely to purchase from someone who doesn't have a sincere, heartfelt belief in the brilliance of the product they are selling.

"Sell it to me again," he says now, appearing in front of the stand. "Come on, Eden – your mum told my mum you're super reliable. We need to shift this stock today and I want to leave you on your own for a few hours."

After only a couple of hours of Jimmy's presence, it would appear that he has many annoying qualities, but training me using customer service role-play has got to be the worst. But if I can't make this trial shift at Delicious Doughnuts work, then Melissa is going to take that as proof that I'm not ready for a job, so this is my best chance to earn money. Plus, I've only been here a couple of hours, but I already like the feeling of freedom I get from having something other than school and home to occupy my time. I'm not going to let anything jeopardize it. Including my natural aversion to interacting with other people.

"Excuse me." Jimmy is putting on his best "interested customer" face, which probably goes down like a charm when he's in his A level Theatre Studies class. "Please can you tell me about the products you have on offer today?"

I sigh but play the game.

"Certainly," I tell Jimmy, waving my hand expansively across the stand before launching into the patter he has been making me memorize since half-past eight this morning. "Over here we have the ring doughnuts and over here are the filled doughnuts. You can choose from a variety of fillings such as jam, custard and cream, and here at Delicious Doughnuts we have a cornucopia of toppings for your every whim, including Cinnamon Sensation, Apple Crumble, Strawberry Surprise and

Chocolate Crème." I pause to take a breath. "We also offer a personalized messaging service where, for a small and very reasonable fee, I can delicately hand-pipe a message to a loved one on top of a sugar-glazed doughnut ring."

This is a big, fat lie. Despite my attempts, my hand-piping skills are not in the slightest bit delicate, and I am living in terror that someone will request a bespoke doughnut during my shift.

"Anything else?" Jimmy asks, giving me an encouraging nod. I try to think about what else I'm supposed to be saying.

"Our bestselling doughnut is the Toffee Fudge Delight," I offer, trying to make my voice less flat. "And it is, indeed, a delight."

Jimmy shakes his head, snapping instantly out of *interested customer* character and back into *narked-off boss*.

"You forgot to mention the special deal," he snaps. "The once-in-a-lifetime, get-it-while-it-lasts, buy-two-get-the-third-free deal." He waves his hand in my face. "Come on, Eden. Get with the programme."

"Sorry," I say, as he pointlessly rearranges the Peanut Butter Bliss. I'm not though. From what I can tell, Delicious Doughnuts has a "buy-two-get-the-third-free" deal every day. It's hardly what a person would call "once in a lifetime".

Jimmy finishes his display and then turns to me, pulling his striped apron over his head.

"I really have to be somewhere important ASAP," he says, fixing me with a stern expression that looks totally ridiculous on his seventeen-year-old face, especially because he's really not supposed to be leaving me alone on my first shift. "Have you got this, Eden? Can I trust you not to run the business into the ground while I'm gone? You need to remain super vigilant at all times and we'll rendezvous back here at twelve hundred hours."

Jimmy's second most irritating quality is his obsession with playing online war games and the way he seems to think that army phrases are compatible with doughnut selling.

I give him my best customer service smile and adjust the badge on my apron so that it's clear for all to see. *Eden McCoy. Doughnut Dealer.* It makes me feel like I'm part of some kind of baked goods cartel but if wearing this is what it takes to get Jimmy to leave me in peace, then I'll do it.

"I'll be fine," I tell him.

Jimmy places his apron underneath the stand and picks up his rucksack. "Don't forget that I'll be doing an inventory when I get back and if there's a single product unaccounted for then it's coming out of your wages. Got that?"

Jimmy's third most irritating quality is his refusal to

use the word *doughnut*. It's either the *product* or the *stock* or the *asset*.

"Got it." I wave him goodbye and watch as he dashes to the main entrance, where he's met by Chantelle, a gorgeous girl who I recognize from our sixth form. He slings his arm over her shoulders and says something that makes her laugh and then they're gone, up the escalator and away, for a few stolen hours of freedom.

Despite slight nerves about my first day on the job, I'm happy on my own, just me and the doughnuts, cloaked in the invisibility of the service industry. Here I can busy myself, trying hard to forget the events of yesterday that I cannot take back.

Given who clearly runs the account, it was no surprise that no post has appeared on *Woodford Whispers* about Mikki. I lurked online for a while last night, just in case, half-wanting to know if anything came up and half-wanting to live in blissful ignorance. But the lack of an "official" post hasn't stopped people talking about it.

A couple of daring jibes about Mikki's shock dethroning sprang up under the post about Mary. The comment "Still not the most entertaining race of the day" gathered almost a hundred likes. @footballrules added "Where's the video of the 800m??? Absolute scenes", and one reckless keyboard warrior asked, "Anyone else waiting for a replay of Mikki biting the dust? 👀". Luckily, I didn't spot anyone using my name. There was obviously no comment from any of the Glossies, or from the @trooth-hurts account, which fuels my suspicions that the anonymous account is owned by Bea. All I can hope for now is that something big and awful happens to someone else and fast, to draw all the attention away from sports day.

I am aware that thinking this does not make me a particularly nice person.

The first hour at the stand passes slowly. I check we have enough boxes ready to go and spend a thrilling five minutes shooing away a fly that takes an unhealthy interest in a Rainbow Sprinkle. At just after eleven o'clock I get my first customer and, while my heart beats like a muppet playing the drums, I get through the experience and serve up a box of three Chocolate Crèmes and three Strawberry Surprises without any kind of mishap.

It's almost twelve o'clock when they start coming in. First thing this morning it was mostly the pensioners, then the mums with young children and then only now, once they've had their Saturday morning lie-ins, do the kids from my school arrive. I guess I'd know this if I'd ever hung out at the shopping centre at the weekend. As they flood through the doors, a riot of shrieks and shoving and flicky hair, I reassure myself that everything is going to be fine; that I'm going to be even more invisible than I am at school behind the doughnut stand.

It isn't only Melissa I lie to.

It takes approximately thirty seconds for me to realize that things are not, in fact, going to be fine. A group of girls standing by the water fountain are looking in my direction, muttering furiously to each other and then one of them points right at me. I turn away and busy myself with organizing the paper bags. One of the girls has probably just asked the others where the best snacks can be bought, and that was why she was pointing over here.

A moment later, a group of boys from my year stroll past, and I am forced to look up. Jimmy has enforced upon me the need for constant surveillance to ensure that wayward teenagers don't pilfer the product, and I need to stay alert.

"All right, Eden?" One of them, whose name is Jake, or maybe Jack, looks at me and nods as he walks past, and I have to steady myself on the stand to narrowly avoid pitching head first into a pile of Blueberry Bursts. We have never exchanged so much as a word. I didn't think he even knew my name. Why is he greeting me?

I take a deep breath and try to pull myself together. I'm overreacting. This is not a thing.

And then the Glossies are strutting through the doors, walking through the crowds of people who instantly move out of the way. I just have to stay where I am, blend into the background like always and do my job. There is zero chance of them heading in my direction – Glossies don't eat carbs in public.

"Nice race, Eden!" calls a vaguely familiar voice, and it's probably my imagination but it feels like the entire shopping centre grinds to a halt. "You should definitely join track."

It's Riley, relentlessly cheerful as ever, waving as he walks by with Hope and another boy from the team. Hope gives me a small, grateful smile with her eyes, and then they head off in the direction of the sports shop.

I'm sure Riley was intending on being nice, but it's a niceness I could do without because once again he's shoved me into the spotlight. The Glossies have noticed me, and I can tell immediately that they are not happy. Autumn and Mikki are shooting me death glares that make my skin tingle. Mikki mouths something, and even though I'm no expert at lip-reading, it's fairly clear she's not sending me bright blessings.

Next to them, Bea stands very still, gazing at me. It feels awkward and I look away, but when I turn back, she's still staring. The hairs on the back of my neck stand on end, and I pray for Jimmy to come back and save me from whatever fate awaits me. Then Autumn grabs Bea's arm and, after throwing me one last threatening look, starts to guide her away. Bea hesitates for a moment and then lifts her hand, giving me a dainty finger wave. I don't know what that's supposed to mean but my stomach twists. It can only be a bad sign.

My phone beeps for the hundredth time this morning. Jimmy has made the personal phone use policy extremely clear and under normal circumstances I would stick to the rules. But these are not normal circumstances and Jimmy is not here. Sliding off the stool, I duck down behind the stand, pull my phone out of my back pocket and discover a whole load of new notifications from *Woodford Whispers*.

My heart leaps into my mouth. They're clearly feeling brave and have decided to risk the fury of Mikki. But it's even worse than that. They're tagging me.

@footballrules: Did you all see Mikki getting thrashed by **@just-eden**???!!! That girl can run! She made Mikki look like a snail.

@bonbon01: She left her standing! I thought the 800m was supposed to be Mikki's event? She always wins it.

@footballrules: That's cos nobody has the guts to beat

her... Lol.

@trooth-hurts: You want to be careful, saying stuff like that.

@footballrules: Makes you wonder what Eden is capable of, that's all I'm saying. Mikki better watch her back!

@alwaysautumn: Don't be ridiculous. It was a total fluke. Mikki would win if they raced again.

@kacey789: I mean, **@just-eden** was really fast. She's kind of come out of nowhere, right?

@daisychain: I've never even really noticed her before.

@ethan-is-king: It's always the quiet ones you have to watch!!

@trooth-hurts: That I agree with. Who knows who or what Eden will challenge next? Everyone should watch out. She's always seemed a little off to me.

It's bad.

It's really, really bad.

Suggesting I'm out to challenge anyone – let alone one of the Glossies – is the most dangerous rumour that has ever been spread about me.

Jimmy eventually returns, full of remorse for missing his own rendezvous deadline by a whole fifteen minutes, but I can't even enjoy his discomfort, because the worst thing that can possibly happen has happened.

For the first time since being ghosted in Year Seven, I have been seen. I am on the radar.

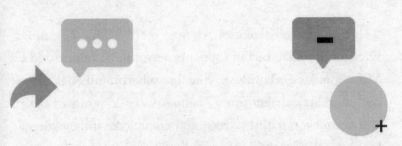

Act Like A Girl

I'm not going to lie. There have been times in the past where I've wondered what it might be like to be one of the sparkly people. Sometimes, in the very darkest hours of the night, I've wished I was someone different. Someone braver, bolder. Someone who just wakes up, gets up, eats some breakfast and then just – gets on with the day. A day spent laughing with a group of friends, texting a cute boy, messing around with a sports team, hanging out at the park or the shopping centre or hosting a giant sleepover. I've wondered what it would be like to be one of the girls who make everything look so freaking effortless.

But, of course, now the spotlight of attention has swung right on top of me and I would very much like for it to focus on someone else, as rapidly as possible.

It's a strange sensation, being seen. Don't get me wrong — it's not like I'm suddenly about to be nominated Most Popular Girl in Year Nine, but when I walked down the corridor this morning, people were looking *at* me and not *through* me. It's stressing me out. Like if they keep looking, they might figure out more about me than I want them to know. About the only thing keeping me sane is the knowledge that someone else will no doubt come along in a moment and be thrust centre-stage and I'll be able to retreat into the safety of the wings. Today's news is tomorrow's fish and chip paper, that's what Melissa says. I'm very much hoping that she's correct.

Anyway, until that time, the only option I have is to hide out in the girls' toilets at break. I can't avoid the Glossies in lessons but I'm doing everything I can to keep out of their way the rest of the time.

The door to the toilets opens and I freeze.

"Have you started on your essay for Mrs Lipscott yet?" I recognize the voice — it's Britt, a girl from my science class, and I relax slightly. It's not the Glossies.

"Are you joking?" her friend replies. There's a clattering sound and I imagine the contents of someone's make-up bag falling into one of the sinks. "God — that's the second eyeshadow I've broken this week."

"I don't even know what I'm going to do mine on,"

says Britt, and then the door to the cubicle next to mine slams shut. I lift up my knees, just in case anyone looks underneath to check who's in here, and pray for them to leave.

"Who cares?" The second girl turns on the tap. "We've got ages."

"Yeah — but she said that they were going to use it to decide which set we go into next year," calls Britt from the cubicle. "And my mum will go spare if I don't get invited to do triple science at GCSE. Have you got any toilet paper in there?"

The second girl doesn't reply and then there's a sudden banging on the partition beside my head.

"Hey! Can you pass me some toilet paper?"

Right. She's talking to me.

Quickly, I grab a handful of the nasty toilet roll that bears more resemblance to tracing paper and shove it under the partition.

"Thanks!" There's the sound of flushing and then the door opens and both girls start muttering quietly over by the sinks. I glance at my phone — there's only two minutes until the bell rings and I really need them to get lost so that I can leave here and get to my next lesson on time.

"Are you OK in there, hon?"

There's a tapping at my door.

"Yeah – you've been in there for ages. Do you need us to get a teacher?"

I've literally been in here for all of three minutes. What does a girl have to do to get some peace and privacy?

"I'm fine," I call back. "Thanks though."

"Eden? Is that you? Are you hiding?"

"Oh my God – has it already happened? Are you all right?"

The questions are fired like shots, and I know that I have no choice. Sighing, I stand up and unlock the door.

"I'm fine," I repeat. "Has *what* already happened?"

The second girl turns out to be Daisy, another girl from some of my classes, and she's staring at me with the bright, hungry eyes of someone who's spotted some drama.

"Everyone's talking about what happened on sports day – and about what's going to happen next."

I feign nonchalance and brush past her towards the sinks, trying to stop my skin from reddening. "I don't know what you're on about. I won a race – it's not a big deal."

Daisy makes a weird sound, something between a laugh and a snort. "Yeah, if you say so!"

Britt nudges Daisy with her elbow and then catches my eye in the mirror as I wash my hands. It's the kind of look that a person might give to someone who is unwittingly about to plummet off the edge of a cliff and there's nothing that anyone can do about it, except retreat to a safe distance.

"We just heard that Bea was looking for you, that's all," Britt says. "I'm sure you'll figure out what to do."

Daisy snorts again and then starts rapidly gathering up her make-up. "Well, no offence but if Bea is going to find you in here then I think we've got other places to be."

"No offence taken," I say weakly, trying to process what is happening.

As they head towards the door, Britt pauses at the last moment and turns to look at me.

"Maybe stick to well-populated places," she advises. "You know, just until they move on."

And then they're gone, leaving me stranded in the deserted toilets, wondering why on earth Bea is looking for me, and what she's going to do if she finds me.

The bell rings and I wait until the stomping of feet outside quietens. It's a fine line, balancing it just right so that I don't risk bumping into the Glossies while ensuring that I'm not too late for class, so I move fast, launching my way out of the bathroom and into the corridor.

There is nobody around as I rush to collect my English folder from my locker.

The pink envelope is the first thing I see when I open the door and I recognize her swirly, elaborate handwriting immediately.

I pause, staring at it for a moment, not wanting to touch it. I know, more than I've ever known anything in my life, that I don't want to read the contents; that once I've read the words there will be no unreading them. If I was strong then I'd rip it up and throw it straight in the bin without even opening it.

But I am not strong.

Putting my rucksack on the floor, I reach in and tentatively pick it up, holding it between my thumb and forefinger. I am running late for class but I don't leave. Instead, I lean against the lockers and, after checking that there is nobody around to see me, I open the envelope and unfold the piece of paper inside.

Monday 25th June

Dear Eden,

Wow, it's been a while, hasn't it? I'm going to get right to the point here because I've got a lot on right now and this whole thing needs to be dealt with quickly.

I know that you've seen by now what people are saying about what happened on sports day. Everyone has. You made a mistake, Eden. You shouldn't have beaten Mikki in the race. <u>When Mikki runs, Mikki wins.</u> Being the star of the track team is part of who she is at Woodford High. But you and I both know this isn't really about running or sports day. It's about reputations. And the thing about reputations is that they're fragile. They take time and care to build, and they can be destroyed in seconds. Mikki cannot be seen to fail. She especially cannot be seen to lose to - how did she put it? - "the wrong kind of person".

People talk about the butterfly effect - the idea that something as small as the flap of a butterfly's wings can trigger a chain of events that causes a tornado somewhere else in the world. One tiny change can alter the course of everything else.

You're the butterfly, Eden. You're the tiny change that nobody saw coming. You've disrupted the status quo and Mikki is not happy. She's convinced that the only way to put things back to the natural order of things is to remind

everyone of where you belong - which, in her
opinion, is out of the picture.

I swallow hard, trying to focus on what Bea is telling me. About the only thing I understand is Mikki's opinion of where I belong. She's not wrong about that. And if Bea is that bothered about Mikki's reputation then she should maybe stop posting inflammatory comments on *Woodford Whispers* under a stupid misspelt pseudonym.

So, we need a plan and thankfully, I've already
put something in motion. Mikki was getting ready
to exact all manner of humiliating revenge upon
you but I've managed to convince her there's
another way to rescue the situation. I explained
that if you joined us, you could be an asset to
our group instead of a threat. And it's exciting,
yeah? We get to hang out again, after all this
time. Let's put the past behind us.

I clench my jaw, feeling my teeth grind together. Put the past behind us? As if it's that easy, as if she didn't completely discard me?

The problem is, Mikki and Autumn need to see that you're worthy of joining us. I know - it's all a bit tragic, but, essentially, you can't become one of us without some kind of public trial friendship challenge. We'll call it a test.

This has got to be a wind-up. I glance around, checking to see if they're spying on me to witness my reaction, but the corridor is still empty. A *test*? I see that she wrote "public trial" at first before crossing it out, and I can't help sensing that feels closer to the truth. Like I'm framed for a crime, facing my prosecution. Or a witch about to be burnt at the stake.

The rules are easy. Just follow the instructions when you're given them. It's one tiny thing to prove to the girls that you can be trusted. It'll be a laugh! And then everything can go back to normal for Mikki - with the added bonus that this time, you'll be with us.

And one last thing, Eden. I've gone out of my way to give you this opportunity. Don't blow it, OK? Mikki is on the hunt and unless you want to be her prey you need to step up. I strongly suggest that you follow my lead.

That's the only way for you to stay out of the firing line.

 I'll talk to you properly once you've completed the test. And don't worry. The girls may hate you right now, but they'll come around once you've shown them you're one of us.

Bea xx

I shove the note back in the envelope and ram it deep inside my rucksack. As I trudge up the stairs, I feel a hysterical laugh bubbling up inside me.

It's hard to know what to focus on first – Mikki and Autumn's seething desire to humiliate me, Bea's sudden, oh-so-diplomatic invitation to be "one of them", and the looming, mysterious threat of what is about to be asked of me is a heady mix.

This truly is Bea Miller at her worst.

"Eden McCoy!" Mr Danes glowers at me as I finally enter my English classroom. "I warned you yesterday what would happen if you were late again. What's your excuse this time?"

I shrug and walk to my chair, ignoring the sniggers that follow me, just as I ignore my spluttering teacher telling me that I now have a demerit on my file and that I should consider myself lucky it's not more, after that little display of disrespect.

Sure, Mr Danes. I'm the luckiest girl in the world right now. That's exactly what they're going to write as my epitaph.

I sink into my seat and lower my head on to the desk.

There was absolutely no doubt in Bea's words; no hesitation or consideration about whether I, in fact, *want* to be "one of them". I seethe silently.

I can't even decide if it's a serious offer, or if the whole thing is one big joke designed to punish me for daring to embarrass Mikki. Regardless, I'm certain they'll issue me with this so-called "test". I think it's safe to say that whatever they instruct me to do, it won't be "a laugh".

I keep my head down, the noise in my head drowning out the sound of Mr Danes droning on about *Lord of the Flies* and misuse of power. Finally, the bell rings, signalling the end of the lesson and the room fills with the sound of chairs screeching across the floor as everyone starts to move. I wait until they're all gone and then get up slowly, my bones feeling like I've aged fifty years in fifty minutes.

I've worked so hard to avoid any kind of trouble or attention. I have no idea how to handle the fact that trouble and attention have found me.

★

Melissa is on a later shift and isn't due home until eight o'clock. I'm glad. I need some space to figure out exactly what I'm going to do and how I'm supposed to deal with this insane situation. After school, I pull on my trainers and go for a run to clear my head.

The more I think about, the more convinced I am that it's not a joke. I've heard whispers about this kind of thing before. Autumn joined our school at the start of Year Eight and there was talk of some initiation test that she had to pass before she could hang out with the Glossies. There was another girl, Piper, who was part of their group back then, but she got kicked out when Autumn joined. She left at the end of Year Eight and went to another school, presumably after the constant backstabbing on *Woodford Whispers* got too much for her.

After my run, I make myself a bowl of cereal and take it up to my room. It's small but it's about the only place that I can truly relax, safe in my solitude among my fairy lights and running girl posters and my wonderful prickly cacti.

Slumping on to my bed next to Midnight, I spoon cereal into my mouth. I need to calm the hell down and get rational about this.

"So, here's the thing," I say, around a mouthful of cornflakes. That's the good thing about having a cat as your best friend – they really don't care about social norms.

"Bea has sent me a letter saying that she wants to be my friend again, and she *claims* she doesn't know why we stopped hanging out in the first place."

Midnight looks up me, her eyes narrowed. I nod back at her in agreement. It was Midnight's fur that I drenched with my tears when Bea ditched me at the end of Year Six. Now that I've burnt through my anger on my run, some of that old sadness rises to the surface. I've noticed this before and it sucks – it's far easier to be angry than to be sad.

That party was all anyone had been talking about for ages. Jessie Perkins, the coolest, most popular girl in our year, was holding a "Goodbye Year Six" event at her house, one week before the end of term. There was going to be a disco and a chocolate fountain and a bouncy castle and a swimming pool and, if the rumours were to be believed, a tiny Shetland pony in the garden. She invited the entire year. Well, almost the entire year. Bea and Jessie had been involved in an argument over something ridiculous that seemed totally important back then – and Jessie refused to invite Bea to the party. So, when I received my invitation, I told Jessie I wouldn't go unless Bea had an invite too.

And that was fine. Bea told me over and over again that I was the best, most loyal friend in the entire world and that we'd have a much better time eating pizza and watching YouTube at my house than at Jessie Perkins' rubbish party. She even gave me a necklace with a tiny, silver star charm hanging from the chain, just like the one she always wore. I lapped up the glowing feeling of having made Bea happy and I wore that chain every single day.

Then it came to the night of the party, and Bea didn't turn up. I sat by the front window, waiting for her for an entire hour before my mother phoned Bea's mum. Mrs Miller told her that she wasn't sure how the miscommunication had happened but that she'd just dropped Bea off at Jessie Perkins' party.

And suddenly everything was not fine.

I spoke to Bea just one more time after that night. I needed to understand why. But all Bea said was that she'd made things up with Jessie, and that Jessie had invited her to go to the party after all. I asked her why she hadn't told me and given me the chance to go too, and she'd shrugged and said that as I'd spent so long trash-talking Jessie Perkins, she "didn't think it would be my thing".

Jessie Perkins was cool, and now, since the sudden friendship that bloomed between them, Bea was cool by association. But I was not. I was the kid on the outside — the one who wasn't at the party. The one who couldn't join in the conversations about dive-bombing each other in the pool, or dipping marshmallows into chocolate sauce, or jumping so hard that the bouncy castle deflated, or the stupid, pointless, cute miniature pony.

So, I took one step back, and then another, and before I knew it, I was standing with my back against the wall, hidden in the shadows. And nobody seemed to notice me go, not even my former best friend. The star necklace Bea gave me was consigned to the small wooden box on my desk, and I haven't looked at it since. Just like Bea hadn't looked at me until last week.

"I know," I tell Midnight, blinking rapidly and wiping my hand across my eyes. "She's a joke. But the facts remain. Apparently I am going to be given some kind of test."

I let Midnight lap up the rest of my cereal milk, then she stretches out beside me, resting her head on my leg.

"I've got a very bad feeling about this, Midnight," I tell her, stroking her sleek fur.

Bea has always loved a prank. One time in Year Six, when we were still friends, she brought a bag of googly eyes into school, and we stuck them all around the classroom. We thought we were so damn funny, and they were still turning up at the end of the school year. But I think I can assume that whatever my instructions are going to be, they won't be as mild, inoffensive or harmless as googly eyes.

I reach down to put my bowl on the floor and then grab my phone. Sports day was three whole days ago but

I'm still being tagged in random comments about how unbelievable it is that I beat Mikki and how everyone wants a "rematch".

Opening up *Woodford Whispers*, I scroll through various posts. One is slagging off a teacher nobody likes, and another spreads a vicious rumour about a kid in Year Eleven who hasn't been in school for a few weeks. According to *Woodford Whispers*, she is either a) pregnant, b) in prison, c) on holiday in Tenerife or d) any combination of the above.

And there it is. Like they were just waiting for me to come online. A ping and a number in the top right-hand corner, alerting me to a notification.

@trooth-hurts: So, I've heard a certain someone thinks they're above the rest of us all of a sudden.

@footballrules: Do you want to be a bit less cryptic? Or do we have to guess?

@ethan-is-king: Is there a prize?

@trooth-hurts: Maybe – but only for **@just-eden**. And only if she makes the right choice.

What? I haven't said a single thing that could make anyone think that this could be true. Is this Bea's twisted way of trying to make me do what she wants?

@footballrules: Love a bit of drama on a Monday evening.

@virtuallyviolet: Just because Eden beat Mikki on sports day doesn't mean she's better than anyone else.

@kacey789: Totally. And I'm not being funny, but I wouldn't go up against any of that group.

@daisychain: Me neither 🙈

@trooth-hurts: Well, let's hope **@just-eden** is as clever as you and does what needs to be done.

@bonbon01: If she's got any sense then what needs to be done is disappear back where she came from, am I right?

I quite clearly need some help here and while my options are fairly limited, I do know a few people who might be able to offer some semblance of guidance. I swipe to the

Cactus Club chat and start typing.

17:32 **@just-eden**: Hey. Anyone around? I could do with some advice.

17:33 **@TKOcactus**: Always. You know me – I'm always awake!

17:33 **@just-eden**: Yeah, you might want to do something about that. Sleep is kind of critical for human function, you know?

17:34 **@TKOcactus**: Critical-schmitical. What's up?

17:35 **@just-eden**: You know that girl I told you about? Bea Miller?

17:35 **@TKOcactus**: Yeah.

17:36 **@just-eden**: She wants us to be friends again.

17:37 **@TKOcactus**: Sweet.

17:39 **@just-eden**: Not sweet. I'd rather hang out with a clan of hyenas than spend a single minute with her and the Glossies.

17:40 **@TKOcactus**: So don't be friends with her. What's the big deal?

17:41 **@just-eden**: She wants me to do some kind of stupid test to prove my worth as a friend.

17:42 **@aussiekid**: What? That's messed up.

17:43 **@just-eden**: Right? I'm not playing her crappy game and she can't make me.

17:44 **@aussiekid**: This is the girl who rules your school, yeah?

17:44 **@just-eden**: 👍

17:45 **@aussiekid**: So she probably can make you. If she's that powerful. Or at least make your life hell if you don't do what she wants.

17:46 **@just-eden**: That's exactly it though. It's all about what she wants AGAIN. And now she's started posting anonymous comments on our heinous school gossip page and stirring everything up to make it even worse.

17:47 **@TKOcactus**: So what do you want?

17:47 **@just-eden**: I want her out of my head.

17:48 **@aussiekid**: Have you considered a lobotomy? I've heard they're very effective.

17:50 **@aussiekid**: Or perhaps visit a hypnotist and ask them to eradicate all thoughts of her from your brain?

17:51 **@TKOcactus**: So what are you going to do?

17:52 **@just-eden**: I don't know. But whatever it is, it won't be what she wants me to do.

17:53 **@TKOcactus**: Sounds like a solid plan.

17:54 **@just-eden**: Thanks – you've been as helpful as ever.

17:55 **@aussiekid**: We're here all week…

Trust Like A Girl

"Eden! Wait up!"

It's Wednesday, and the bell for fourth period is about to ring at any moment. I turn and see Hope racing down the corridor towards me. She gave me that small smile at the shopping centre on Saturday that in reality could have meant anything from "thanks for helping me out yesterday" to "nice doughnuts" but we haven't actually spoken to each other since sports day. I pause at the door to the changing rooms, unsure why she would want me to wait for her. We're not in the same PE lesson.

"I was asked to give this to you." She screeches to a halt in front of me and thrusts a lime-green envelope into my hand. I glance down and my heart does a small flip in my chest. Here it is. A second letter. I am truly blessed.

"Who asked you to give it to me?" I mutter, not looking her in the eye.

She hesitates for a brief second, but it's long enough to confirm what I already know.

"Sorry," she says and when I look up, her face is creased in sympathy. "I wanted to say no, but you know what they're like."

I nod. I don't blame her. I do know what they're like.

"What's going on?" Her voice is quiet, and she keeps glancing anxiously around the corridor. "What's in the envelope? They've clearly got a problem with you, Eden. What are you going to do?"

I don't reply. Instead, I join her in scouring the corridor, as if Bea and the Glossies might be about to leap out from the cleaning cupboard. She's making me even more nervous than I already was. This is why other people suck.

"At least you're fast!" she trills, in what I suspect is an attempt to add some levity to this dire situation. "You can just run every time they come close."

But I have a feeling I can't run away from this situation. The truth of it hits me harder than anything I have ever known.

"But seriously, what *are* you going to do?" Hope repeats.

I shrug and reply without thinking. "Nothing."

Hope's timid eyes widen and then she nods.

"That's actually very smart," she tells me, putting her hand on my arm. "Like those animals that freeze to avoid being detected. Those girls are like cats with a mouse, but they'll get bored if you don't give them anything to chase."

Before I can say anything, the bell rings, startling us both.

"I'm going to be late for class," Hope tells me, and with one last, sympathetic smile, she's gone.

I tear open the envelope quickly this time and scan the contents fast, like maybe it will be more palatable that way.

"McCoy!" The shout snaps me back into reality and I look up to see Miss Robinson marching down the corridor. "You've got three minutes to get changed and out on that track. And now I know how fast you are, I expect to see some commitment to this lesson. Hurry up!"

She opens the door to the changing rooms and gestures me inside. I have no choice but to ram the envelope into my bag and scurry past her into the fug of body odour and deodorant, the sound of thirty-four Year Nine girls all screaming to make themselves heard bouncing off the tiled walls.

Bea looks up as I enter but says nothing and I dump my bag at the other end of the changing room, hoping that the presence of Miss Robinson will keep things civil.

"Right – everyone who is ready can head out," the

teacher barks. "Anyone not out there in the next two minutes and thirty seconds will be coming back at twelve-thirty to complete their laps."

She stomps out towards the exit and the room quickly empties in a mass exodus of girls desperate not to lose their lunchtime. I pull on my shorts and try not to catch the eye of anyone walking past, which isn't hard because nobody appears to want to be anywhere near me. Trouble is contagious, they all know that.

Bea waits until everyone has gone and then strolls past where I am sitting.

"This is your chance," she says, as casually as if she's telling me the time. "Just wait until they've all gone and then do it, OK? Simple."

She squeezes my arm like she's giving me a pep-talk and leaves. I finish tying my laces and then pull out the envelope again. The letter is crumpled after being hastily shoved back into the envelope, but the words are still loud and clear.

To: Eden
Target: Kacey
Test: Hide her school uniform in the
      showers during PE
Time: Wednesday 27th June

I'm not sure what I was expecting from my test, but it wasn't this. I don't know what Kacey has to do with anything – although I have seen her popping up on *Woodford Whispers*, generally being given a bit of a hard time. But regardless, my imagination already conjured much more horrifying potential challenges than this. If anything, it's a bit pathetic. What are we, five-year-olds? Nobody is going to be the slightest bit amused or entertained by me hiding Kacey's clothes and it'll take her all of thirty seconds to find them. The whole thing is ridiculous, and clearly designed to make me look weak and biddable. If I do this, then the joke is utterly on me – which is probably the purpose, of course. And I have no intention of being their puppet.

My legs start to tingle but I grit my teeth and resist the urge to run. From now on I'm dealing with my problems a new way. Hope said that doing nothing was smart, and I don't know if she's right but I do know that I need to do something different. Instead of flight, I'm going to freeze, just like a squirrel or a rabbit when confronted with an intimidating predator. I'm going to stand still, let it wash over me and wait it out. I'm not going to do what Bonnie said and disappear back to the shadows where I came from – I'm going to try and disappear in plain sight.

Before I can even think about talking myself out of it,

I walk across the room and stuff the envelope into the top of Bea's rucksack. It's the closest I can get to telling her I won't play her game without actually saying the words. Then I head outside to join the rest of the class on the track, trying to convince myself that when the mouse stops running, the cat will move right past it and start stalking something else.

Bea catches up with me halfway round the first lap.

"Did you do it?" she asks, already out of breath. "Is it mission accomplished?"

"No." I keep running.

Please get the message.

Please leave me alone.

"So, what are you waiting for? Everyone's out here — you can sneak back in and get it done!"

I should just keep my mouth shut. I'm silent for ninety-nine per cent of the average school day. I should just keep running and pretend she doesn't exist, just like she did with me.

"What's your problem with Kacey anyway?"

Way to go, Eden. Excellent job of staying quiet.

"Oh, Eden." Bea drops to a jog, and I reluctantly slow down so I can hear her answer. "It's not about *Kacey*, is it? It's about you."

I shake my head. Of course. Kacey is just collateral. "I'm

not doing it." I can feel my heart pounding in my chest, and it's not got anything to do with the exercise.

"You're making a mistake." Bea's voice holds a clear warning. "I'm trying to help you. You don't want to see what happens when Mikki has it in for a girl. If you do this, you're showing everyone that you're one of us."

I slow further and meet her eye. "And what if I don't want to be *one of you*?" My mouth is moving even though my brain is screeching at it to shut the hell up.

Bea raises her perfectly sculpted eyebrows. "So, you'd rather be a loner than hang out with us? Is that really what you're saying, Eden?"

"Y-yes." My voice wobbles, like the traitor that it is. "And before you say it, I don't think I'm *better than you* or *above the rest of you*, so you can stop spreading nasty rumours about me online, please."

Bea glances around, like she's checking nobody can hear us, then reaches out to touch my arm. She's changing tack. "Look. I know things haven't been great between us, but it'll be different from now on. We'll have so much fun – like old times, but with all the amazing perks of being the most popular group in school. Surely you want friends again, Eden?"

Why is she trying to persuade me? Why does it even matter to her?

And then the penny drops. I remember what Bea said about the butterfly effect, about the fragility of reputation. It's power games, all of it. Now she's stuck her neck out and persuaded Mikki and Autumn to test me, she can't fail. She needs to prove to them that she was right – and I'm not playing. The feeling gives me a tiny but much-needed boost of courage.

I shrug her off me and shake my head. It's all the response she needs, and her face falls.

"Well – just remember I tried to help you, OK? None of this is on me – you're bringing it entirely upon yourself."

I open my mouth again to tell her where she can shove her help, but then decide my feet can do the talking far better than my voice can right now. As I grind to a halt and watch Bea sprint away to where Mikki and Autumn are waiting, I can only hope and pray that doing nothing is going to be enough.

The forty-five minutes of PE are over too quickly. Miss Robinson blows her whistle and sends us all back to the changing rooms, where the sound of sniggering hits me as soon as I cross the threshold. My skin prickles with a familiar sensation of paranoia. I'm no stranger to being whispered about but this feels different. By the time I enter the changing room the sniggers have turned into full-blown raucous laughter, the air fizzing with expectation, and my heart is in my throat. I keep my eyes fixed ahead and walk across to the bench, thirty-four pairs of eyes following my path as I open my bag.

"Very funny." I try to keep the tremor out of my voice. "Where are my clothes?"

The laughter stops abruptly, and nobody will meet my eye. I stand up and realize that the chortling and hilarity has been replaced with the sound of running water.

My head whips round to look at Bea. She's standing in the corner of the room with Mikki and Autumn, releasing her hair from its ponytail and letting it cascade across her shoulders while her face radiates such fake innocence that there can't be a single person in the room who is unaware that this is her doing.

I know exactly where my school uniform is.

Cheeks burning, I have no option but to walk over to the shower area, which is unused and neglected but apparently still functional. I'm braced for what I'm about to discover but still, the sight of my school skirt, jumper and shirt lying in a puddle of tepid, musty-smelling water is quite a shock.

This isn't fair. My test said nothing about drenching Kacey's clothes. I was just supposed to hide them.

Frantic whispering and a few snorts of muffled awkward laughter start up again as I turn off the shower and gather my soaked clothes. To my horror, when I turn I see several phones pointed in my direction. I ignore them, even though my pulse is racing, and will my face to stay neutral as I walk back to the bench, leaving a dripping trail of humiliation behind me.

"Kacey!" cries Autumn, in mock outrage. "I can't believe you turned the water on poor Eden's clothes. That's awful!"

I lift my head and stare at the girl whose clothes I naively spared from a lesser fate. She flushes and looks away, towards the Glossies.

"But you said that I should—" she starts before Bea interrupts her.

"It's kind of funny though, right?" She starts giggling and the tension in the room instantly dissolves as everyone rushes to laugh with her. Bea can command the vibe of any room at Woodford High. "And no real harm done, hey, Eden? You can just go to lunch in your PE kit."

I glance down at the tiny running shorts and fitted top that the PE department insists all the girls wear in the summer months and try to suppress a shudder.

"No snitching, yeah?" says Kacey. "It was just a joke."

"What's she supposed to say to the teachers about why she's not in uniform though?" Mikki's voice is fake-thoughtful as she looks at Autumn and I brace myself for the double act that is about to come.

"She can just tell them that she's men-stru-at-ing," Autumn suggests, sounding out the word as if it's rude, "and that she's had a little *situation*." She gives a snide smile as the room erupts into hysteria. If the whole soaking-wet-uniform situation was funny, then the idea of anyone confessing to being on their period is the goddam hilarious cherry on top. Last year, a girl in my art class had a slight leakage accident that resulted her being called Red for an entire six months. It might be a completely regular, monthly occurrence, but it seems being on your period is still something that needs to be hidden unless you want to be ridiculed.

"What's going on in here?" yells Miss Robinson from the doorway. "I've got lunchtime gym club in three minutes so hurry up and get moving."

It breaks the spell. Everyone launches themselves into action while I do my best to wring the wetness out of my clothing. Britt silently hands me a plastic carrier bag which is the kindest thing anyone has done for me in ages – then scurries away after being treated to a seriously dirty look from Autumn as she glides past, her stupid squirrel and acorn folder clutched to her chest as if it contains state secrets. Which isn't out of the question. As well as all of her schoolwork, that folder probably holds more gossip and ammunition than TMZ.

Mikki waits until most people are ready to go before issuing her final strike.

"Kacey! Sit with us at lunchtime, yeah? That's cool with you, Bea — yeah?"

Bea glances at me and then nods.

The message is loud and clear. I failed my test and the strike against me has been approved and validated. But at least it's over. They've had their revenge and I've been punished for daring to beat Mikki on sports day.

I wait until the room is empty and then pick up my rucksack, ready to ram the carrier bag and its soggy contents to the bottom.

The crumpled lime-green envelope is lying neatly at the top and, even though I know I shouldn't engage, I can't help myself. The word Failed has been slashed across the writing in red pen but that's not what scares me. It's the note written at the bottom, also in red.

> Don't worry — you've got a second chance. Date of next challenge to be confirmed. You've got this, girl!

I was wrong before. This is far from over.

This is just the beginning.

Smile Like A Girl

"Eden! Come and set the table, please. Supper's nearly ready."

Her voice floats up the stairs, under the crack between my firmly closed door and the carpet and into my room.

I do not want to set the table. I do not want to eat. I do not want to make small talk with Melissa. Most of all, I do not want to leave my room.

18:12 **@just-eden**: I knew there would be stuff online. There always is if anyone does something even a tiny bit embarrassing.

18:13 **@aussiekid**: Totally. Our school had a kid go

viral cos someone filmed him popping his spots in the school bathroom.

18:13 **@TKOcactus**: Why did he think that was a good idea though?

18:14 **@aussiekid**: Right? Don't put yourself in a position where you can be shamed like that.

18:15 **@just-eden**: Erm – it's not that easy. Not when it's happening to you.

18:16 **@aussiekid**: Sorry, Eden. I didn't mean it like that. What have they put online?

18:16 **@just-eden**: Photos. I guess I should be thankful there isn't any video footage.

18:18 **@TKOcactus**: There you go then. That's not so bad. Also – they're idiots.

It *is* bad.

The photos they've posted on *Woodford Whispers* are close-ups. One photo shows me looking like I'm about to start sobbing, which isn't fair because I managed not to cry until I got outside the school gates. A creepy old man coming out of the newsagent's told me to "*cheer up love, it might never happen*" and "*people will like you better if you smile*".

But if the photos are grim, the comments are worse.

@bonbon01: Looks like Eden is trying out for a triathlon but forgot it's her that needs to get wet, not her uniform!

@footballrules: Why are her clothes soaked? Did she wet herself?

@trooth-hurts: Look at her FACE!!! Priceless #teammikkiforever

At least I have my Cactus Club chat:

18:20 **@aussiekid**: Shall we distract you by talking about the orange spot problems on my cactus?

18:21 **@just-eden**: They won't stop commenting on the post. I don't know how to stop it.

18:22 **@TKOcactus**: You can't stop it. I'm sorry. It sucks, I know that.

I flick back to *Woodford Whispers*. The comments are still rolling in. Mostly streams of laughter emojis, with a sprinkling of grimaces and embarrassed faces. I spot one vomiting icon too. But some people are using their words.

Cringe! She looks like she's going to actually cry.

Is this the girl who won the 800m? 👀

Not the face of a champion 😆

"Eden! I called you ten minutes ago!" My mother's voice has an impatient edge.

I close the chat without signing off and put my phone in my pocket. Then I stare at myself in the mirror, making sure that my face isn't portraying how I'm really feeling. Running my hands across my cheeks, I blink a few times before taking a deep breath and walking downstairs. Warm, delicious smells hit me as soon as I step into the kitchen and for some reason it makes me want to cry again.

"How was your day?" Melissa asks, as I grab the knives and forks from the cutlery drawer. "Anything exciting happen?"

I wonder what she'd do if I actually told her. Maybe I should. Maybe I should tell her that my clothes were deliberately soaked, and I had to spend half the day in the school nurse's office, pretending to have a headache that was *just* bad enough to avoid being sent to class but not so bad that they'd insist on calling home. Perhaps I should tell her that the whole school now have access to photos of me being brought low and are commentating freely. I could tell her that today was bad but that tomorrow promises to be worse.

"It was a tricky shift today," she continues, before I can say anything, and I notice how tired she looks, dark circles beneath her eyes. "I'll spare you the details but I'm glad to be home with you, put it that way."

She bends down to pull a pasta bake out of the oven and I see how tense her body is, how taut her shoulders. When she straightens up, she winces slightly although I don't think she even knows that she's doing it. She catches me looking and gives me a big smile and I swallow down the words. She's got enough to deal with at work, and being the only adult in the house doing the job of two. She needs me to be OK.

"School was fine," I tell her, passing her a plate. "Nothing exciting happened because nothing exciting ever happens."

"Perhaps that's not the worst thing." Melissa piles my plate high with pasta and tomato sauce. "Sometimes *exciting* can be more hassle than it's worth."

She has no idea how right she is.

We sit down opposite each other at our little kitchen table, and she starts telling me some long-winded story about Joyce and her new air fryer.

I nod half-heartedly.

"Although, like I said to her, it might be a bit of a hassle to make your own, but at least she knows exactly what's in them and—" She breaks off and gives me a pointed look. "Do you need to get that?"

I shake my head.

"No."

My phone pings again and I pull it out, cursing myself for not silencing it before I came downstairs.

"Eden?" She puts down her fork and rests her chin on her hands. "Is there something that you want to tell me?"

And this is the moment. I could tell her about what happened.

"Is someone trying to contact you?" she asks, her eyes sparkling. "Is it a *boy*?"

And the moment is gone as quickly as it arrived.

"It's not a boy, Melissa," I snap, and then I remember that I'm supposed to be trying to make things easier for her. "I mean, it's a lot of boys. And girls." I take a breath and start again. "It's just a few kids from school."

My mother picks up her fork and gives me an approving

smile. She is almost as obsessed about the subject of my social life (or lack thereof) as she is about my academic prowess (or lack thereof). At least she hasn't attempted to throw me a party, since our epic argument over the last one.

"It's good to have friends," she says. "Maybe you could invite a few of them back one day? I'd love to meet them."

I dig as deep as I possibly can and smile back, and on the table my phone vibrates with yet more judgement.

I eat quickly and, once the washing up is done and she is settled in front of the television, I make my escape. There are so many comments I can't read them all, but the general consensus seems to be that a) I am a loser and b) I probably had it coming. I scroll through, feeling confusion and despair swirl together in the pit of my stomach. I don't even know who most of these people are, but some of the comments sound so *angry*. Like they've been waiting for me to get my comeuppance for a while.

Eventually, when I can't take any more, I turn off my phone and bury it in my sock drawer. It's dark now and I heard my mother trudge tiredly to bed half an hour ago. But I can't sleep, and I can't think about anything else, so I turn off all the lights and sit on the floor, my knees pulled up to my chin. Midnight glares at me moodily from the end of my bed. She knows I'm not following my usual routine but I ignore her, instead staring at the closed drawer as if it contains a dangerous creature that is waiting for me to relax before it makes its move.

Nyctophobia, a fear of the dark, is one of the most common phobias, right up there alongside a fear of heights, circus clowns and being alone. Apparently, it's some evolutionary thing that stops us from becoming victim to predators and whatever other scary things might be lurking out of sight. I don't wish to minimize anybody else's life experiences but seriously, of all the things to be phobic about, fearing the dark has got to be the most ridiculous.

As far as I'm concerned, in the dark, you may not be able to see, but you also can't be seen. And if you can't be seen, you can't be targeted. You can be left alone.

I look around my dark little room, which up until now has felt like a safe space, and then I crawl across to my sock drawer and pull out my phone. When I turn it on I have sixty-four new notifications and one new message from someone called @trackstar09. I click on the icon and open it up, blinking in the harsh light as I see the captain of the track team's profile picture on the screen.

22:13 **@trackstar09**: Hey! How're you doing?

I am too tired to even bother trying to make sense out of this. Riley probably sent it to the wrong person. Everyone who's been commenting on *Woodford Whispers* has been doing me the favour of tagging me, just to make absolutely sure I see all their kind and generous opinions. Maybe he clicked on my name by mistake instead of one of my tormentors when he was scrolling through the comments. Maybe it's meant to be some kind of sarcastic joke.

I put my phone on charge and then drag myself to the bathroom, where I splash some water on my face and clean my teeth. The person looking back at me in the mirror looks a complete mess and I force my features into a smile, spending a few moments going from slack-faced to beaming grin and back again. If I'm going to get through this in one piece, then I'm going to have to perfect the art of showing the world that they cannot hurt me.

And apparently the best way for a girl to do that is to smile, smile, smile.

Lie Like A Girl

Jimmy is on one today. He's been talking non-stop since I got here while glancing over at the main entrance every five seconds. I determined in the first two minutes of my shift that he and his on-again-off-again girlfriend are off again and so I've been letting his prattle wash over me and focusing on getting through the next four hours with as little drama as possible.

However, after the new envelope that was delivered at the end of school yesterday, I am aware that this is entirely wishful thinking.

A girl can dream.

When I went into school on Thursday there were the usual sniggers and whispered comments. But I had my headphones clamped over my ears and my music turned up. On Friday, I sat in all my classes with only minimal smirks and snide comments muttered in my direction. I was starting to wonder if I was going to make it to the weekend without any further stress.

They waited until I was walking down the corridor, the main exit firmly in my sights. Then Autumn appeared by my side, like an ethereal being magicked into existence. She pulled the purple envelope out of her ever-present folder and thrust it at me before I could really register what was happening. You have to hand it to them for their excellent sense of dramatic timing, I'll give them that.

"Customer," Jimmy hisses now, and I stop yawning and direct my brightest smile towards the family who have materialized in front of the stand.

"Welcome to Delicious Doughnuts! How may I be of service today?"

I have politely tried to tell Jimmy that this is a ridiculous thing to say. *How may I be of service?* suggests that I am offering a plethora of choices and may be called upon to address a variety of needs – not just shove a doughnut in a bag and hand out change from a fiver. He's having none of it. Apparently, the entire Delicious Doughnuts franchise has a script that should be followed with as much fidelity as if we are appearing in a West End production of *The Lion King*.

The Tannoy system which pumps music into the shopping centre switches to a new song and suddenly I am not sitting in the food court, waiting to flog doughnuts to shoppers. Instead, I am standing at the side of my primary school hall, laughing and cheering as Bea leaps on to the makeshift stage and grabs the karaoke microphone. We'd been daring each other to volunteer for the whole evening and, just as the school karaoke-disco was about to end, she plucked up the courage and dashed onstage. She'd chosen an upbeat song which was pitched far too high for her, but she didn't care – she opened her mouth and went for it while I whooped and whistled and filmed the entire thing on my new phone. I still have that video and I can still remember the joy and excitement of just *being*.

Being with my best friend.

Being happy.

Being blissfully unaware of the way she was about to betray me.

"Eden!" Jimmy hisses again out of the side of his mouth, and I realize the family are ready to order.

"What an excellent choice," I tell them, picking up the tongs and placing a Strawberry Surprise and a Toffee Fudge Delight in two separate bags. These kids don't look like the kind who can share nicely. "You all have a delightful doughnutty day!"

They wander off and I turn to Jimmy. "Is that definitely in the script?" I ask him. "It seems kind of – weird? And *doughnutty* is not actually a word."

He frowns at me. "Yes, Eden. Why would I get you to say it if it wasn't in the script?"

He has a point. I'm paranoid. Presumably not *everybody* is out to make a complete fool of me.

"More customers at eleven o'clock," he mutters. "ETA in five seconds."

This boy needs to rein back on the video games.

"And don't forget to push the Luscious Lemon this time, OK?"

"Fine," I murmur, picking up the tongs from the tray in front of me. "Welcome to Delicious Doughnuts! How may I—"

The words freeze in my mouth as I look up and see the three people standing in front of me.

It's happening now, then.

"—be of service?" completes Jimmy, leaping in like a consummate professional. "We have a wonderful range for every taste and palate and you're in luck because, for today only, we have an amazing, once-in-a-lifetime, buy-two-get-the-third-free deal!"

They turn their gaze on my boss, their smiles as bright as the sunshine and just as deadly if he were to get too close. He grins back, and then a movement over by the main entrance catches his attention.

"Today's special is the Luscious Lemon," he says. "My assistant will tell you all about it."

"We'd like a box of nine doughnuts," simpers Autumn, her voice more sugary than any of the products on my stand.

"I'll be right back!" Jimmy tells me, tearing off his apron. "I've just got to do a thing." And then he's gone, AWOL, and I spot Chantelle loitering by the water fountain.

"We'd like a box of nine," snaps Mikki, just in case I didn't hear the first time. "Hurry up, there's a good girl."

I say nothing. I am a possum, playing dead. They'll give up and go and it will all be fine.

"Hmm, what to choose?" Autumn steps forward, tapping one immaculately painted orange nail on a Blueberry Burst.

"Please don't touch the merchandise," I whisper, and it's a shame that Jimmy is currently deep in conversation with his apparently on-again girlfriend because he'd be super-proud of me right now. If my voice was loud enough for anyone to hear, that is.

"Bea?" Mikki shoots her a look. "What flavour do you want?"

Bea gazes at the doughnuts and then shrugs. "I don't care."

Mikki frowns. "You have to choose one. It's *buy-two-get-the-third-free*, remember?" She mimics Jimmy's enthusiastic expression which makes me want to lean over and ram a doughnut right in her hole, because it's one thing for me to ridicule Jimmy in my head, and something else entirely for them to mock him. "We each choose a flavour – that's what we agreed."

"Fine." Bea gives Mikki a look. "I'll have that lemon one."

"And I'll have toffee and Autumn will have rainbow," says Mikki. She stares at me. "We want three of each, *please*."

"Box them up!" adds Autumn, clapping her hands excitedly like a little kid.

I shake my head and Autumn stops clapping.

"I'm not doing it," I tell them. "Please just go."

"Are you sure you want to do that?" asks Mikki. "You got the note, right?"

She's not really asking. Mikki and Bea were standing on the other side of the corridor when Autumn presented the envelope to me, watching my every move.

"I got the note," I say, my voice low. "And I'm asking you to leave."

"It's just one tiny test," trills Autumn.

"Just do it, Eden," says Bea, finally looking at me.

I gulp, but I'm not going to give them the satisfaction of seeing me wobble. "No."

Mikki raises her eyebrows. "Fine." She turns to Bea pointedly. "I told you she'd bail."

Bea stares right back at Mikki, who gulps slightly. "You'll get your doughnuts, OK? Chill out. Don't you trust me?"

They hold each other's gaze for a long moment, and then Mikki looks away.

"Of course I do," she murmurs. "Just as long as Eden understands the rules, yeah? As long as she knows what will happen if she even thinks about telling anyone about this little game – this can all stop being a bit of fun like *that*."

She clicks her fingers, and my stomach drops at the unsubtle warning.

Autumn laughs. "This is so great, right? And we've got loads more ideas to keep this going if you don't complete the test this time, so don't worry!" She pats her shoulder bag, and I see the ever-present folder sticking out of the top.

She links one arm with Bea and the other with Mikki before shooting me a bright smile. "Now, don't say we didn't give you a chance!"

I genuinely cannot tell if Autumn truly thinks this is all

a merry lark, or if she's play-acting her sickly, saccharine performance. I've always thought Mikki was the more terrifying of the two, but I'm starting to think that Autumn might be even more dangerous.

They turn as one, like a three-headed, six-legged creature and sweep across the food court.

"And you all have a delightful doughnutty day!" I mutter quietly.

I watch as they glide up the escalator, their laughter hanging in the air like mustard gas, and then I sink back on to my stool and wipe my slightly sweaty hands on my apron. Mikki called it a game and that's fine. I'm just not going to play. They came, they saw, but they did not conquer. I stood my ground; I did not run away, and they left.

My tactic is working. I just have to stay strong until they get bored.

The next thirty minutes are busy and, while I try to keep a lookout for the Glossies, I'm distracted by a constant stream of customers. I sell out of the Luscious Lemon, which I'm excited to tell Jimmy about if he ever returns, and have finally cleared the small queue which built up when a lady requested that I hand-pipe her son's name on to a Sugar Glaze. I totally messed it up and then she refused to buy it, so I had to fob her off with a Chocolate Crème.

It still tastes delicious though, even if I do have to crouch on the floor behind the stand to enjoy it.

The sound of someone sniffing gets my attention and I hurriedly wipe my mouth clear of the evidence before standing and launching into my well-rehearsed spiel.

"Welcome to Delicious Doughnuts!" I say, re-energized by the sugar. "How may I be of service?"

"We'd like three toffee, three rainbow and three lemon, please." Britt and Daisy are in front of me. I glance around but there's nobody else from school in the food court. A box of nine doughnuts costs more than most kids can afford to spend and I know that this is wrong. But I have no choice. I can't exactly refuse to serve them, just because I'm suspicious.

"We're out of the Luscious Lemon," I tell Britt, who placed the order.

She looks at Daisy, who shrugs.

"Get chocolate instead," she says. "Chocolate is good."

I pull out a box, carefully placing each doughnut into position. Daisy is jiggling from one foot to the other and now I can smell threat in the air. Not that I can do anything about it except let this whole thing play out.

"Here you go," I say, handing Britt the box. "That'll be—"

But I don't get to tell her how much it will be because

she's opened the lid, taken out a Chocolate Crème and squished it right into my face.

It is fair to say that of all the things I was anticipating, I absolutely did not see this coming. The whole thing takes me by surprise and I stagger back, my eyes closing instinctively. Which means that I don't see the second doughnut – the Toffee Fudge Delight – as it makes contact with my cheek. My eyes flash open and I bring my hands up in defence, just a split-second too late to deflect the Rainbow Sprinkle as it is mushed into my forehead.

"No!" I shout, the shock giving my voice a surprising volume. "Stop it!"

Britt laughs giddily, like she can't quite believe what she's doing, and turns to look at Daisy who has her phone in her hand, filming.

"Doughnut attack!" Britt yells, turning back towards me, brandishing a Chocolate Crème in one hand and a Toffee Fudge Delight in the other.

I duck behind the stand, my arms crossed above my head to protect me from an aerial onslaught. I can hear both girls laughing and the sound of feet pounding across the food court.

When I tentatively raise my head above the parapet of the doughnut stand, I see them racing away, zipping between the other shoppers and dodging prams.

And then Jimmy appears.

"Eden? What is going on?"

Excellent. Almost as excellent as the tears springing from my eyes.

The attack.

The filming.

The deep and utter shame.

"Eden?" Jimmy prompts, staring at my sugary face in shock.

"They… They didn't pay for them," I admit shakily, pushing myself to my feet, wiping my hand across my face, which is hot with embarrassment. It comes back covered in icing sugar and a whole lot of sprinkles.

"I—"

"I know you're going to have to take it from my wages," I add, my voice flat. "I get it."

Looking very much out of his comfort zone, Jimmy reaches for a wodge of the blue tissue paper we use for wiping up mess and hands it to me. I focus on cleaning up my face, wiping away the tears along with the sprinkles.

"You do know how much a box of nine costs, right?" he asks awkwardly. "It's pretty much half your wages for today."

"I know," I mumble.

"Are you – uh – OK? What was all that about?" he

asks, but then we're both distracted by the sound of voices coming from across the shopping centre.

The Glossies are descending the escalator, chatting and laughing like they haven't got a care in the world. They reach the bottom and start walking towards us with the remaining doughnuts that Britt has presumably just handed to them. A Chocolate Crème for Bea. A Rainbow Sprinkle for Autumn. And a Toffee Fudge Delight for Mikki. I'd be marvelling at the hitherto unseen sight of the Glossies eating carbs in public if I wasn't so utterly devasted by what has just happened.

To: Eden
Target: Jimmy the doughnut king
Test: Give Bea, Autumn and Mikki free
      doughnuts
Time: Saturday 30th June

I refused their test and so once again, they've flipped it on me but changed the rules to make it one hundred times worse. Just because they can.

"That was delicious!" Autumn smacks her lips together.

"Hi, Eden!" calls Mikki, smirking at me as they waltz past. "You've got a little something on your face, hon." My hand flies up of its own accord, wiping away a missed splodge of icing before I can stop it. I want to tell them that I hope they choke, but I don't because I am unable to speak or think or do anything except stand here.

Bea just sails by, saying nothing. The queen doesn't have to say a single word. She just has to exist.

"Who are they?" Jimmy asks.

I stagger back to my stool and stare at the floor, trying to maintain some tiny element of composure.

Don't say we didn't give you a chance, they told me. And now I know the rules of their game.

Complete the test or be tested upon.

Do something to the target or become the target.

This isn't going to end until I either cross the battle lines and become like them – or I somehow withstand their attacks long enough for them to retreat.

"They, Jimmy, are the enemy," I reply. "And the terms of engagement have just been firmly established."

Talk Like A Girl

My breathing is all over the place. I've usually settled into a rhythm by now but I'm struggling today and even though I've been out for fifteen minutes, nothing is going right. My legs feel heavy, as if my veins are flowing with lead and not blood and my feet keep landing badly on the pavement.

I don't know what's wrong with me.

I totally know what's wrong with me.

Slowing to a walking speed, I give up and turn back in the direction of home.

The gates to the park loom large in front of me and I've taken the turn before I've really thought about what I'm doing. My mother will be home soon, and I haven't got the energy to pretend that everything is OK. The path divides into two and I head down the left-hand side, scanning the area to make sure that there's nobody here. The kids' play park is usually heaving with people, but it's past five o'clock on a Sunday and everyone has probably gone home for their tea. Apart from a dad, trying to manoeuvre a fractious toddler into its pram, the place is empty. I reach the swing gate and hold it open for the dad, who gives me an exhausted nod of thanks before pushing the pram through.

I wait until I'm sure they're not going to come back and then I wander over to the swings, sitting down and letting myself swing gently back and forth, trying to give my head chance to settle.

The video of the doughnut attack already had more than one hundred and twenty likes by the time my shift ended yesterday. *Woodford Whispers* was buzzing with hilarity about the entire thing, and some computer genius managed to create a photo collage taken from the footage, showing me in a variety of unflattering poses including a zoomed in image showing sugar strands scattered across my face like rainbow freckles. Kieran started referring to me as *Sprinkles* and by the time I went to bed last night, my actual name appeared to be obsolete.

Eden is dead.

Long Live Sprinkles.

I still had icing sugar in my hair when I got home. I have

never felt so small and out of control in my entire life.

But as bad as this latest humiliation is, the reason my brain is louder than a rock concert right now is the knowledge that this is going to keep happening. These are not pranks; I know that. The definition of a prank is *a trick that is designed to be funny but not cause harm or damage*. The purpose of the tests the Glossies are setting me is the opposite of that. I am being punished for defying them, and the entire objective is to humiliate and hurt me. My stomach twists with dread at going to school tomorrow.

My phone buzzes and I pull it out of my pocket, braced for whatever bile is about to aimed in my direction. I saw a post earlier on *Woodford Whispers* that showed a picture of my head photoshopped on to a doughnut body and the words "*Have a doughnutty day!*" scrawled underneath. I can't be one hundred percent certain who did it, but Bea is always being praised in our graphics class for her editing skills, so it was probably her.

The latest notification is not me being tagged in a new post though. It's another message from Riley.

17:23 **@trackstar09**: Hey, Eden. I just wanted to say sorry you're having a hard time & I'm really sorry if volunteering you for the race on sports day was the wrong thing. Hope you're doing OK.

I stare at the screen and try to process the words. I've never spoken a single word to Riley, but this is the second message he's sent. Maybe the first time wasn't a mistake or a joke, like I thought?

I type out a few words and then quickly delete them. It's probably better to say nothing. It could still be a trick. Riley seems OK but I don't know him.

I push myself off the ground and make the swing go a little higher, holding the chain with one hand and my phone with the other. What's the worst that can happen if I send a message back to him? Everyone is already laughing at me. One more thing isn't going to make any difference.

Letting the swing slow, I take a deep breath and then tap a response, hitting *Send* before I can change my mind. I've tried to reply with something that is succinct and not stand-offish; something that portrays me as being open to communication but also as a person who is not to be messed with.

17:29 **@just-eden**: Thanks.

Yep. Think I've nailed it.

His reply comes seconds later.

17:29 **@trackstar09**: How are you doing?

I slam my feet on to the floor, forcing the swing to come to a complete standstill. OK, so I'm really doing this? I'm going to have a message conversation with the captain of the track team.

Swiping across the screen, I scroll through his profile. There are a few photos of him and the rest of the track team, either hanging out at meets or mid-race action shots, and a couple of motivational quotes about running but he clearly isn't living his life online and there's not a lot of content. I like that. My own profile has a photo of the sun setting and a picture of someone else's dog. I don't like to give anything away and it seems Riley is the same.

Putting my phone back into my pocket, I grab hold of both the chains and push hard off the ground, driving the swing into action with my legs.

The swing arcs forward and I feel the wind on my face. *I could message Riley back.*

It hurtles backwards, flinging me into the unknown. *What's the point? I don't need anyone else. Plus, if he hadn't pushed me forward for the race none of this would have happened.*

Forward again, my body held in suspension as I reach the swing's zenith and hover for a perfect second. *He was trying to be nice. Maybe I don't have to do this on my own?*

And backwards, my stomach flipping over as the Earth's force pulls me back down. *Who am I kidding? Even if I do message Riley, it's not as if having one person to talk to is going to make this any better. And I already have the Cactus Club chat group.*

Backwards and forward, swinging higher and higher. In science last term, Mrs Lipscott taught us about Newton's first law of motion. She told us about pendulums and Galileo Galilei and gravitational constants. She spoke about inertia and how, in physics, it refers to the ability of an object to stay moving unless it is stopped by an outside force – but that the word is also used in psychology to imply that someone is maintaining the status quo or lacking the desire to change.

I am a pendulum, propelled by my own strength and gravity.

I have inertia – I can keep going for ever but I'm also stuck.

Sticking out one leg, I drag my foot on the ground, letting the friction slow me down.

And then I jump. I jump forward because sometimes a person has to make a change if they want things to be different.

I'm out of breath by the time I reach the garden gate, but it feels good. My run home was perfect – my feet hit all the right spots on the pavement and the rhythmic pumping of my heartbeat was louder than the thoughts in my head.

"There you are!" Melissa opens the front door, her face twisted in worry.

I straighten up, dragging air into my lungs.

"Sorry," I gasp. "I lost track of the time. Is it late?"

She glances at her watch and then shakes her head. "It's fine. I was just wondering where you'd got to. You didn't leave a note."

I wince and give her an apologetic look. I'm not allowed to leave the house without scribbling a message on the notepad on the fridge. It's the one rule that she insists on and I've never forgotten before. Then again, I've never been this preoccupied before.

"Sorry," I say again. "Were you worried?"

She steps aside, ushering me into the house and giving my shoulder a quick squeeze as I pass by.

"A bit," she confesses. "Does that make me an insufferable, overprotective mother?"

I shake my head and then bend down to unlace my trainers.

"You're allowed to be worried," I tell her. "Next time I'll leave a note."

"You'd better," she calls, heading into the kitchen. "By the way, I got you a present."

I kick off my shoes and follow her. My mother doesn't

do random gifts. I get something for my birthday and when it's Christmas, and maybe an egg at Easter if she's remembered to get to the shop in time, but that's it.

In the kitchen, she is pulling something out of her bag. She turns to face me, hiding whatever it is behind her back.

"Joyce and I saw this when we were on our coffee break," she tells me. "I wasn't sure if it was the kind of thing you'd be interested in. But then I told Joyce about all the running you do and how you only wanted trainers for your birthday, and she said that she thought you might like it. So, I took a chance." She hesitates for a second, the worried look back on her face. "It's nothing special or anything – I've probably made too much of a big deal of it now."

She removes her hand from behind her with an embarrassed flourish and presents me with a running magazine. "Ta-dah!"

I stare down at the front cover, which shows a young woman in shorts and a vest, launching herself over some moorland with the caption *"Don't Stand Still."*

"It's fine if you don't like it," she says. "It was just a thought. I can take it back and get you a copy of *New Scientist* if you prefer."

"I love it." I look up at her and for the first time in a long time my smile feels real. "Thank you. It's perfect."

"Right." She picks up an onion and starts peeling it. "That's all good, then. Tea will be ready in half an hour, so you've got plenty of time to shower and then set the table."

I nod, and then head upstairs. The shower always needs at least five minutes to warm up, but I don't need that long. I'm not going to overthink this. I'm going to send something out into the universe and see what comes back.

Putting the magazine carefully on my bed, I take my phone out of my pocket and send my reply.

18:12 **@just-eden**: Things aren't exactly great but I'm OK. Just been for a run which helped.

Once again, his reply comes quickly.

18:13 **@trackstar09**: Do you know why that thing with the doughnuts happened?

Of course Riley has seen the video and pictures, but it still stings to see him mention it.

18:14 **@just-eden**: Yeah. Cos some people are awful.

18:15 **@trackstar09**: I'm sorry.

18:17 **@just-eden**: It's not your fault. I just have the misfortune to have landed on the radar of the worst people at Woodford High.

I don't know what's come over me. I would never say this stuff to anyone in real life.

There's a pause, then:

18:19 **@trackstar09**: Hmm, a couple of them can be pretty awful, I agree. OK – so shall we talk about something else?

I exhale in relief. That doesn't sound like the words of someone who is about to grass me up to the most dangerous girls in school.

18:20 **@just-eden**: Sure. But I should probably warn you, my chat repertoire isn't exactly wide.

18:21 **@trackstar09**: Ha! That's OK. Neither is mine. But I can always talk about Netflix. Have you seen that show about the kids who all have different magical strengths and spend most of the time trying to kill each other?

18:23 **@just-eden**: Yeah, sure – deadly powers etc but I'd still rather take my chances with them than the kids at Woodford High.

18:24 **@trackstar09**: Imagine if the entirety of Year 9 suddenly got miraculous skills. I'd want to be able to move at warp speed. What about you?

"Eden!" My mother is yelling at me up the stairs. "Are you out of that shower yet?"

18:25 **@trackstar09**: It's an important decision, I get that. You can take your time to answer...

"I'll be down in a minute!" I shout back, throwing my phone on the bed and pulling off my running kit.

I grab a towel, then, just before I dash to the bathroom, I pick up my phone and tap out my reply.

18:27 **@just-eden**: Easiest question in the world. I'd choose invisibility, every time. No questions asked. That way nobody would ever see me fail.

18:28 **@trackstar09**: Hmm. That's very deep... But

then again, nobody would ever see you win, either –
have you thought about that?

18:29 **@just-eden**: I wouldn't mind having Wednesday
Addams' powers. Brilliant at everything with a few
psychic visions thrown in for good measure.

18:32 **@trackstar09**: I mean, now you mention it, I can
see the resemblance between you and Wednesday. If
she wore tracksuits, that is. You could really lean into
that look, Eden.

18:33 **@just-eden**: Lol. Only if you dress as Thing! Got
to go now. Bye.

18:34 **@trackstar09**: See you.

And I think about those words. I think that maybe, in
a small way, he does see me. The feeling is warm and
unusual, and it wraps me up, a bit like my invisibility cloak
used to do.

Throw Like A Girl

The third test arrives in a baby powder-blue envelope that reminds me of the trendy tracksuit that Bea posted a picture of herself wearing.

> To: Eden
> Target: Violet
> Test: Take her lunch
> Time: Monday 2nd July

Violet is on the basketball team and spends every lunchtime on the outside courts with her friends. She's never had an issue with me, nor I with her – but after the doughnut attack, I know none of that really matters. Either I take Violet's lunch or my own lunch will be sacrificed.

It's the Hobson's choice of lunchtime – humiliate or be humiliated. I get to choose.

It's a warm day but the canteen is still heaving with kids. I was complaining about the disgusting offerings from the school kitchen last night and when I woke up this morning, Melissa had surprised me with a lunchbox of food left on the kitchen table before she went to work. She must have got up extra early to make it. I will admit it made the beginning of a day I was dreading marginally better – until I read the contents of today's envelope.

I did briefly debate smuggling my lunch into B Block but our school has a zero-tolerance rule about food only being consumed in the canteen and, while I might be scared of the Glossies, I have no desire to spend the next week in after school detention with Mr Danes. I'm not part of the Cactus Club chat group for nothing, obviously. My plan is to hide in my usual corner of the canteen, eat fast and then attempt to find a new place to hide.

My plan is rubbish.

They approach me the instant I sit down, Mikki and Autumn standing guard while Bea sinks down opposite me. I pick up the carefully wrapped packet of sandwiches and try to look unbothered.

"Violet is outside," Bea tells me. "Her lunch is just lying next to her bag. It literally couldn't be easier, Eden."

For a second, I think about that. What if I did just get up and grab Violet's unattended lunch? Could all of this really be over? No more horrible posts on *Woodford Whispers*. No more streams of spiteful comments, no more corridor laughter and burning shame. For a moment, it's tempting. Really, really tempting.

But I don't want to take the food someone else is planning to eat. I don't want to make Violet feel the way I feel. And most of all, I don't want to give Bea the satisfaction of breaking me.

I put the sandwiches down and look up. "I saw on *Woodford Whispers* that Kieran thinks Violet is the hottest girl in Year Nine. Is that why you've chosen her?"

The words are out before I can stop them. My mouth needs to shut the hell up.

A flash of surprise crosses Bea's face as my comment hits home. Autumn sniggers and then slaps her hand across her mouth. Mikki glances across at her, her face scrunching up ever so slightly, but Bea is too focused on me to pay attention to whatever is playing out between her henchwomen.

"Listen, I'm trying to help you," she mutters, her eyes boring intensely into mine as she leans across the table towards me. "Just do the damn test, OK?"

I don't reply and after a few heavy seconds Bea sighs and stands back up.

"Do it," she says to Mikki, and then she turns around and sweeps towards the exit.

Mikki raises an eyebrow at Autumn but pulls out her phone and taps at the screen. I hear the pinging sound of a message being sent and then Mikki flashes me a hideous grin.

"It's your funeral," she tells me, smirking sideways at Autumn.

My legs jiggle under the table and I place my hands on my knees to stop them. I will not run. I won't give them the satisfaction.

I am solid.

I am unyielding.

I am still.

They both laugh and then turn to follow their queen, who is disappearing out of the door. I relax slightly. Surely if anything was going to happen then they'd stick around? There's no way they'd risk missing out on watching the test. Anyway, Violet is outside.

I stare down at my lunchbox and the food that my mother lovingly packed for me. I should text her and say thank you. There's no need to be such a miserable cow to her all the time. She's only absent a lot because she works so hard. And she only pressures me about my future because she's trying to make things better for me than they were for her.

I've just pulled out my phone when the doors burst open and a whole load of kids come flying through.

Violet is not outside. She is here, tangled up with the rest of the basketball team, all arms and legs as they run through the packed canteen, bouncing a ball between them, and turning the relatively calm hall into instant chaos.

"Throw it to me!" yells a boy and the ball sails through the air, over the heads of a table of Year Eight kids who squeal and duck.

"Now to me!" calls someone else and the ball is dribbled around a pile of rucksacks before being flung close to the table where the football boys are sitting.

"Pathetic!" shouts Kieran. "Let us have it if you want to see some real skills!"

The basketball kids jeer back at him and then one of them throws the ball with such force that Kieran has no choice but to fling himself on to the table or risk being smacked in the face.

"Tosser!" he screeches, as the ball rebounds off the canteen wall with a loud bang and straight into the hands of one of the girls.

"Come and get it, then!" she goads Kieran.

"Hold me back, man!" Kieran tells Ethan, who makes a half-hearted effort at hanging on to his arm. "I'm not kidding – hold me back."

The girl laughs and then throws the ball to Violet, who dribbles it between tables and towards the corner of the hall where I am sitting, completely stunned.

Violet comes close and our eyes make contact. A look passes between us that feels a bit like solidarity and for the briefest of seconds I think she might not do it. But then, in one fluid movement, she tosses the ball to one of her friends and leans down, grabbing my sandwiches in one hand and my apple in the other.

"What on earth is going on?" shouts Linda finally. "Get that ball out of here right now!"

"I've got it!" calls Violet, waving her spoils in the air. "Let's go!"

She sprints away, towards the doors, her every step recorded by one of the many phones being brandished in her direction.

"Violet's got Sprinkles' lunch!" cries Kieran, clearly delighted to have an opportunity to move on from his own embarrassing run-in with the basketball team. "It's game on!"

The room moves as one. It would be a thing of beauty, like watching symmetry in action, if I wasn't frozen to the spot, barely able to breathe.

"Just let it go," whispers a voice, and I sense Hope sliding into the seat beside me. "I've got a cheese sandwich that you can share if you're hungry."

And it's as if her words unlock me. I'm suddenly unfrozen and as the blood rushes to my hands and feet, I realize something else.

I do not *want* to let it go.

I put my phone back into my bag and then I'm up and pushing through the throng of kids trying to get out of the door, elbowing someone in the ribs and squeezing in between two others.

"Let Sprinkles through!" laughs Kieran, and suddenly the crowd parts and I can make a run for it. Out of the canteen, down the corridor and then on to the concrete area that divides the main school building from the sports hall.

"Over here!" yells a voice and up ahead I see the basketball team, sprinting away. A group of kids jostle me from behind and I'm off again, racing towards the courts with no single clue about what I'm going to do when I get there. I fling myself in through the mesh gate and then screech to a halt, watching as Violet throws my packet of sandwiches towards one of the other girls.

"Did someone call for Uber Eats?" she yells, tossing it to another kid and laughing.

"Fruit order coming through!" shouts another member of the team, but he misjudges the throw and my apple crashes into the metal fence, where it disintegrates on contact. The crowd gathered behind me lets out a cry of approval and I wonder where all the teachers are and whether they'll rouse themselves from the staffroom for something as paltry as my lunch being sacrificed.

"Come on, you guys." A voice rings out and I turn to see Autumn stepping forward, waving her damn folder in the air to get everyone's attention. "That's enough now. Give Sprinkles back her lunch."

I frown. This is all moving too quickly for me to figure out what her aim is, but I do know that she's got no intention of shutting this down without a big finale.

"Fine." The boy with my sandwiches in his hand gives me a nod. "Come and get it." And then he's unwrapping the packet and holding up a piece of paper, his face lit up with delight. "Oh my God! Listen to this, everyone!" His words silence all the chatter. "Sprinkles' loser of a mum has written her a note and put it inside her sandwiches. Do you all want to hear what it says?"

I know immediately what it is, even though I haven't seen one of these since I was in Year Three and she'd put a funny little message in with my lunch.

This. Cannot. Be. Happening.

"*To my darling cutie-pie Sprinkles!*" His high-pitched voice, presumably an attempt at impersonating my mother, fills the basketball court, followed by a ripple of laughter.

"Have a wonderful day at school and enjoy playing with all your lovely little friends."

He glances up at the crowd. "What friends would they be, then?" The laughter increases from a ripple to a torrent, and he smirks and keeps pretending to read.

"Mummy is so proud of you, and I can't wait to see you later so that we can have a marvellous, wonderful, fabby time together at home. Love you, from Mummy. Kiss."

And I know that there are now two rational pathways that I can take. I can either turn and run away or I can freeze and act like none of this bothers me.

I choose a third, irrational path. And it's the path that leads from where I am currently standing towards the boy posing in the centre circle, one hand clutching my note and the other holding out my sandwiches like an offering to the gods. Because even though my mother's unwise attempt at making me smile has just given my tormentors yet more ammunition against me, I can't let this go. Not now they've brought her into this.

My feet start to move, one step and then another and I can feel the glare of five, ten, fifteen, twenty, more, more, more phones at my back but I keep walking. He waits until I'm right in front of him. Until I have stretched out my hand and let my fingers curl towards the sandwich, one half of my brain screaming at me that this is ridiculous; that I have no intention of eating it anyway so what the hell do I think I'm doing – and the other half howling back that this is my damn sandwich and I refuse to let them beat me.

"My mother made that for me," I tell him, so quietly that nobody else can hear. "Give. It. Back."

"Ooh! Did Mummy make your lunch?" he calls, in a fake falsetto voice, and I grit my teeth, determined not to give him any more ammunition.

He waits until my fingers are almost touching the bread and then he acts, whipping back his arm like lightning and hurling my lunch towards Violet, who catches it and races down the court towards the hoop.

"Slam dunk!" bellows Mikki and now I freeze because there's no point in doing anything else. All eyes are fixed on the sandwich as it arcs through the air and hurtles through the hoop before splattering to the ground beneath.

The gathering of Year Nine let out a jubilant roar of appreciation.

And then it's done. The boy pushes past me, dropping the note as he goes, and I pick it up before turning to watch as everyone just leaves. Some alone, some in pairs, some in small groups. Conversation turns to late homework or the science essay that's coming up. Phones are pocketed and remnants of lunch shoved into mouths. I am invisible again as I read the note that my mother lovingly wrote in the early hours of the morning.

The irony is almost funny.

Have a good day, Eden.
Love Mum ☺

Lose Like A Girl

By the time I get home from school, *Woodford Whispers* is flooded with video footage of me running after Violet. Some genius has slowed down a clip of the end game and I watch as my sandwich curves through the air to the sound of slow-motion roaring, speeding up again as my lunch hits the ground with a miserable splat.

The comments start to pour in, an unstoppable tide that threatens to sink me.

@trooth-hurts: Thanks for providing the lunchtime entertainment **@just-eden**.

@ethan-is-king: Best hoop I've seen scored all year!!!

@alwaysautumn: I mean, it's super cute that **@just-eden**'s mum puts a note in her lunchbox. My mum used to do that when I was six.

@silverbullet: She runs like she's six. Did you see her arms flailing all over the place? I thought running was supposed to be her "thing"????

@footballrules: Think you could beat her in a race, do you? 👀

@trooth-hurts: Mikki could totally take Eden and you all know it.

@alwaysautumn: Exactly.

@kacey789: I feel bad for laughing cos, you know, food waste and starving people and everything – but that was genuinely funny!

@ethan-is-king: Out of interest, why do you have it in for **@just-eden**?

@trooth-hurts: She's annoying. And strange.

Like – who hangs out all on their own for years on end?
I'll tell you who – psychopaths. And weirdos.

@silverbullet: Preach.

All I can do is sit on my bedroom floor, holding a reluctant Midnight in my arms and my breath in my chest.

They're just words. Nobody ever drowned in words.

I'm lying. Again. Right now, I would rather be battling a raging storm at sea than going under right here in my own bedroom.

And then – a life raft.

16:33 **@trackstar09**: You OK?

16:34 **@just-eden**: I guess.

16:34 **@trackstar09**: So that's a no, then?

16:35 **@just-eden**: *shrugs*

16:36 **@trackstar09**: It wasn't OK, what happened at lunch. Why is all this stuff happening to you?

16:38 **@just-eden**: You wouldn't believe me if I told you.

16:38 **@trackstar09**: Try me?

Mikki said this would all get so much worse if I told anyone about what is going on, but I'm going under here. I need someone to talk to.

16:39 **@just-eden**: Promise you won't tell anyone?

16:40 **@trackstar09**: Promise.

16:42 **@just-eden**: The Glossies want me to be in their group. But I have to pass a test first.

16:42 **@trackstar09**: The Glossies?

16:43 **@just-eden**: You know – Bea and her underlings. Anyway, Mikki & Autumn hate my guts but for some reason Bea wants me to join them. So I have to prove my worth by passing a test – and the tests are all about me doing something horrible to someone else. With me so far?

16:45 **@trackstar09**: I think so. But why is rubbish stuff happening to you, then?

16:47 **@just-eden**: Because if I don't do the test, it gets done to me, but worse. Like a twisted forfeit.

16:49 **@trackstar09**: OK. So let me get this straight. You could stop all of this crap if you just do one of their tests?

16:50 **@just-eden**: Yep.

16:50 **@trackstar09**: I don't want to state the obvious here. But wouldn't it be easier to just do it?

16:53 **@just-eden**: Probably. But I'm not going to make some other kid feel awful and humiliated, just to play some stupid game of Bea's. Can we talk about something else now, please?

17:02 **@trackstar09**: Sure. What are you having for tea?

17:03 **@just-eden**: Seriously? After my lunch got destroyed?

17:04 **@trackstar09**: Sorry! It's been a bit of a day – cut me some slack?

17:05 **@just-eden**: OK, fine – I'm having whatever Melissa picks up on her way home which is probably going to be either pizza or frozen lasagne.

17:06 **@trackstar09**: Who is Melissa?

And just like that, we're talking about stuff that actually matters. I tell @trackstar09 a bit about my mother and how it's just the two of us.

He asks me why I call her by her name and I pause, wondering how to explain how everything changed between us. How starting secondary school without a single friend felt like I had walked through a doorway and left being a little kid behind. I couldn't bear to confess to my mother exactly what had happened with Bea, but at the very start I did try to talk to her about my loneliness. She just told me that it was the same for everyone starting big school. She told me that the friends would come.

It was the first time that I realized that my mother was as big a liar as me.

The hardest part was trying to figure out why, even though I didn't feel like a child any more, in some ways it felt like I needed her more than ever. She was working more shifts and it started to feel like I hardly saw her. Instead of spending lots of evenings with Bea like I did at primary, I spent long hours alone with Midnight and my cacti. And the time I did spend with my mother, she seemed fixated on my *potential* and the *adventures* that I'd have once I got my incredible grades. I saw how work and money stressed her out, and I went along with her goals for me, tried to seem OK, tried to be one less thing for her to worry about. The more I didn't tell her how I felt and how alone I always am, the more the space between us grew too.

It's impossible to put into words how deserted I felt; how I still feel. It's hard to explain that calling her *Melissa* helped me make that leap into a world where I had to look out for myself.

It's impossible to confess that seeing her stiffen every time I use her name makes me feel a bit more in control, like I'm telling her that everything is not OK without actually saying the words – as if one day it might change things.

It's impossible to say any of this stuff when everyone else seems to be fine and doing life like it's no big deal.

But something about @trackstar09 makes me want to try.

17:14 **@just-eden**: Things aren't always that great between us. She won't understand all of the stuff that gets me down. I call her Melissa cos it makes it easier not to care that she doesn't really know me. Does that make sense?

17:16 **@trackstar09**: I totally get it. I don't tell my parents the important things either. My mum's answer to everything that goes wrong in my life is "you've had too much screen time".

17:17 **@just-eden**: Exactly! My leg could be falling off and Melissa would blame it on my social media use...

17:18 **@trackstar09**: It's just simpler not to tell them anything.

★

We bump into each other as I walk into school the next morning. I glance at him, and our eyes connect. I feel a flood of nervous excitement. I don't do this. I don't have friends I say hi to. But we sent messages to each other for a while last night and the possibility of a genuine friendship in school seems, for the first time in for ever, like it might be not such a bad thing. He gives me a quick grin, pushing his floppy fringe out of his eyes and I stop, my mouth opening in a greeting.

"Eden! There you are!"

My heart sinks. Bea appears in front of me, her eyes flashing with something that could be either excitement, fear or too much coffee on the way to school.

"I've been looking everywhere for you!"

I crane my neck to peer around her but it's too late, Riley has been swept up in a crowd and disappeared down the corridor with Hope and a couple of other kids from the track team.

"Look, I think you'll agree that everything on *Woodford Whispers* is getting a little out of hand," Bea tells me quietly, linking her arm with mine and tugging me towards my locker. "And it's so unnecessary. You don't want this; I don't want this."

I plant my feet on the ground and look at her in disbelief. "You don't want this? You could end this with a click of your fingers."

She gives a tiny sigh and pulls me forward. "You've been given another chance. This one's super easy, Eden – and you don't even have to *really* do anything cos it's all online. Which doesn't really count, if you think about it!"

I let her drag me through the crowd of people, keeping a lookout for Riley as everyone parts at our approach.

Once again, Bea demonstrating immaculate timing in her goal to mess up my life.

"Bea! Love your hair today, girl!" Daisy smiles and gesture at Bea's two immaculate French plaits. I self-consciously pat my own hair with my free hand – I got up late again and just had time to scrape it back into a ponytail, which I can already feel is starting to escape from its elastic band.

"Call me later, yeah?" Kacey makes the "call me" sign, followed by a cheesy thumbs up.

It's like walking through Woodford High with a celebrity – if the celebrity made people feel utterly terrified.

"Here we go!" chirrups Bea, as we arrive at my locker. She lets go of my arms. "Just do it," she adds more quietly. "The longer this goes on, the harder it will be to recover."

I turn my back on her, trying to ignore the barely veiled threat. Bea doesn't get to tell me what to do.

Test four is waiting for me inside my locker, the envelope a subtle lemon-yellow. I debate not opening it at all, but forewarned is forearmed and all that. Glancing around to check that Bea has gone and that nobody is watching, I rip it open and pull out the note inside.

To: Eden
Target: Hairy. Hope. Daisy. Britt.
Test: Post a rumour on Woodford Whispers.
       The faker, the better.
Time: Tuesday 3rd July

I slam my locker door closed and give myself a pep talk as I walk slowly towards my form room. It's OK. At least I know what the test is going to be. They're going to post a rumour about me on *Woodford Whispers*. And it can't be any worse than what is already happening in the comments section, night after night. I can handle this.

It's not real. It can't hurt me.

Hashtag *and-other-lies-I-tell-myself.*

"Are you going to do it, then?"

Mikki and Autumn. They've been waiting for me under the stairs, out of the view of any passing teachers. I look around but Bea is nowhere to be seen – she's sent her flunkies to put the pressure on. I try to push past but Mikki isn't having any of it, blocking my path with her tiny body and massive, terrifying force field.

"You have to do it today," Autumn tells me, blowing a bubble with her gum. I smell the sweet, sickly smell of cherries and take a step backwards, but there's no point in running off. There's only one way to get to my form room and the impatient Mr Danes, and it's in front of me.

"Excuse me," I say, stepping to the side.

Autumn creases up with laughter and Mikki allows a rare smile to form on her usually blank face. Her teeth are tiny, and I'm reminded of a fox.

My rabbit-in-the-headlights strategy is not proving very effective.

"Are you going to do it?" Mikki stares at me, her face impassive again. Her allocated smiling time has clearly been used up.

I shake my head. "No." My traitorous voice cracks. I clear my throat and try again. "No."

"Excellent." She moves aside and gestures me towards the stairs. "I was hoping you'd say that. Autumn – do what you do best."

"Hang on a minute." Autumn looks confused. "Don't we have to give her the rest of the day? I thought those were the rules?"

Mikki rolls her eyes. "Is there the remotest chance that you're suddenly going to develop the guts to do this?" she asks me.

"I'm not doing it," I confirm, holding tightly on to the handrail.

"There you go!" Mikki tells Autumn. "There's no need to wait until tonight cos she's not going to do it anyway.

She's made her choice and we have to respect that."

"You do know what's going to happen to you if you don't, yeah?" Autumn calls after me as I start up the stairs, trying not to break into a run.

"Just leave me alone," I mutter, picking up speed. "Freaking losers."

"What did you just call us?" Mikki's shout bounces off the walls.

Damn it. I didn't think I'd said that out loud.

It's too much for my legs, who despite me willing them to be strong, take it upon themselves to hurtle me up the rest of the stairs and through the door at the top, where I crash straight into Mrs Lipscott and her armful of science coursework.

"Watch out!" she shrieks, as papers tumble fall to the floor. "Eden McCoy! What do we always say about running in the corridors?"

"Sorry, Miss," I splutter, dropping to my knees and starting to gather up the work. The door opens behind me, and I don't need to look up to know who the fake gasping is coming from.

"Oh my life!" simpers Autumn, her feet coming into view. "Are you OK, Miss?"

"I'm fine," sniffs Mrs Lipscott. "Thankfully."

"We told Eden to slow down," says Mikki, kneeling

beside me and reaching across for a folder. "But she seemed to be a bit *upset* about something."

"Is that true?" asks Mrs Lipscott, her voice softer now. "Eden? Is everything OK?"

I swallow my words. There's no point in telling this teacher, any teacher, anything. They're the same as everyone else – they just see what they want to see.

"Here you go, Miss." Autumn puts her stupid squirrel folder down and retrieves some papers that have fluttered across the floor. "Is that a new dress that you're wearing? It looks lush!"

Mrs Lipscott's cheeks flush a deep pink and she starts wittering on about "*What, this old thing?*" and "*What a lovely thing to say*" and "*Thought it was too young for me, but you've really made my day*" and blah, blah, blah. I crawl towards Autumn's folder, half-wondering whether I can get away with stealing it, and then Mikki is right beside me, using Autumn's distraction to make her move.

"Watch out, McCoy," she hisses into my ear, giving me a sharp jab in the ribs with her elbow. "Nobody calls me a loser and gets away with it."

"What's this about being a loser?" snaps Mrs Lipscott, her teacher radar picking up on the tension despite Autumn's best efforts to divert her attention elsewhere.

Mikki looks up and opens her mouth. And even though

I still feel like I'm drowning in the Glossies' threats, something inside me sparks. It's just a flicker but it's there.

"Mikki was a loser on sports day," says a voice, making both of the Glossies gasp. I can hardly believe it's come out of my mouth. "She was just saying that she's not used to that."

I stand up and hand some papers to Mrs Lipscott.

"Failing to win a race does not make a person a loser," she tells us, frowning. "It's the taking part that—"

"But Mikki accepts that her winning streak is over," interrupts the voice, overriding my brain. "From the top the only way is down."

Hopefully the opposite is true too. I can only dream.

Although from the expression on the other girls' faces, it is more likely that I have just unleashed my own, personal Armageddon.

It starts just before third period is about to begin. It's raining, there're a couple of minutes of break left and Mr Danes has popped out of the room to finish his photocopying. Everyone is milling about or slouched in their chairs, chatting and scrolling through their phones. And then the air trembles with the buzz of thirty-four phones on silent, all vibrating to alert their owners to a new drama.

Kacey is the first to react.

"Have you seen this?" She shows her phone to the girl sitting next to her and stabs furiously at the screen. I sit very still, not even getting my phone out of my bag. Maybe what I don't know can't hurt me.

"OMG!" gasps someone else, and just like that, the mood changes. It's as if the lights dim and the temperature drops and I'm suddenly trapped in the eye of the storm. And then the room is alive with mutters and whispered comments. Kieran slopes over and sits down on Violet's desk and then I hear my name being mentioned by a group of kids who are gathered in the corner of the room, which shouldn't come as any kind of surprise but still makes my heart beat faster in my chest.

"This is wild!"

"What the hell?" Kieran looks over at me, his eyes confused.

"Damn, Sprinkles – I didn't know you had it in you!"

"I mean – it's always the quiet ones you have to watch out for!" yells Ethan. "I've said that before!"

My stomach starts to churn but I force myself to stay calm. It's the next test. I just have to sit it out. I can do this. I'm braced.

"I haven't done anything," I mutter pointlessly. "What does it say?"

"You should know," snaps Bonnie. "Not going to lie though – I would not have thought you'd do something like this!"

I hold my hands up in the air, like I'm under arrest. "Do something like *what*?"

"Nice try." Kacey glares at me. "It's right here in black and white."

"You can't get out of it now," says Daisy. "You should have thought about the consequences. Did you think we wouldn't work out that it was you? How clueless do you think we are?"

"So @trooth-hurts was her all along?" calls a girl from the back of the room. "That's just weird – especially when you think what she's been saying online."

"Yeah." Kacey shoots a look in my direction. "Didn't she just refer to herself as a psychopath?"

My feet are desperate to carry me out of the room, but my body is incapable of leaving the chair. I sink down low into my seat and pull out my phone.

@trooth-hurts: Right – I've had enough of being treated like garbage and that doughnut attack was a step too far, so let's start talking real truths about the kids at Woodford High, shall we? And who better to start with than our very own Queen Bea, who apparently has her sights set on a certain Year Nine boy **@footballrules** 😌 I mean, he's the latest in a long line of hook-ups – this girl likes to have fun with a capital F-U-N, and by that I mean FAKE, UGLY, NARCISSIST. She'll take **@footballrules** and wipe the pitch with him and then, once she's done, put him back on the bench. Which is where he belongs, to be fair – especially if his hook-up skills are as dreadful as his football skills. Saying that, he'd have to be Premier League to be as good as **@BeaKind**. That girl has had a LOT of practice, if you know what I mean. But don't despair **@football-rules** – I'm right here 👻 #hidinginplainsight #callmesprinkles #girlsjustwanttohavefun #pickme #truthhurts

I don't want to read any more. I would never say anything like this, let alone write it on social media. Surely nobody is going to believe that @trooth–hurts is me?

A quick glance around the room confirms that in fact, yes – the overwhelming majority of my classmates think I'm behind the awful, anonymous account, despite the fact that I have also been the victim of their nasty comments.

Which presumably means that @trooth–hurts isn't Bea, either. Unless she's decided that the damage to me will be worse than it is to her? And if she's prepared to do this to her own reputation, then just how far is she prepared to go to destroy mine?

Violet is staring at me with real dislike in her eyes. "I know that Bea and the others can be a lot sometimes but it's only a bit of fun. This is just plain evil."

"It wasn't me," I try again. "I wouldn't—"

"Mikki just posted a comment," interrupts Kacey. "Apparently Bea is raging. She's using #girlcode and told us all to post in support."

"So has Autumn," adds Daisy. "They're right – this is totally out of order. Girls shouldn't say that kind of thing about other girls."

"Can you believe that?" asks Violet, throwing a dirty look in my direction. "I didn't think she was like that."

"I think it's obvious what she's *like*," calls Bonnie, who for some reason really seems to hate me. "Two-faced troll."

"It's pretty funny though," says one of the boys, clearly reading his phone and not the room.

"It's pretty psychopathic," snaps Kacey.

Ethan laughs and turns to grin at Kieran, who is looking slightly shocked. "What d'you reckon, mate? You going to trade off Bea for Sprinkles?"

Kieran blinks and then seems to recover, screwing his face up in disgust. "You think I want to hook up with *that*?" I flush, staring down at the table so that I don't have to make eye contact. "I'd rather take my chances with Bea 'The Slapper' Miller."

The girls in the room erupt in fury at his slur, the spotlight momentarily off me and firmly focused on the boys who are now making foul comments about what someone *else* has said about Bea.

I stand on shaking legs and start to walk towards the door. There is literally nothing that I can do to make it stop. There is nowhere to hide. They can say what they like about me online, pretend to be me – and I am powerless to stop them.

They are invincible, untouchable, undefeatable.

"Someone should report her," says Bonnie, glancing up at me as I walk past her desk. "She should be blocked."

"Yeah – or muted," adds Kacey, glaring at me. "Like, permanently."

I ignore them all, willing my feet to keep moving towards the doorway. Whatever the tiny spark was that fired in my belly when I was talking to Mrs Lipscott, it's been extinguished by the avalanche of despair that has crashed down upon me.

I push through the classroom door, praying that Mr Danes won't choose this moment to return, but the corridor is free from teachers. Moving quickly, I head to the stairwell and then pause. Voices are floating up from the floor below and while I can't see them, it's obvious who it is. Quietly, I tiptoe to the railing and peer over.

"Don't worry about it." Mikki tries to put an arm around Bea, who jerks away, hands on her hips.

"Do I look worried?" she snaps. "I'm not worried. What I am is confused. Please do enlighten me as to how a post slut-shaming me in front of the entire school has made its way on to *Woodford Whispers*."

She rounds on Autumn.

"What the hell were you thinking?" she demands. "Why on earth did you allow that post to go on the site?"

My brain splutters, trying to make sense of what they're saying. Autumn being the admin for *Woodford Whispers* is not exactly a big reveal, but Bea appears to be genuinely angry, which means that she is as surprised about this as I am. Which means that someone else is behind the @trooth-hurts account. I don't really know what to think about that. As much as I dislike her, the thought of anyone reading this stuff about themselves makes me feel kind of sick.

"I was trying to protect you," whimpers Autumn, cowed in the face of Bea's fury. "It was obviously written by Eden. I thought you should know how much she hates you, and just how far she's prepared to stoop to hurt you. There's no way that we could have predicted she'd spread a rumour about *you*, Bea. That wasn't the instructions for the test."

"But why didn't you just show me when she sent it in to *Woodford Whispers*?" Bea's voice is cold, and I feel a shiver run down my spine. "We could have kept it quiet. And even if she'd posted it on her own account, nobody would have seen it. She doesn't have any friends."

"Autumn messed up," soothes Mikki, putting her hand on Bea's arm. "She knows that. But honestly, I think she was just trying to make sure that everyone knows what a nasty piece of work Eden is. People have seen that she's been the target of a few *jokes*, and the last thing we want is anyone starting to feel sorry for her. Right? People should know what kind of a girl she is, Bea. You can't keep protecting her – she quite clearly wouldn't do anything to protect you."

It wasn't bloody me! I scream at Bea.

In my head.

"At least you know the truth now." Mikki links her arm through Bea's. "You tried to give Eden a chance and she threw it back in your face. We can't let her get away with this – you know that? Let us deal with it, OK?"

Bea's shoulders sag and she sighs. "Fine. I was wrong. She isn't who I thought she was."

"At least you've got us," chirps Autumn, moving

around to flank Bea on the other side. The three of them move away and I wait until the door to the first floor has closed before scurrying down the stairs and along the corridor towards the nurse's office, picking up the pace until I push through the door to safety.

As safe as a dead woman walking can ever be, anyway.

Breathe Like A Girl

16:03 **@just-eden**: Hey! How was your day?

16:15 **@trackstar09**: 😬

16:16 **@just-eden**: Well, it can't have been as bad as mine.

16:18 **@trackstar09**: You reckon?

16:19 **@just-eden**: Absolutely.

16:23 **@trackstar09**: Well, I guess you put a target on your back when you started slagging off Bea.

16:23 **@just-eden**: What?

16:26 **@trackstar09**: You must really hate her, huh?

16:29 **@just-eden**: I can't believe you think I'd actually do something like that. Do you really think I'm behind that awful **@trooth-hurts** account?

16:37 **@trackstar09**: Oh God – I'm sorry, Eden. Seriously. Everyone is saying it's you and I guess I just believed them.

16:52 **@just-eden**: Whatever.

16:53 **@trackstar09**: I'm so glad it wasn't you, Eden, and I really am sorry I doubted you. But you do hate Bea, right?

16:55 **@just-eden**: Pretty much. But I would never do something like that. Even if she is a cow.

16:56 **@trackstar09**: So who do you think wrote the post?

16:57 **@just-eden**: I don't know. But whoever

@trooth-hurts is, they clearly hate Bea.

17:09 **@trackstar09**: That's really sad, don't you think?

17:10 **@just-eden**: No – an abandoned kitten is sad.
Bea made her choices. I'm not wasting a moment of
sadness on her. Now, real talk. Jam or custard?

17:14 **@trackstar09**: What are you on about?

17:15 **@just-eden**: In a doughnut? Come on – you must
have heard about my speciality subject?

17:16 **@trackstar09**: I might have heard a few rumours,
Sprinkles. (Too soon?)

17:17 **@just-eden**: You're an ass. Which flavour?

17:19 **@trackstar09**: Is this a trick question? Cos you
know that there is only one answer, right?

17:20 **@just-eden**: Choose carefully or this friendship
might be over before it even gets going.

17:26 **@trackstar09**: Are we friends, then?

17:27 **@just-eden**: Depends on what you answer about the doughnuts…

17:29 **@just-eden**: Sorry – I didn't mean to make this weird. I know we're just chatting.

17:30 **@trackstar09**: It's not weird. I like talking with you. I haven't got many people to talk about pointless stuff with and just have a laugh with after a tough day. My friends don't always feel like people I can trust, you know?

17:32 **@just-eden**: Really? I always thought you had great friends on the track team – Hope and everyone. And hey, I don't talk about pointless stuff!

17:33 **@trackstar09**: Whatever! Jam, by the way.

17:34 **@just-eden**: Our friendship lives! Unlike me once I step foot in school tomorrow.

17:36 **@trackstar09**: It'll be OK. Maybe I can help? See if I can pick up any intel from Bea, Mikki or Autumn about what they're up to. I see Mikki a lot through track. Then maybe I can warn you if I hear of anything?

17:41 **@just-eden**: Thanks, Riley.

17:42 **@trackstar09**: No worries. I can try being "undercover"! Probably best not to let them see us chat at school though so they don't realize I'm on your side.

17:43 **@just-eden**: Yeah, I guess. I'm used to being on my own so it won't make much difference.

17:44 **@trackstar09**: You're not on your own, Eden.

And just for a short time, I believe him. I understand why people bother to make the effort to have friends because, for one hundred and five minutes, I feel part of something; protected.

And then they make their next move.

The backlash is brutal. You'd think I would be getting used to it by now. But the goalposts keep moving – whenever I brace myself for the next onslaught, they mix it all up and I'm sideswiped by a fresh new layer of hell.

This time, it's not on *Woodford Whispers*. The link is on there, to make sure everybody can find it, but I have apparently reached the heady heights of my very own hate page. And a whole ton of very civic-minded people have tagged me, just to ensure I am included in this evening's sport, which is to annihilate me.

I Hate Eden McCoy.

As titles go, it's straightforward and to the point. There's no risk of a person ending up here and expecting to find videos of kittens or recipes for red velvet cupcakes.

It's still a surreal horror to be faced with photos of myself that I've never seen before, posted for all to gawk at. There is a highly unflattering one being used for the profile picture, which looks like it was taken in my maths class. My eyes are half-closed and I'm scowling, a perfect fit for the devil horns which have been edited on to the top of my head.

I'm trying to be OK. I'm trying really, really hard to squash down the panic and terror that I can feel swirling in the pit of my stomach. But as I scroll down the page and see the comments, it's impossible to stay calm.

They hate my attempt to undermine the most loved girl in school.

But it's not just that.

They hate my "superiority complex".

They hate my belief that someone as popular as Kieran would be interested in hooking up with someone as gross as me.

They hate my face.

They hate my voice.

One person hates the way that I walk.

There is no part of me that isn't being picked apart, vultures pecking at the carcass of my body and soul. Soon all that's going to be left is an empty, hollow shell.

I am not OK.

And it just keeps coming. It's death by a thousand likes.

Riley messages me. He offers to comment on the account and defend me, but I ban him from getting involved. The only way to make this stop is to let it run until it has no more oxygen. And in the meantime, I have to figure out a way to keep breathing.

I try to distract myself. I try to find ways to put down my phone. I pick up my trainers and start to put them on before throwing them into the corner of the room – I've barely got enough air in my lungs to do up my laces, never mind go out for a run. I pick up my tiny watering can and attempt to give Colin a drink, but my hands are shaking too much and I overload his pot with water. It's not good for him to get too wet, I know that – but the damage is done now.

In the end, I sit down at my desk and stare at my reflection in the mirror, gazing at my "ugly face" with its "too-big nose" and "too-low forehead" and "disgusting spots" and "bushy eyebrows". Before today I thought it was just a face. Now I can see that it's a whole list of imperfections and flaws. I might never have known if they hadn't pointed it out to me.

It's late when Melissa gets in from work. I hear the front door slam and then her voice calling up the stairs. She's brought us takeaway and it's going to get cold if we don't eat it immediately. I yell that I'm not hungry, which is the honest truth, and she orders me to come down.

I leave my phone on my bed and trudge downstairs. I tell her I'm fine, which is a big, fat lie. Then I push curry around my plate, pretending to eat, the whole time wondering how many more new comments, or even new photos, will have been posted by the time I get back to my room. Wondering what new things they will have found to hate about me.

"I'm worried about you," Melissa tells me once she's finished eating. "How was school today? You know that you can talk to me, don't you, Eden? Sometimes it's easier to figure out a solution to something when there's someone to help you." She leans across the table and takes hold of one of my hands and it's like something comes undone inside of me. Maybe, if there is the tiniest of possibilities that talking about this with her might help, it's worth a shot?

I take a deep breath and drag my last bit of courage up from my toes.

"There *is* some stuff going on," I confess. "I didn't want to hassle you with it, cos you've got a lot going on with work and everything, but it's starting to get a bit much."

"Tell me, Eden." She squeezes my hand and I continue, feeling emboldened.

"Some kids at school … took photos of me and put them online," I say. "And there's some video of me on there too, and—"

"What do you mean?" interrupts Melissa, her forehead creasing. "What kind of video? What were you doing?"

She probably doesn't intend to sound accusatory. It's probably just the way it came out of her mouth, spiky and panicked.

"I wasn't doing anything!" I remove my hand from her grasp and clench my fingers into the palms of my hands. "Why would you instantly assume I've done something wrong?"

"That's not what I meant," she says, and the lines on her forehead deepen. "I mean – what do the videos show?"

"Just some stupid pranks a few of the girls pulled." I make my voice sound casual. "The pranks aren't the worst thing though. It's what everyone is saying about me online."

"What are they saying?"

I inhale and try to get a grip. Why is it so hard to put this into words? "They're making nasty comments. About how I look and what I'm like and stuff like that."

"Oh, honey." She sighs and shakes her head. "I'm so sorry. You know why they're doing it though, don't you?"

Don't say it. Please do not say it. It's ridiculous and patronizing and it couldn't be less true.

"They're just jealous of you, Eden." She smiles at me sadly. "It was the same when I was at school and it hurts, I know that. Girls should be there for other girls, but it definitely does not always work out that way."

"They are *not* jealous of me!" I snap back. This conversation was a big mistake. They aren't currently voting online to decide whether the fact that I have never been kissed is because a) I think I'm better than everyone else or b) I'm a reclusive, friendless weirdo, because they're *jealous* of me.

"So let me help you," says my mother, ever the solver of my problems. "I can contact school and ask to speak to your Head of Year, see what they suggest?"

"God, no!" My head snaps up in alarm. "Don't do that. They'll do an assembly on e-safety and cyber-bullying, and it'll just make it fifty thousand times worse."

She frowns again. "I don't think that's true, actually. But I won't talk to school if you really don't want me to."

I exhale loudly. "I really don't want you to."

"Then I won't." She stands up and jerks her head at my plate. "Are you finished with that?"

I nod. I've managed a few mouthfuls, enough to keep her from giving me a hard time, but it's gone cold now. I get up and head over to the other side of the kitchen, where I start prodding the remnants of curry into the bin.

Melissa starts running hot water into the sink. "I suppose the only positive thing is that cyber-bullying is preferable to real-world bullying."

She doesn't notice me freeze, mid-scrape.

My mouth drops open. "What do you mean?"

She squirts some washing-up liquid into the water and swirls it with her hand, making bubbles. "Well – you can't avoid real bullying, can you? If there's someone in your face, threatening you or hurting you or saying unkind things then it's impossible to ignore them. At least if it's online you can just not look."

You. Can. Just. Not. Look.

I can feel it, bubbling up inside and threatening to spill out of me. An uncontrollable torrent of hysteria and terror and fury, gushing from my hateful mouth, eyes, nose, ears.

You can just not look.

She has no idea. She has zero knowledge that she has just said the single most insane thing that I've ever heard. She has no clue that the words she's just spoken have made me feel more alone and untethered than ever.

You CANNOT *just not look*. Not when more eyes are scrutinizing your image online with every minute that passes. Not when people you know, and people you don't, are making comments, passing judgement on every aspect of your person. Not when occasionally, maybe one in every thirty comments, someone will say something in defence, or marginally less damning, and you can cling on to their words like a lifeboat in an ocean of negativity.

You cannot *just not look* because *they* are looking. They will say it anyway, and how will you know, how will you prepare yourself to face them, if you don't log on?

"Eden?" She's still talking. "I do get it, you know. I was a teenager once too and I know how mean some girls can be. Boys seem to just have a fight and then it's out of their system, but it can be so much more complicated with girls – we juggle so many different pressures, I suppose. It will pass though, honey, and I really think that if you give yourself a break from the internet and put your phone down for a change, it will help."

She smiles, clearly pleased with herself for administering some top-quality parenting, unaware that of all the kids in Year Nine, I probably spend the least time on social media. Actually – *spent* the least time. It was one thing having a casual flick through *Woodford Whispers* when there was no chance of my name being mentioned: quite another now that I'm the unwitting main character in this hideous drama.

"My *phone* is not the problem, Melissa," I hiss, my teeth clamped together so tightly that the words struggle to escape. "Why is your go-to reaction to blame me and my phone?"

"I'm not blaming you!" Her voice has an edge now – she's annoyed that I'm not accepting her brilliant advice. "I'm just saying, social media has a lot to answer for. And that maybe, if you're finding it an unpleasant place to be, then you should limit your usage for a bit."

She's right. Social media *does* have a lot to answer for. But the same could be said of just about anything, couldn't it? Most things have a positive and a negative side.

Besides, Melissa is a hypocrite. She's had a Facebook account for years and it was only when I outright banned her from putting up photos of me that she stopped sharing embarrassing posts about our life. She says she only goes on to find out what her old friends are up to these days or to arrange a rare night out with her work colleagues – but the fact remains that she probably has less understanding of how to keep herself safe online than anyone my age.

"Fine." My shoulders slump in defeat.

There's no point in trying to explain because she won't get it. She won't understand that my phone is both my lifeline and my noose. Sure, it's showing me all these bad comments, but without it, I wouldn't have my friendship with Riley. I wouldn't be able to chat to kids in Perth or Tokyo about life, the universe and how not to kill a cactus plant. I wouldn't have endless entertainment, an escape from reality, a galaxy of information and knowledge at my fingertips. Where does she think I'd learn everything that I need to survive if I didn't have my phone? School? Don't make me laugh.

So all I can do now is shut up, keep it all to myself, and "accept" her advice. If she takes away my phone, then I will truly be isolated.

Fight Like A Girl

School is grim. The old days of lessons just blending one into another are over. Now I'm on heightened alert, constantly vigilant for the next test. They should be getting over this by now. Why the hell aren't they getting bored? Running didn't save me and neither did my feeble efforts at standing still and letting it wash over me.

I walk through the school corridor, and people stare at me from a safe distance. Nobody wants to catch some of the fallout when the next drama hits.

If I had any humour left then I'd laugh at the fact they have no idea how much mess *would* have been headed their way if I had decided to actually carry out any of the tests.

There's no moment of reprieve. Test number five arrives in an envelope of deep bottle-green. Of course it does, because officially I did not pass the last test. But there's no way the Glossies are doing this so that I can join their group; that's abundantly clear. This is all about punishment for a crime that I didn't commit. I could try telling Bea that it wasn't me who wrote that stuff about her, but there's no point, not when the entire school (minus Riley) thinks that I'm @trooth-hurts. I don't bother to check if anyone is around before ripping it open and when I've read the note, I shove it deep inside my rucksack. I walk as fast as I can towards the stairs, feeling multiple sets of eyes boring deep holes into my back.

"Cow," mutters one girl as I pass by.

"If you've got something to say, then you should say it to Bea's face," hisses another. "Don't hide behind a screen, you loser."

I ignore them. What good would it do to claim innocence now? They've all decided I'm guilty. Plus Mikki said that this would all get so much worse if I told anyone – and one thing I know about the Glossies is that they don't make threats they don't intend to keep.

The morning drags on for what feels like for ever. I zone out in science and Mrs Lipscott threatens me with extra homework. I put my head on the table in English but it's a substitute teacher and they're too busy dealing with Kieran and Ethan's impromptu indoor football match to bother about me. I make it all the way to the end of fourth period and then, as the bell rings to signal lunchtime, my phone vibrates. The substitute teacher gathers her bag and leaves the room like there's a fire beneath her desk and now it's just us in here.

My mother's words pop into my head.

I could just not look.

Yeah, right. Everyone's phone is now in their hands, their faces lit up with the light from the screen.

"Oh my God." Violet's voice is quiet. "Have you all seen this?"

"Ooooh," mutters Daisy from behind me. "I know she posted that stuff about Bea but this is a *lot*."

The air in the room has a sudden uneasy feeling – like it's being stretched taut, and I have a horrible sense of déjà vu. Unlike last time there was an online attack though, nobody speaks and for the first time in ages, people are looking everywhere but at me. I pick up my phone and tap my notifications and there it is.

The list that the note in the bottle-green envelope instructed me to make but I never would, not if they gave me a day, a week, a month, a year.

Top 10 Grossest Girls in Year 9
Eden McCoy with her repulsive face

Eden McCoy and her uptight attitude

Eden McCoy and her ugly laugh

Eden McCoy with her scruffy hair

Eden McCoy in her cheap trainers

Eden McCoy the embarrassing loner

Eden McCoy with her vile personality

Eden McCoy and her loser mother

Eden McCoy with her cringeworthy life

Eden McCoy the total bi—

I slam my phone back in my pocket, unable to take any more.

"That's not OK." I look up and Hope is standing in front of me. "It's not OK, Eden."

And she's right. It's not.

I'm not.

I'm up in seconds, my chair spinning out of control behind me.

"Eden!" calls Hope but I've already gone. Out of the classroom and along the corridor to the stairs, pushing my way through the crowd of kids who are making their way to the canteen. I want to scream at them to get out of my way but I'm saving my words for *them*.

I sprint past the lockers, my eyes searching as I run. I push through the double doors at the end and out into the yard and there they are. Two of them, anyway, which is good enough for now.

"Hey!" I slow as I get closer to them, my heart pounding in my chest. "I want to talk to you."

Mikki turns to look at me, her face as impassive as ever.

"Do you have an appointment, Sprinkles?" she asks, making Autumn splutter. "No? Then I'm afraid that you're going to have to leave."

"You have to stop," I tell them, trying to keep the tremor out of my voice. "You've made your point. You win, OK? Everyone hates me. Now no more tests. It's over."

Mikki folds her arms. "Or what?"

"If … if you send me another test then I'm going to show it to Mr Danes," I say, trying to sound like I mean it.

Mikki laughs, and it sounds like one hundred fairies dying. "Sure," she says and then suddenly, before my brain can compute what is going on, I'm lying flat on my back on the ground, and she is holding down my arms. She is shockingly strong for someone so tiny.

Autumn seizes the opportunity to sit on my legs and now I'm pinned, my heart racing.

"Get off me!" I yelp, kicking my legs in a pathetic attempt to shake her off. "What are you doing?"

"Snitches get stitches," says Autumn, giggling like a

maniac. "What were you saying about telling Mr Danes?"

"To be fair, Autumn," says Mikki politely, as if we're engaging in pleasant conversation, "she hasn't *actually* snitched. Yet. What she needs is a warning."

Autumn nods thoughtfully. "Good point."

Mikki leans forward and hovers above my face. I see what's coming and twist my head from side to side, trying to dodge it, but there's no escaping.

The warm, thick strand of saliva stretches out of her mouth, lingering for a nerve-racking second before plopping down on to my cheek near my ear, where it starts to ooze slowly across my skin and into my hair. I keep my head very still now, partly to avoid diverting the drool's journey towards my mouth and partly because I am truly frozen. I'm not playing dead this time. I couldn't move even if they weren't still holding me down.

Autumn is speaking but I can't hear her. From my position I can't see much, though what I can see is several pairs of feet. Pairs of feet belonging to people who are standing right here in complete silence, watching my humiliation.

"*We* decide when this is over," hisses Mikki. "And I warned you what would happen if you tried to go against us." Then she grins at me and finally lets go of my arms.

And now I move, my hands flying to my face, wiping

away the disgusting evidence. Autumn releases my legs and the two of them stand up. I push myself into a sitting position and look around, matching feet to faces. Kieran and Ethan. Kacey and Bonnie. And over there, right at the front with Bea beside him, is Riley. Doing nothing.

"Did anyone get that on camera?" asks Ethan, pulling his phone out of his pocket and breaking the stillness.

"Put it away," mutters Riley. "Not cool, man."

He shakes his head and then turns, as if he's disgusted by the sight before him, with Bea close behind. And out of everything that has just happened, this hurts the most.

"You're not on your own." That's what he told me. That's what I let myself believe. But I *am* on my own. As I sit on the ground and watch everyone move off, bored now that the action is over, I realize I have known the answer to my problem for a while now. And that, as nobody is coming to rescue me, I have to be strong enough to rescue myself.

Flight didn't work, and nor did freeze.

It's time to take some positive action.

It's time to fight back.

Strong Like A Girl

16:01 **@trackstar09**: Are you OK?

16:08 **@trackstar09**: Are you there, Eden?

16:13 **@trackstar09**: Eden?

16:24 **@just-eden**: Where were you when I needed some help earlier?

16:25 **@trackstar09**: I had no idea they were going to do that to you. Honestly.

16:29 **@just-eden**: I'm not suggesting you should be able to predict their actions. But a bit of back-up might have been nice, you know?

16:30 **@trackstar09**: I know. I'm sorry.

16:31 **@just-eden**: How could you just stand there?

16:32 **@trackstar09**: I didn't know what to do. And I guess I got scared.

16:38 **@trackstar09**: Eden? I truly am sorry. I know you'd never stand by & let someone else be treated that way.

16:45 **@trackstar09**: You're really brave, you know? Way braver than any of them.

16:47 **@just-eden**: Brave or stupid.

16:48 **@trackstar09**: No – definitely brave.

16:58 **@just-eden**: Whatever.

I silence my phone and throw it on my bed. I'm still angry with Riley but what he's said whirs around my head. It's true that I haven't done the tests on anyone because I can't imagine treating anyone the way the Glossies treat people.

So why the hell am I letting them hurt me?

The spark flickers inside of me again and this time, I let it burn.

Riley is deep in conversation with Hope when I walk into school the next day. They look up as I near and then Hope puts out her hand to stop me from walking past. I reluctantly lower my headphones, letting the tinny sound of my music float out into the corridor.

"Are you OK?" she asks, her voice low. "What happened yesterday was really bad."

I glance at Riley. His face looks concerned but he's doing a good job of acting like he doesn't really know me. Presumably even Hope doesn't know that we've been chatting.

He kept on messaging late into the night, pleading with me to still be friends, but I ignored him and poured out my sorrows to my Cactus Club chat group instead. I'll let him off the hook when I'm ready.

"Did you tell anyone about the post?" he asks me now. "Your mum? Or a teacher?"

I resist the urge to roll my eyes. He knows I can't talk to anyone about this stuff. We've previously discussed how badly it went when I tried to tell Melissa what's been going on. We both know any adult intervention is going to increase the outpouring of nastiness, and besides, what I need now is to fuel the flames of my own fury, not risk it getting extinguished.

I focus my attention on Hope, in the mood to confront someone, anyone. "Why are you even talking to me? Nobody wants to come anywhere near me after that post about Bea was put on *Woodford Whispers*."

"Eden, we know you didn't write that." Hope gives me a small smile. "There's obviously been a targeted campaign against you since sports day. You should join track. Come and hang out with us."

Riley nods and I feel a small rush of something warm in my stomach.

"Maybe sometime," I say cautiously. "But not while Mikki is on the team."

Hope wrinkles her nose. "Watch this space," she says, and it is so out of character for her that a laugh bubbles out of me. Maybe I've got her all wrong. Maybe she isn't as timid as I thought. She grins at me and then turns to continue her conversation with Riley, who gives me another nod. I relent and nod back, then head towards my locker, headphones firmly in place and music blasting into my ears.

Test number six is waiting to greet me when I open my locker. It's an orange colour that reminds me of embers, which seems fitting for my current mood. Ripping open the top, I see today's challenge.

> To: Eden
> Target: Bonnie
> Test: Destroy her science essay
> Time: Friday 6th July

OK, then. Opening my rucksack, I put the envelope deep inside and then walk slowly down the corridor, my brain whirring with options and possibilities. They made a mistake giving me twenty-four hours to prepare. I'm not worried about what happens next because this time I'm finally going to do what I should have done in the first place.

The Glossies aren't going to know what's hit them.

I can tell that something new has happened as soon as I step foot inside my tutor room. I turn off my music and then make my way towards my desk, letting the words wash over me.

"I heard that Bea left the group," calls a girl from the back of the room.

"I heard she had a huge fight with Mikki and Autumn," says Daisy, from her seat behind me. "Apparently Bea was angry about something they did."

"They weren't sitting together on the bus after school yesterday," adds someone else. "Bea was on her own at the front."

It's true that Bea kept her distance more than usual yesterday, leaving Mikki and Autumn to do her dirty work. Perhaps she's still mad at Autumn for allowing the post to be published on *Woodford Whispers*. Anyway, good. If the Glossies are less of a united front, maybe it will be easier for me to fight back.

Either way, I'm not rolling over and accepting this any more. If they go up against me again, they will meet the new Eden.

And she is a girl who is ready to scorch the earth.

She is ready to burn it all down.

Smart Like A Girl

"What time did you get to bed last night?" asks Melissa, yawning as she enters the kitchen. "And did you get it finished?"

I nod. I stayed up for hours writing my science essay but I'm not tired. There's too much adrenaline flowing around my body for that. It turns out that deciding to become a girl who is ready to say it like it is makes a person feel all levels of hyped up. Now I just need to put that feeling into action.

"You really shouldn't leave it until the last minute," she says. "It's not like you to be so behind with your work."

I rinse my dirty cereal bowl in the sink and turn to face her.

"It was pretty much already done," I lie, not in the mood for a lecture. "I just wanted to make sure that it was as good as it could possibly be before I hand it in today."

She nods approvingly. "Well, I'll be rooting for you to get a good grade," she says. "Aren't they basing the sets for next year on this essay?"

"Yep." I dry my hands on a towel. "They're only inviting the top thirty kids to do triple science for GCSE."

"You definitely need to get into that class, Eden," she says, "If you're going to have any chance of getting accepted for medical school."

I close my eyes and take a deep breath.

"I'd like to do triple science." My throat feels scratchy, but I remind myself that I am the new Eden – I can stand my ground. I can do this at home as well as at school. "But... I'm not sure I want to be a doctor. I'm kind of more into animals than people. I might want to be a vet. Or maybe a biologist. Or a zookeeper. Or an animal rescue worker. Or work in a pet store. I don't know. But not a doctor."

I brace for disaster, but Melissa looks at me and nods.

"I can totally see you doing any of those things," she says. "You don't need to decide now, you know. You've still got plenty of time."

"Aren't you disappointed in me?" The words escape before I can claw them back. "All you've ever talked about is me going to medical school and doing the things that you didn't get to finish."

"Disappointed?" Her face drops and she takes a step towards me, putting her hand on my arm. "Eden – the only way you could ever disappoint me is if you don't do the things that make you happy." She pauses, and I see her swallow. "I thought that being a doctor was what *you* wanted – that's the reason I've been pushing you towards it. It's not about what I want. It's about what you want for yourself."

I blink. Is that it? Was it that simple, all this time? All I had to do was tell her what I was thinking, what I was feeling? I ask myself why I didn't say something earlier and I can't seem to find a reasonable answer.

"Hey – I was thinking." She pats my arm and then moves past me to get to the kettle. "What do you think about us doing something together after school tonight? There's a couple of new films out and I wondered if you might like to go and watch one and then grab something to eat afterwards?"

"Is it Christmas already?" I joke, and then wish I hadn't when a shadow crosses her face. In my defence, I'm still trying to process the knowledge that my mother doesn't have my life all mapped out for me. "I mean – yeah, I'd like that."

She sighs. "I know things have been a bit tough around here lately. But I'm thinking we can change that, you know? I've been offered a different position at work, and it'll mean more responsibility, but with some ability to do less shift work." She smiles at me. "So hopefully the increase in wages and the decrease in utter exhaustion will make a difference. I know I've not been here as much as you need me to be, and I'm sorry, Eden."

I smile. I have to admit it's nice to hear. Suddenly our frustrating conversation about all the online stuff doesn't seem like such a huge barrier between us. Melissa doesn't always get it right, but she does try. And clearly it helps when I do a better job of telling her the truth.

"You've been fine," I tell her. "We're fine."

And as I say it, I know that it's true.

"We might not be great." I put a piece of bread in the toaster and press down the handle. "But we *are* fine – and that's a good start."

Melissa laughs and reaches out to ruffle my hair with her hand.

"That's my girl," she says. "And how's it going at school? Has taking a break from social media helped at all? Are things any better with those girls?"

I pause. I'm nowhere near ready to share all of that with her. But still, when I reply it feels true.

"I'm handling it," I say.

My plan is in motion.

★

I told Riley about the sixth test last night, and he messages me again this morning.

07:32 **@trackstar09**: Are you actually going to trash Bonnie's essay?

07:34 **@just-eden**: Maybe.

07:34 **@trackstar09**: Eden! Just tell me already.

07:36 **@just-eden**: Forget that I said anything, OK?

07:37 **@trackstar09**: You do know you can trust me, don't you?

07:38 **@just-eden**: Well, I did. Until you said that. Now you sound totally dodgy.

07:39 **@trackstar09**: 🙁

07:41 **@just-eden**: Jeez, some people are so sensitive. 😛

07:42 **@trackstar09**: Yeah, well, don't do anything stupid.

07:45 **@just-eden**: Chill out. I have a plan.

I'm reluctant to share my plan, because I know nobody can be trusted, not really. Just when you think you've made a connection with a person, you turn around and there they are, watching you get beaten down.

I know he wants me to tell him more though, and there's a part of me that wants to share my plan – a quiet bit of my brain whispering that it might be good to have someone to talk it through with; someone to tell me it's going to work out; someone to cheer for me…

08:03 **@just-eden**: OK, fine. I'm not going to trash Bonnie's essay. Even though she's awful to me & probably deserves it.

08:04 **@trackstar09**: What are you going to do, then? If you don't do the test they're going to destroy your essay. That's the way it works, right? That's what you said they'll do if you don't follow their orders?

So, I tell him. I outline my strategy in all its glory and swear him to secrecy. And Riley agrees that my plan is audacious and bold and utterly genius.

★

The corridor outside the classroom is buzzing with tension. It's deadline day and most people were up late, either putting the finishing touches to their essays or frantically starting them, depending on what kind of school-life balance they've got going on.

Our instructions were to choose an area of science that interests us and then write an informative report, explaining what we discovered. And when I say write, that's exactly what I mean. For some ungodly reason, Woodford High has decided that the youth of today are losing the skills of yore, and so this assignment had to be written out by hand, every painstaking word of it.

My work is tucked safely away inside the new folder that I dashed out of school to buy yesterday. It's brown and orange with squirrels and acorns scattered across the front, which is not my vibe at all, but needs must. It's currently hidden inside my rucksack, which I'm clutching to my chest. I can't risk anyone seeing the folder or taking my project before I've had a chance to enact my plan. I might have met Mrs Lipscott's deadline but the deadline for the test is upon me.

"What did you write about?" asks Hope, walking over to stand beside me.

"I looked at how different animals react to stress situations," I tell her, keeping a careful watch on anyone who gets too close. "You know – whether they choose flight, freeze, fawn or fight when they're threatened by a predator. You gave me the idea, actually."

"That's cool." Hope winces. "I hope mine is going to be OK. I really, really want to do triple science at GCSE."

"What's yours on?" I ask, shifting my body slightly so that I can get a clear view of the rest of the class.

"Oh – well, not much."

I look at her. "Come on – I told you about mine."

She glances around to check that nobody is listening, almost as if she's embarrassed. "I looked at how we might use advances in molecular science to create a vaccine for the common cold. Do you think it'll be enough to get me into triple science?"

A couple of kids start messing around, pushing each other about and getting suspiciously close to where I'm standing. I tense when I see that Bonnie is behind them. I just need a few more minutes – that's all.

"Eden?" Hope taps my arm. "Do you think my essay sounds OK?"

"Sure," I tell her, not really listening. "Oh, good – she's finally letting us in."

Ahead of me, Mrs Lipscott is opening the door and ushering the first kids in the queue into class.

"It's deadline day!" she calls in a sing-song voice. "I

want you to put your essays in front of you on the table and then we're going to go around the class, one by one, so that you can give us all a quick summary of what you've been working on."

There's a universal groaning sound and then we're moving forward and into class. I glance at my watch. Things are about to get interesting in three, two, one…

Ping.

"OMG!" gasps Violet, who is ahead of me. "Have you seen this?"

"I got tagged into it too," says Britt. "Check it out."

All around me, kids are grabbing their phones and logging on.

"Whose is that account?" calls Ethan.

I keep walking, into the classroom. The Glossies are standing near their bench, outwardly still a trio, although from the hostile body language Bea is emanating, the other two probably wish they'd skipped this class today. The sight of Mikki and Autumn makes me shiver slightly as I walk past, remembering how it felt to be held down by them, powerless to stop them doing whatever they felt like doing to me. And then I remind myself that I'm not ever going to allow that to happen again, and I harness that feeling, letting it fill my veins and give me strength to carry out the rest of my plan.

"It's from someone called @glossygirl," says Kacey. "It could be a bot. She doesn't have any other posts or any friends – but she's tagged a few of us into this post."

That's what you think. She has got one friend, actually.

"Phones away, please!" calls Mrs Lipscott, shooing the last kids into the room. "If I see a single device then I'm going to be confiscating it until the end of the day. You have been warned! Now – sit down and essays on display."

I glance across at where the Glossies are gathered, my pulse racing as I watch Autumn put her trademark folder down on top of the bench. She has been as predictable as I expected, and the final piece of my plan just fell perfectly into place.

"I've forgotten mine," whines Ethan, inadvertently buying the rest of the class (including me) a few more precious seconds, as Mrs Lipscott summons him to her desk and proceeds to give him a lecture on the importance of committing to his education.

"Nice pic!" says Kieran, turning to look at the Glossies. "Looking sharp, ladies."

"What are you talking about?" snaps Mikki, reaching for her phone. "What picture? I can't see anything."

"I'll tag you in," offer Kacey oh-so-helpfully.

"Share it with me too!" calls someone else.

And just like that, my tiny act of rebellion starts to grow.

I was quite pleased with the image. It captures their group dynamics really well, if I say so myself, and the additional edits and photoshopping really add that extra something special.

A giant hammer added to a scowling Mikki's hand, smashing repetitively up and down on top of a cartoon image of a girl.

A speech bubble coming out of Autumn's lips, containing nothing but poo emoji after poo emoji, as if she's defecating from her mouth.

A magnificent, bejewelled crown set on top of Bea's head, her arm waving imperiously in the air.

But it's the caption that really makes it work.

How do you know if we're lying? Our lips are moving...

"Whoever this @glossygirl is," says Violet, "She clearly hates all of you."

"What is going on?" breathes Autumn, her face crumpled up in confusion as she stares at her phone. "Who would dare do this to *us*?"

"Someone with very little regard for their own safety," snarls Mikki.

Everyone starts talking and the Glossies move closer together. Well, Mikki and Autumn do. Bea is still standing slightly apart from them, her eyes briefly finding mine across the crowded room. I think for one, awful second she's going to ruin my plan by somehow drawing attention to me. But then she glances at her phone and waves it in front of the other two girls.

"Have you seen what someone has put in the comments?" she murmurs, ushering them towards the door where they can't be heard. "I can't believe that they would say something like that about you, Mikki."

Perfect. I hoped that this would happen. All I had to do was light the touch paper – the rest of Year Nine will keep fanning the flames, at least for another twenty seconds which is all I need.

At the front of the room, Mrs Lipscott is still admonishing Ethan for his lack of responsibility. Over by the door, the Glossies are huddled in a protective group, frantically muttering to each other. Everyone else is staring at their phones, or tapping at them furiously. There is never going to be a better time than now. Moving as silently and ghost-like as I can, I pull my newly purchased folder from my bag and drift across to the bench where the Glossies always sit. It takes seconds to do what needs to be done and then I'm back in my seat, essay in front of me and the folder stashed safely in my rucksack.

Let the fun begin.

Mrs Lipscott finally finishes with Ethan and claps her hands.

"Quieten down," she warns. "And I'm serious. Any phones that are visible in five seconds are being locked in my cupboard. That's five, four, three…"

There's a flurry of activity as everyone stashes their phones in bags and pockets and then sits down. Essays are displayed on tables and the room quietens as Mrs Lipscott takes the register.

I must admit, I'm curious about exactly how this is going to go down. My favourite guess is something involving the elements. Fire would be my choice. There's something very fitting about fire. I'm not sure Bonnie has the guts for that though – I'm probably going to have to settle for something less dramatic.

"We'll start at the front," states Mrs Lipscott. "Hope – can you please tell us about your essay?"

Hope stands and I can see from here that her legs are shaking. She quietly explains what she's been working on, and my mouth drops open when I hear just how much of a genius she clearly is. The rest of the class slump in their seats, as the standard is set ridiculously high. Hope finishes and then turns to look at me. I give her a thumbs up and a huge grin, feeling bad that I wasn't paying attention to her earlier.

"And now we'll head to the back row. Bea — let's hear from you next," instructs Mrs Lipscott.

Bea pushes back her chair and stands.

"My essay is about the hive culture," she says. "Particularly the queen bee and how she's totally misunderstood."

"Are you kidding me?" murmurs Mikki, loud enough for those of us closest to hear.

Bea ignores her and continues. "Everyone thinks that the queen rules the hive, but that's not true. Sure — she lays all the eggs but she's at the mercy of the worker bees. They feed her and keep her alive while she's useful to them but the instant that they detect she's failing, it's all over for her. The other bees decide when they want a new queen, and they'll get rid the old queen without a second thought. They surround her and won't let her move and eventually she overheats and dies."

She sits down, glancing at Mikki and Autumn. "It's super harsh and totally unforgiving."

Interesting. I see she failed to mention the fact that the queen is the only bee who can sting again and again and again, without harming itself.

"Thank you, Bea," says Mrs Lipscott. "Britt — you're up."

Britt starts to talk and then the next and the next, and

I'm starting to think that Bonnie might have chickened out, when she raises her hand.

"My drink tastes weird," she tells the teacher. "Please can I refill it from the tap?"

"Yes, yes – just do it quietly." Mrs Lipscott flaps her hand. "Do carry on, Kieran. Your account of how you have investigated the optimal number of hours it takes to *rank up on FIFA* is absolutely fascinating. Who knew that online gaming was so scientific?"

Kieran grins, missing the thick layers of sarcasm, and continues to drone on about what a skilled gamer he is.

Bonnie weaves between the tables, unscrewing the top of her bottle as she heads across the room. My heart starts to beat faster in my chest, and I force my face to remain bored and still. She mustn't suspect a thing. None of them can.

She gets nearer and I zone out Kieran's voice, focusing purely on Bonnie. Later, people will tease her for falling over her own feet because there is nothing on the floor – Mrs Lipscott keeps a very tight rein on her classroom and all coats and bags must be stashed under the tables. Bonnie scuttles towards me, getting closer and closer.

And then, just as she reaches me, she trips.

Win Like A Girl

I see it all in slow motion.

Bonnie losing her balance and lurching towards me.

The hand holding the bottle thrusting forward, the contents flying out in one, beautiful, blackcurrant-squash-coloured arc, landing squarely on the essay in front of me.

I half-got my wish, then. It *was* one of the elements.

"Oh my gosh!" Bonnie gasps, as the world resumes its normal speed. "I'm so sorry, Eden."

She clasps her hand to her mouth as we both stare at the purple liquid seeping through the pages. For a brief second she looks genuinely shocked, as if she can't quite believe what she's done.

"What's happening back there?" calls Mrs Lipscott. "Is everything OK?"

"Oh, this is terrible," says Mikki, appearing behind me. "Look – Eden's essay is ruined." She can barely keep the joy out of her voice, and I force myself to keep facing the front. If I have to see her smug face right now, then I'll give it all away and ruin the surprise.

"What?!" Mrs Lipscott strides briskly across the room, pushing through the kids who are starting to stand up and crane to look in my direction. "How on earth did this happen?"

"It was my fault," wails Bonnie, and I hope that she's intending to do GCSE drama next year because she's highly convincing.

"Don't blame yourself," says Autumn, coming to give her a reassuring hug. "It could have been any one of our essays. This kind of thing just happens, doesn't it?"

This is too much, even for me, and I let out a snort of laughter which I have to rapidly disguise as devastation when everyone looks at me.

"I don't know what to say." Mrs Lipscott shakes her head. "Do you have a backup copy anywhere, Eden?"

"Of course she doesn't!" calls Violet. "You made us write them out by hand."

"Oh, yes." The teacher looks at me with sympathy. "I'm so sorry that this happened. You'll get an extension to rewrite it, obviously."

"*Obviously*," repeats Autumn. "I mean, that's only fair, isn't it, Miss?"

"And this is why we do NOT move around the room with unsecured liquids," snaps Mrs Lipscott, glaring around at the rest of the class. "This could have been entirely avoided."

She marches back to her desk, leaving me with the soggy mess of papers on my table.

"I'll help you with that," says Mikki, raising her voice so that everyone will hear her being helpful. "Sorry, Sprinkles – I think this all needs to go in the bin."

She picks up the pieces of paper and scrunches them together, ensuring that even the pages that weren't too damaged are now wet and illegible.

"I might be able to salvage some of it," I protest feebly, as she dashes across the room and rams the entire thing into the bin, where Autumn is already waiting to block Mrs Lipscott's view.

"Oh God – sorry!" yelps Mikki, as she shoves the project right down into the bin. "Someone's left a banana milkshake in here." She retrieves her arm and waves the papers in the air, and I watch as a large splodge of something thick and yellow oozes across the title page. "Do you still want to try and save it?"

"No," I say sadly. "It's completely trashed."

Mikki smirks at Autumn.

"We'll get rid of it for you," Autumn calls to me. "It's the least we can do."

And then Mrs Lipscott is telling the Glossies to sit down because time is running out and there are still several more people to go. Mikki drops the essay back into the bin with a mic-drop flourish and then they saunter back to their places. I resist the urge to look over at them. Instead, I dab some splashes of juice off the table and sit back.

And I wait.

We sit through one kid talking about the fascinating world of the earthworm and another who has attempted to explain how the entire planet's energy can be supplied using orange juice – and then it's time.

"Autumn." Mrs Lipscott adjusts her glasses and stares towards the back of the room. "You're up. Tell us all about your essay and why you chose this particular topic."

Autumn stands and clears her throat, pulling the brown and orange, squirrels and acorns folder towards her and opening it up.

"OK, so my essay is all about—" she starts and then she stops. And stares. And it's my turn to put my hand to my mouth because I can't laugh now.

"Carry on," says Mrs Lipscott impatiently. "We need to get this done before lunchtime."

"This isn't my essay." Autumn's voice is confused. "I don't understand – I didn't write this. This isn't my handwriting."

"What do you mean?" snaps Mrs Lipscott. "Is that your folder?"

Autumn nods. "Yes. But this isn't my essay. She pulls out the pages, holding them closer to her face as if that will somehow make a difference. "This project is about stress or something. It isn't mine."

"Let me see that." Mikki grabs it out of her hands and riffles through the pages. The room is silent, the sort of silence that happens just before a storm.

"This is Eden's!" Mikki's voice is shaking, but not with terror. She glares across at me and I give her the tiniest smile.

"What?" Mrs Lipscott walks across the room, and I internally beg her to speed up because now Mikki's hands are shaking too, and I know it's only a matter of time before my precious essay is ripped into a thousand pieces. "Let me see that."

She reaches out and takes the papers from Mikki and I exhale.

"Yes," the teacher confirms. "This work has got Eden's name on." She turns to Autumn, an accusing look on her face. "What was it doing in your folder, may I ask?"

"I don't know!" squeals Autumn, looking first at Mikki

and then at me. "But where's my essay? What have you done with it, Eden?"

I blink rapidly and then hold my hands out in front of me. "I don't know what you mean. I haven't done anything with your essay."

And yes – it's possible that I linger ever so slightly with an emphasis on the "I".

Mikki gets it first. She always was the smarter one of the Glossies. Her face pales and her eyes flicker towards the bin but she doesn't say a word.

I'm going to have to bring this home myself.

"There must have been a mix-up," I say, trying to sound confused. "But I don't understand how."

"Did you leave your essay anywhere?" asks Mrs Lipscott, frowning. "Maybe Autumn picked it up unintentionally?"

"That must be what happened," I agree. "I did leave my essay in the girls' toilets at break-time. Although I have no idea how it ended up in Autumn's folder – it's a bit of a weird thing to happen."

"It's obvious what's happened," snarls Mikki. "Eden took Autumn's essay."

"I just don't get it," I say again, and the wobble in my voice isn't entirely fake. I resist the urge to look down and make sure that the duplicate folder isn't visible in my bag – if that gets discovered then the whole game is up.

"Hmmm." Mrs Lipscott stares first at me and then at Autumn. "That seems unlikely, given the circumstances."

I let out a silent breath of relief. One of the benefits of having been invisible for the last three years is that teachers don't tend to suspect you of criminal activity.

"Everyone check to see if you have Autumn's essay in your folder," orders Mrs Lipscott, sighing heavily. "Just to be sure."

There's a lot of noise and rustling of paper and murmured snorts of laughter as everyone goes through the pointless motions of looking for Autumn's work. Bea catches my eye and I hold her gaze until she looks away and then I sit very still, enjoying the unfamiliar feeling of power.

"Has everyone checked their folders?" calls Mrs Lipscott.

The room rings with a resounding: "*Yes, Miss.*"

"And does anyone have Autumn's work?" she asks.

A chorus of enthusiastic "*No, Miss*" bounces off the wall.

"And does everyone else have their own essay in front of them?" she enquires. "All except for you, Eden, and you, Ethan – don't worry, I haven't forgotten about you in all this drama."

Ethan groans as everyone else confirms that they have the correct work.

"So, whose essay is in the bin, then?" Hope asks the completely unnecessary yet killer question and if I could blow her a kiss without being seen, then I would.

"I think it's probably fair to assume it is Autumn's," says Mrs Lipscott, and the room erupts. She yells for quiet and threatens a whole-class detention and eventually, the room settles down again.

"I have no idea what is going on," she tells us, glaring around the lab. "And whatever it is, I do not like it. But it ends right here, right now. Eden – you appear to have had a stroke of good luck." She hands me my work and starts to walk back to her desk.

"What about me?" wails Autumn. "It isn't good luck for me!"

"We're moving on now, Autumn," snaps the teacher, clearly having run out of patience. "Eden. As you now have your work back, please can you tell us about what you chose as your topic?"

I don't do this. I don't speak out in front of other people. I don't take risks. I don't let myself be seen.

I push back my chair and stand up.

"Yeah, OK." I clear my throat and try to push my nerves to one side. "My project looks at the behaviour of different animals when they are put in a stressful situation. Some animals choose flight – they run away as fast as they can, like a zebra when it's faced with a lion trying to kill it. Its heart rate gets faster, and its blood pressure increases, and it will run for its life."

I pause and look around the room. "Some animals choose flight in a different way though. They might not run away but instead they change colour and try to blend in, so they don't attract attention to themselves. So, you could say that blending in and trying to be like everyone else is a form of flight."

I let my eyes briefly rest on Violet and Kacey, and then move on.

"Other animals freeze when they're stressed. Chickens do this, and so do rabbits. Some predators are more interested in the chase than the actual kill, so playing dead is a cunning way to get them to lose interest." I take a breath. "Unless they are prepared to come for you no matter what state you're in – in which case freezing can go horribly wrong."

"This sounds like a fascinating essay," says Mrs Lipscott, glancing at the clock on the wall. "I'm looking forward to reading it. Right then, up next is—"

"There's another fear response," I say, talking over her and glancing at Daisy. "The fawn response. Nervous dogs sometimes do this, tucking their tails and licking a person or another dog to try to placate or appease a perceived threat. So, trying to make the predator feel good about themselves in the hopes that they will fix their sights on someone else." I let my eyes flicker around the room again. "Then there's the final response."

And now my gaze is firmly on the table of Glossies. "Some animals have had enough of being terrorized. They don't run away, and they don't play dead. They don't try to please or suck up or abandon their principles to stay safe." I let a small smile creep across my face and deliver my punchline. "They fight. They do whatever it takes to survive. They'll battle to the very end if that's what it takes."

And then I sit down.

"Yes, thank you, Eden. Now, hurry up, last one before the bell rings..." Mrs Lipscott motions to the next kid.

"Good job, Eden," whispers a voice, and I can't tell where it comes from although for a split-second I think it sounds like *Bea*. Then I notice that Hope grinning at me, and I smile back, and mouth, *Thanks*.

But I'm not stupid. I know that the story doesn't end here.

I've declared my decision to fight and I'm not expecting the Glossies to just take off into the sunset. It's like I said – I'll battle until the very end if that's what I need to do.

I just hope I have what it takes.

Dare Like A Girl

"We have a new special today," Jimmy tells me as soon as I've stashed my bag beneath the doughnut stand and put on my apron. "It's kind of a mash-up between our product and a carrot cake."

"That sounds like a food crime." I grimace and look at the offending items, which are stacked high at the front of the stand. "Vegetables have no place on a doughnut. What's wrong with people?"

"I know, right?" Jimmy sits down on his stool and shakes his head. "What next? The cabbage-nut?"

I think about it for a moment. "How about the mushroom-nut?"

"Gross." He grins at me. "Although not as bad as the broccoli-nut."

"And definitely better than the pea-nut," I tell him.

"No." He puts his hands over his face. "That is cursed, Eden!"

We both start laughing and it takes a few minutes to get a grip. I've noticed this more and more recently – whatever I'm feeling seems to be at maximum levels, so if I'm laughing then I'm almost hysterical. If I'm angry then I can feel a volcano erupting inside me. And if I'm sad, it's as if the whole world has gone into black-and-white mode and there's no colour left in anything. Basically, everything feels like a *lot*.

"So," I ask once we've both calmed down. "What is the name of this incredible new product?"

Jimmy snorts. "Twenty-four *Carrot* Gold."

I groan. "Please don't make me say that to any customers! I'm begging you, Jimmy. My life is challenging enough right now without adding that kind of humiliation to my day."

Jimmy stops smirking and looks at me seriously. "What happened with those girls after last week?" he asks.

I ended up telling him all about it after the Glossies had strolled off with their stolen goods. He was pretty great about it, actually – there was no way that he could let me off paying for the box that was taken but at least he applied my employee discount, so I got to take home a bit of my wages that day.

I shrug and use the tongs to start rearranging the doughnuts into a pleasing pattern on their trays. "Oh, you know how it is," I say, aiming for casual. "Kids like that – they get bored after a while and choose a new target."

"Hmm." He isn't convinced.

"OK, fine. It's like this," I tell him, picking up a Rainbow Sprinkle and placing it on an empty tray. "This is me. I'm the target."

Next, I pick up three Peanut Butter Bliss doughnuts and line them up close together, facing the Rainbow Sprinkle. "These are the Glossies. They are the enemy and all they want is to terrorize me into submission."

I glance up at Jimmy, who is leaning forward on his stool, taking it all in. I carry on.

"OK, so I've mostly been trying to keep away from them and ignore what they're doing."

"Playing defence," confirms Jimmy, nodding sagely.

"Maybe," I nod. "Or maybe what I've been doing is hiding."

"Oh." Jimmy scowls. "Defence is only a good tactic if you're prepared to use a little fire power when it's needed. If you hide then they can pin you down and that's no good – you need to be ready to mobilize at any moment."

"There has been some pinning down," I agree. "And it was not great."

"So, what you need to do now is change your tactics." Jimmy stands up and takes the tongs out of my hand. "We need to review your strategy and find their vulnerable points." He pushes the Peanut Butter Bliss doughnuts apart, putting space between them. "You gear up and you move out and then, when they are least expecting it, you strike. You infiltrate their camp and you kick some doors down, you get me?"

Jimmy manoeuvres the Rainbow Sprinkle in between two of the Peanut Butter Bliss.

"Sure, but then what?" I sigh.

Jimmy says, "You *stop* them. Full stop."

I roll my eyes. "Like it's that easy."

Jimmy pushes the Rainbow Sprinkle right up against one of the other doughnuts. "Did I say anything about easy?" His voice is rebuking, and I sit up a bit straighter. "Nothing about this is easy. But if you don't end *them*, then they're going to end *you*. So, you've got to buckle up and engage." He passes the tongs from one hand to the other and gives me a stern look. "You have to play for your life, Eden!"

And then, before I can stop him, he brings the tongs down, first on to one Peanut Butter Bliss and then the other, smashing them into the tray so that the icing cracks and crumbles and perfect circles become flattened and imperfect, their centres oozing out.

"Jimmy!" I stare at the tray, half-laughing. "We can't sell them now!"

He drops the tongs and reaches into his back pocket, and I watch as he pulls out his wallet and puts the correct money into the cash box. Then he picks up one of the squashed doughnuts and hands it over to me. "My treat."

He picks up the other and we sit in silence for a few minutes, enjoying the delicious nutty flavour mixed with the sweet yeasty dough. It turns out that the people at Delicious Doughnuts do know what they're doing with their taste combinations. Who knew?

"Squashed doughnuts still taste good," I tell him appreciatively, once I've finished it off. "Out of interest, did you have a big CoD campaign last night?"

Jimmy licks his fingers clean and grins at me. "Maybe. Chantelle finished with me again, so I spent most of the night gaming. There's a chance that I'm a bit buzzed right now."

"Nobody would ever notice," I assure him, trying to keep a straight face. "There's nothing even a tiny bit weird about trying to give me bullying advice using a combination of online war games and doughnuts."

He laughs, and then we are rudely interrupted by a young couple who are keen to find out if the Twenty-Four *Carrot* Gold is vegan. I leave them to Jimmy's expert professionalism and gaze around the food court.

And this is when I spot Mikki and Autumn sauntering in through the main entrance and making a beeline straight towards me.

"Eden," Autumn greets me, more quietly and less showily than usual. "How's it going?"

I glance over at Jimmy, but the young couple have moved on to requesting the number of calories in the Luscious Lemon and he is desperately rifling through the folder which contains all the nutritional information. I'm going to have to deal with this without any backup.

"It's going," I say, keeping my voice steady. "How can I help you?"

"We'd like two Toffee Fudge Delight doughnuts," Mikki tells me. I stare at her suspiciously, but she's already got the money ready and hands it over without an issue. I select the stalest doughnuts on the tray and put them both in the same bag as a tiny act of rebellion, and then hand them over.

"What an excellent choice," I say, staring her down. "You all have a delicious doughnutty day."

Go ahead, Mikki. Make fun of what I just said. I will say the word "doughnutty" if I want to.

She says nothing.

"Thanks." Autumn accepts the bag. I wait for a biting comment, but none follow.

I give them a tight smile and then pick up the damp cloth that Jimmy keeps behind the stand to wipe the tongs, which still have squashed Peanut Butter Bliss on them. I clean them and put them back on the tray, but when I turn around, both girls are still standing there, looking at me.

"Was there something else?" I ask. "I have other customers to serve."

Mikki and Autumn look around at the empty food court and then back at me.

"There was just one other thing," says Mikki quietly. She nods at Autumn, who pulls a familiar-looking envelope out of her bag and thrusts it towards me. Part of my brain is vaguely interested to see that the cutesy autumnal folder I bought, and generously gifted to Autumn when I swapped over our essays, is nowhere to be seen. Perhaps it has shared the same fate that her original folder suffered – being shoved into the bins around the back of the school kitchens, along with a whole load of colourful envelopes that were tucked inside it and the contents of which will remain forever unread.

I keep my arms by my sides and stare at them both.

"No."

Mikki steps forward and leans towards me, her voice even lower. "Just hear us out, Eden. You said that you wanted this to stop – well, this is the way. One last little test and we'll never bother you again. You can go your way and we can go ours. And everyone gets exactly what they deserve."

I frown. "How exactly are *you* getting what you deserve? You've made my life miserable but there's been zero comeback on you."

Autumn raises an eyebrow. "You think having to spend most of this weekend and my evenings next week rewriting my science essay is fun? You stole my work, Eden – don't even try to deny it."

I shrug, letting a tiny smile creep on to my face. "What about you?" I enquire, turning to Mikki. Jimmy said that I had to kick down doors to announce my presence – well, here I am. "How are you getting what *you* deserve, Mikki?"

A shadow flits across her face. "Your little friend Hope got me kicked off the track team," she admits in a low voice. "She told Coach I've been winning races by intimidating my opponents into losing and he lost the plot."

"You *have* been doing that," I point out reasonably.

"Winning is what counts," she mutters.

"Some people think actually earning your achievements and being a team player is what counts. But you do you."

This new Eden both terrifies and thrills me in equal measure.

"Whatever." Mikki glares at me, but what I don't understand is why she isn't lashing out, fighting back as usual – and the thought is concerning. Then she nods at the envelope that Autumn has placed on the stand in front of me.

"Look, Eden. Yesterday, you proved you've got a spine, OK? And you've got what you wanted. Autumn and I have both had to deal with consequences because of you. But there's one person who's getting away without any kind of punishment – and she's the reason that any of this happened in the first place."

I stiffen. Mikki is right. Bea is their queen, and they live to do her bidding. It might not have been her who pinned me down in the yard but it's a safe bet to assume that it happened on her orders. In some ways, she's even worse than Mikki and Autumn. Bea is careful not to get her hands dirty, but it all comes from her.

"I thought she was your friend?" I gaze at the girls. "Why would you set her up?"

"She set me up first," says Mikki. "Getting you to run against me on sports day? She knew exactly what she was doing. And nobody embarrasses me – not even Bea Miller."

Autumn rolls her eyes. "Plus, Bea's gone soft," she tells me. "If people think we're off our game, then *we'll* be the target. Bea is a liability."

Oh. It looks like there may be more than one contender for Queen Bee at Woodford High.

"Take the envelope," Mikki tells me. "Do the final test and then walk away. We don't want any more trouble, do we, Autumn?"

Autumn shakes her head. "No. We didn't want to do the tests in the first place, Eden. It was Bea's idea. It's always been Bea."

And despite what these two have put me through, it's true. It's been Bea, right from the very beginning, when we were best friends and she ghosted me at Woodford High because I wasn't the right kind of person for her needs.

"You can choose when you do it," says Mikki. "As long as it's before the Year Nine school dance at the end of next week. We don't want her there."

Silently, I nod at the girls, and they nod back. And then they turn and walk away, and I wait until they're out of sight before picking up the blood-red envelope and carefully, without ripping the edges, pull it open to read test seven.

To: Eden
Target: Bea
Test: Utter humiliation
Time: Before next Friday 13th July (unlucky for some...)

"Oh, my word," groans Jimmy, flopping down on to his stool as the young couple walk away empty-handed. "What kind of a person refuses to buy a doughnut because of the calorific content? If you want to eat clean then go to Sensational Smoothies."

"Right." I'm not listening. My brain is whirring with possibilities.

"What's that?" Jimmy cranes forward to peer at the note. "More trouble?"

I shake my head, shoving the envelope and its contents into my back pocket. "More of an opportunity," I tell him. "It's time to play for my life, Jimmy."

Cry Like A Girl

"Eden? Can I come in?" The knock at the door takes me by surprise and I shove my phone under my pillow.

"Hey." Melissa's head pokes around my bedroom door. "Am I disturbing you?"

"It's fine," I tell her, sitting up on my bed. "I'm about to start my homework."

I'm lying. I've spent the last three days trying to devise a plan and it finally came to me today, during the weekly "Tuesday Sing-up" assembly that Woodford High forces us all to endure. I was silently mouthing the words, like always – and I caught sight of the Glossies. They were standing together in the hall, Autumn and Mikki on either side of the fated queen.

Mikki, head turning from side to side and eyes

narrowed, as if she's daring anyone to challenge her. Confrontational.

Autumn, chewing gum and blowing big, pink bubbles while jiggling from one foot to the other. Bored.

And Bea, standing tall and staring straight ahead, her mouth turned up at the corners in a faint smile of disdain because a girl like her doesn't do anything as embarrassing as sing. Superior.

And I knew exactly how to finish this.

Melissa comes into the room, a steaming mug of hot chocolate in her hands. "You work so hard," she says, setting it down on my tiny desk and giving Midnight a cautious stroke on the head. "I thought you deserved a treat. I put in those little marshmallows you like."

"Thanks." I smile at her, but she doesn't leave. Instead, she walks to the window sill where my collection of cacti is placed, gently touching a finger against each one.

"Do you remember when I bought you your first cactus?" she says.

I glance up at her in surprise. I don't remember and if anyone had asked me, I'd have said I bought it for myself. I don't associate her with my love of these weird, prickly plants.

"No. When was that?"

She turns and smiles at me and then goes back to

looking at my collection. "You were four," she tells me. "We were out shopping at the market, and something had made you sad. I wanted to cheer you up so I told you that you could choose something small from the toy stall."

"What made me sad?" I ask, feeling a vague memory starting to shimmer at the very edges of my mind.

She doesn't turn around this time. "We walked past a family," she says. "A little girl with her parents. And you asked me where your dad was – it was the first time you'd ever mentioned him."

"What did you tell me?" I get up and walk over to stand beside her.

"I told you that I didn't know where he was, and that he was a kind man but not ready to be a dad." She swallows loudly. "I told you that he left when he found out that there was going to be a baby, but that it was OK, because I was your mum and dad all rolled into one and that I would never run away."

There's a pause for a moment and then she laughs. "And then I dried your tears and tried to bribe you with a toy – but you weren't having any of it. There was a plant stall next door, and I couldn't tear you away."

"I remember," I tell her, picking up Cosmo, the cactus I've had for ten years, the one I always think looks like a prickly dandelion clock. I've checked with @aussiekid and @TKOcactus to see if it might be a contender for the Guinness World Record for oldest cactus, but apparently it's not even close. "The toys were boring, but I thought the plants looked exciting."

She nods. "The man on the stall spent ages showing you a beautiful African Violet and he had almost convinced you when you spotted this cactus. And then you asked me why it had prickles, and when I told you it was so that the plant could protect itself, you were insistent that it was what you wanted."

I smile. I do remember this – back in the time when I called her *Mum*, and it was us against the world. I remember thinking that it was the cleverest thing I had ever heard – growing your own self-defence and making it impossible for anyone to get to you.

"I'm sorry if I'm a pain sometimes," I say, the words tumbling over themselves, like maybe they've been waiting to make an appearance for a while now. "I do love you."

She pulls me into a hug, and we stand for a bit, the sunlight streaming in through the window making my hair feel warm.

"I love you too," she murmurs. "My little prickly pear."

"I don't know about that," I tell her back.

She gives me a squeeze and then releases me, stepping back so she can see my face. "My darling Eden," she says, her eyes crinkling at the edges. "You are the dictionary definition of a prickly pear. Spiky on the outside and soft on the inside." She grins at me and heads over the bedroom door. "Don't ever change. And drink your hot chocolate before it goes cold."

She closes the door behind her, leaving me staring at my plants and thinking about what she just said. It's the tiniest bit possible that I have built my entire life strategy on the same model as a cactus plant. I'm not sure if that makes me a genius or a loser. Regardless, I'm ready to let a certain person see my spikes.

Grabbing the drink, I return to my bed and retrieve my phone from underneath my pillow. Then I open the photo album I'd been searching through and swipe through the pictures and videos, reliving everything that has happened since I got a phone for my tenth birthday.

The summer holiday when Mum took us for one week to a caravan in Devon and we spent the entire time either in the sea or making elaborate sandcastles on the beach, before eating fish and chips on the pier.

The day I came home to find Midnight curled up in a basket, waiting for me.

I swipe through photo after photo, documenting birthdays and Christmas and random things that captured my attention.

And then I find it. The entire reason that I'm bothering to take this trip down memory lane. The video taken at the school karaoke-disco.

A video of an eleven-year-old girl, not-so-glossy, scruffy blonde hair flowing down her back and her huge blue eyes grinning at the camera as she grabs the karaoke microphone.

A video of a girl singing her heart out, even though singing is definitely not one of her talents – although it's probably better than the dance moves she is currently executing on screen, and which could be the definition of *dance like nobody is watching*.

A close-up as she reaches for the high note and fails spectacularly but doesn't care enough to stop.

A video full of fun and freedom and uninhibited joy, with not a single thought to what anyone else might think.

A far cry from the cool, collected, pristinely constructed girl she is today, who would definitely not be seen doing anything as uncool as *singing*.

It's perfect.

The birds wake me next morning, just before my alarm clock goes off. I stretch out, enjoying the slight feeling of tension in the backs of my legs. My running has really been improving recently and now that Mikki is off the track team, I'm giving some serious thought to asking Coach if I can join. Not quite yet though. I've got to stitch up this unfinished business before I can move on.

06:54 **@trackstar09**: Morning! How you doing?

06:56 **@just-eden**: Hey! I'm good. Feeling positive about today, you know?

06:57 **@trackstar09**: Why? What's special about today?

07:00 **@just-eden**: Surely the question should really be what's not special about today?

07:01 **@trackstar09**: Huh?

07:03 **@just-eden**: I mean, it's Wednesday. And Wednesday is my day, right?

07:03 **@trackstar09**: What are you on about?

07:04 **@just-eden**: You said that I could have a Wednesday Addams vibe going on, remember?! If Wednesday wore tracksuits 🖤 Anyway, the sun is shining. We should celebrate every day!

07:06 **@trackstar09**: Eden? Have you been taken hostage? Is this your cry for help? Send me a skull emoji if you need me to call the cops.

07:07 **@just-eden**: 💀

07:07 **@trackstar09**: So why are you so full of the joys of spring?

07:09 **@just-eden**: Don't want to spoil the surprise!

07:10 **@trackstar09**: Uh oh. What are you up to?

07:11 **@just-eden**: Trust me – you're going to love it!

07:14 **@trackstar09**: OK, WEDNESDAY, I trust you – but hundreds wouldn't.

07:18 **@just-eden**: Good job I don't need hundreds, then, isn't it? Someone famous once said something about it being better to walk with one friend in the dark than alone in the light. I'd rather be in the shadows with you than out there in the spotlight with everyone else.

07:21 **@just-eden**: Sorry! Am I being a bit full-on again? I think I'm out of practice at this whole friend thing.

07:23 **@trackstar09**: You don't have to apologize for being real. I'd rather be in the shadows with you too. I always feel like I have to put on an act with my other friends.

07:25 **@just-eden**: I know. But I'm sure you don't need to try to be anyone but yourself in front of your friends! They seem really nice.

07:27 **@just-eden**: I'm actually thinking about joining the track team once this is all over.

07:31 **@trackstar09**: I think that's an excellent idea. You're a brilliant runner. They'll be really pleased to have you join them.

07:32 **@just-eden**: What about you? Won't you be pleased?

07:33 **@trackstar09**: Obviously! Now tell me what you're up to & why you're so excited about today, WEDNESDAY.

★

It turns out that bringing someone down doesn't take long.

It is the work of minutes to send the karaoke video to *Woodford Whispers* and now all I have to do is wait for the "anonymous" admin to do their job.

I'm just leaving the house, when my phone pings. I wave goodbye to my mother and then pause by the garden gate.

And there it is. The video of Bea, looking gawky and young and totally un-glossy, is displayed for everyone to see, complete with the *Woodford Whispers* unique brand of sensationalist headline.

Queen Bea or Wannabe? You be the judge.

I gulp, my throat feeling like it has something stuck inside. I've actually done it – I've gone somewhere I told myself I would never go and it suddenly all feels very real, seeing the video posted on a public platform for everyone to see. It's strange and uncomfortable and I quickly shove both the thought and my phone away.

Then I walk slowly to school, every other step punctuated with a ping and a buzz as my phone lights up with notifications. I don't need to read them to know that my work here is done. Woodford High is my battlefield, and I am triumphant, the victor.

I should be feeling great.

Winning is supposed to feel better than this.

So why do I feel like I've lost something?

By the time I enter the Year Nine corridor, the place is packed. Kids are standing in groups, showing each other their phone screens, and laughing at each new comment as it comes in. I walk through the crowd and today it's as if I'm not even here. Nobody is looking at me or shooting me evil glares. Nobody is lurking, wating to ambush me with a test. I am invisible once again.

Just as I reach my locker there is a shout from the door. I turn and stand on my tiptoes to see what's going on and there she is. Queen Bea herself. Instead of her usual polished poise, she's flushed and clearly agitated as she scurries towards Mikki and Autumn. The crowd parts and the corridor goes quiet as people switch their phones to camera mode and hold them up, ready to capture whatever is about to happen.

"How could you be this stupid?" Bea shrieks, advancing on the girls. "What the hell?"

"Hey now." Mikki holds her hands up as if to ward Bea off, wincing. "You're sounding a little off-key there, Bea."

Autumn laughs and Bea rounds on her. "I know what you're trying to do," she hisses. "You're the admin for *Woodford Whispers*. Maybe someone else sent in the video but it was you who allowed it to be posted. It's the second time you've done this, and there's no way you can tell me that it was a mistake this time, so don't even bother. I'm done with you. You're finished."

"What's wrong, Bea?" asks Mikki. "Does the *truth hurt*?"

Bea freezes for a second.

"It's you." She raises one shaking hand and points a finger at Mikki. "You're behind the @trooth-hurts account. I *knew* that it wasn't Eden."

It isn't a question – more a gradual realization of a fact.

I exhale slowly. I knew about Autumn being the admin for *Woodford Whispers*, but I had no idea that Mikki was @trooth-hurts, although it all stacks up. So that means it was her who posted all that stuff about me and Bea, as well as stirring up all that trouble about Kacey and the others.

Damn. Who needs enemies with friends like that?

"Careful," warns Mikki. "You can't go around accusing people of things you have absolutely no evidence of." She looks around at the elevated mobile phones. "We all know that Eden owns the @trooth-hurts account. What I don't get is why you'd want to accuse *me*. Are you in on it with her?"

Oh, fabulous. I wondered when I would get dragged into this. Thankfully, everyone is too engrossed in the unfolding drama to throw much more than a curious glance in my direction.

"What?" Bea's mouth gapes open. "Why would I write rumours about myself?"

Autumn shakes her head sadly. "That's what we've been wondering," she says. "You need help, Bea. Trolling yourself is low, even by your standards."

A murmur ripples along the corridor, as people try to keep up with this latest revelation, although I can see by the look on both Bea and Mikki's faces that it isn't true. Mikki is @trooth-hurts – I'd bet my entire cacti collection on it.

"What have I ever done to you?" gulps Bea. "We were supposed to be friends. You've both taken this way too far. This is complete betrayal."

Autumn flicks her hair over one shoulder: it's Bea's signature power move but right now, Bea's hair is scraped back into an untidy updo that is more mess than bun.

And then a weird thing happens. As Bea appears to shrink into herself, Mikki and Autumn seem to grow. They step forward and even though they don't physically touch her, it feels like they're squishing all the energy out of her and into themselves. For a brief moment I'm reminded of the worker bees, surrounding the queen and raising her body temperature to the point where she dies.

"What's the problem anyway?" demands Mikki, getting up in Bea's face. I hear several camera clicks as the paparazzi of Year Nine record this unprecedented event for posterity. "It's such a *sweet* video." She pauses and looks around, no doubt weighing up just how much she owns the room right now. "Clearly there are sides to you we've never got to enjoy at Woodford High. Maybe you can get up at the school dance and give us all a quick rendition?"

"Oh, yes!" Autumn claps her hands "We all want to hear Bea sing!"

They're good, I'll give them that. For just a second there, the vibe felt like it could maybe shift in favour of Bea. But the Glossies have reminded everyone of just why we're here, and a few kids laugh, breaking the tension.

"Why don't you sing us a tune?" yells one of the boys.

"This isn't fair, Mikki," stutters Bea, and I can tell she's doing everything she can to stay calm. "How would you like it if I posted a video of you sounding like that?"

Mikki smiles. "Oh, hon – I'd hate it. Not that it could happen, on account of the fact that I would never have made such a fool of myself."

"I was a kid," howls Bea, stamping her foot on the

ground in frustration. "This is a really crappy thing to do. Just take it down!"

"It's out there now," Autumn tells Bea, pretending to shake her head sadly. "That's the scary thing about the internet — what goes online stays online. You should know that."

Bea groans and puts her hands to her face. Mikki glances at Autumn and takes a step back from Bea.

"You're sounding kind of desperate," she says, and I can hear the amusement in her voice. "It's just one little video, Bea. Get a grip, girl — you're embarrassing yourself."

Bea's hands lower and for a moment I almost don't recognize her. Her face is twisted in humiliation and it's obvious that tears are building behind her eyes.

"I'm not embarrassing myself," she half-sobs. "You're doing it to me. You're being really mean."

"*You're being really mean!*" mimics Mikki.

"This is *wild*!" howls Bonnie from the crowd. "Like — is Bea for real?"

And the laughter is like an avalanche. It starts with a tiny chuckle and then it builds up and up, rolling over itself and gaining momentum until it's a giggle and then a guffaw and then a whoop and then a full-blown roar of hilarity.

"Can you believe how stressed she is about it though? It's not *that* big a deal."

"Kind of pathetic. She can dish it, but she obviously can't take it."

"I don't know what's more cringe, her awful screeching or how much she's losing it."

"I guess the reign of Queen Bea is well and truly over. Do you think she's really been working with Eden to spread rumours about everyone?"

And Bea stands there, the focus of everyone's amusement and as the tears start to flow, the more they laugh. Because this is what happens. Abject humiliation and embarrassment are sparked by the tiniest of things.

A few people move to the side and suddenly she sees me. I stay very still, unable to look away and then the bell rings. The rest of Year Nine gather their belongings and head to class, but Bea and I stay there, immovable, like two boulders while the river of people flows around us.

She knows it was me who sent in the video; it can only have been me. But she doesn't make any move towards me. Instead, she just stares at me while she cries, her eyes filled with something that looks like betrayal.

And I know that it was her who masterminded all the tests, and I know it was her who let me down from the start. Yet, as I stay exactly where I am, my own eyes are filled with something that I hope looks like triumph but feels an awful lot like guilt.

There is nothing wrong with the video that I sent to *Woodford Whispers* – it was a kid having fun, that's all. The issue is how Bea handles it – that's the real test.

If she had been the kind of person who could laugh it off, she could have ended this day more popular than she began it.

But she isn't doing that. The video alone isn't that funny – it's her reaction that seals the deal.

In the end, Bea is bringing herself down.

It's entirely what I was counting on.

I have never stooped so low or felt so terrible in my entire life.

Laugh Like A Girl

Today was supposed to the best day of my school life. I anticipated floating through the corridors, safe in the knowledge that I have completed the test and simultaneously taken revenge on the girl who tried to squash me.

The reality is a little less Hollywood. There's a squirming sensation in the pit of my stomach.

Bea wasn't in classes for the rest of the day. Someone allegedly saw her red-eyed in the nurse's office just before lunch and the rumour is that she is officially kicked out of the Glossies. I just hope that Mikki and Autumn stick to their bargain to leave me alone now. I've already heard rumours of girls vying for a spot at their lunch table, but a naive part of me dares to hope that without their Queen Bea, they will lose their way.

Not that I want life to entirely return to how it was before. This whole thing has been a mess but even with this knot in my stomach I admit that it's not all been negative. I kicked down some doors and I let them know that I am here – and now I've done it, I'm not sure I want to disappear altogether. Don't get me wrong, the past couple of weeks has been enough drama to last a lifetime, but there are a few things that I'd like to change. And that's because of one person who has been there for me through all of this.

16:08 **@just-eden**: Hey – you there?

16:14 **@just-eden**: Were you around when it all kicked off this morning? I didn't see you.

16:20 **@trackstar09**: I was there.

16:21 **@just-eden**: I can't believe how everyone reacted.

16:28 **@trackstar09**: You sent the video of Bea to Woodford Whispers, didn't you?

16:30 **@just-eden**: How did you guess? She had it coming, don't you think?

16:39 **@trackstar09**: I don't think anyone deserves to be humiliated.

16:40 **@just-eden**: What about the things they've done to me?

16:46 **@trackstar09**: I know they've been awful to you, Eden. But what happened today was bad. They've totally destroyed her.

16:47 **@just-eden**: I thought you wanted me to fight back? She deserved it. I'm sick of having to be the one who just takes it. This one stupid video is nowhere near as bad as being held down and spat on. Or being tested for weeks on end.

17:03 **@trackstar09**: Those things were awful. But there are always 2 sides to a story.

17:13 **@just-eden**: It feels a lot like you're suddenly on her side.

17:28 **@trackstar09**: All I'm saying is maybe it got out of control or something.

17:42 **@just-eden**: So it's OK for ME to be treated like dirt, but I have to be nice to everyone else, yeah?

17:44 **@trackstar09**: That's not what I meant.

17:51 **@just-eden**: Sounds like it.

I stare at my words on the screen, broadcasting my hatred of Bea Miller. I could tell Riley the truth. I could tell him I feel guilty about the video and I wish I hadn't done it. I could tell him that I never set out with the intention of crushing Bea. But telling him isn't going to change anything, so what's the point? Besides, why *should* I be the only one to suffer?

18:20 **@just-eden**: I'm going to go then.

18:21 **@trackstar09**: Wait. Don't. Look, Eden – I don't want to fight. I'm on your side, OK? We're friends.

18:28 **@trackstar09**: I've been meaning to ask if you want to come to the school disco with me, this Friday. There are a few of us from track going. In a group, I mean. You can totally say no if it's not your thing.

18:35 **@just-eden**: It's totally not my thing.

18:39 **@just-eden**: But I'd like to go with you. Thanks.

18:40 **@trackstar09**: Great. Speak later, OK?

18:41 **@just-eden**: OK.

★

Telling Melissa is my first, rookie error.

"Eden!" She puts down her knife and fork and gazes at me in delight. "This is wonderful! Your first school dance at Woodford High!"

"Yeah." I ram a potato in my mouth, already regretting telling her. "It's this Friday night."

Her face drops and she looks at me with wide eyes. "But today is Wednesday. Are you kidding me?"

I raise my eyebrows. "What's the problem? We're not preparing for a mission to Mars here."

"Well, exactly." She picks up her fork and skewers a pea. "Quite frankly, that would be easier."

"So, how was your day?" I attempt the age-old strategy of distraction but she's not falling for it. "I'm a bit worried about Colin, by the way. He's got some brown spots on him – it doesn't look great."

"What are you going to wear?" she enquires, ignoring my cactus concerns. "Have you thought about that?"

I shrug. "Nope. But I have clothes. I'll just find something clean." I think about it for a moment, picturing my bedroom floor with its heaped pile of dirty washing. "Clean-ish."

"Oh, Eden." She shakes her head sadly. "You have no idea, do you? I blame myself – I should have insisted that you go to more school events and socialize with your peers. You're like a baby lamb in a field full of wolves."

Well, that's a bit offensive, even if it is possibly accurate.

"I'll wear what I always wear," I offer, keen to bring this discussion to an end. "My tracksuit."

"You absolutely will not." Melissa's jaw tightens, and I know I am losing this battle. "Do you know what every other girl will be doing right now? They'll be planning their wardrobe and deciding what to do with their hair and make-up and how best to accessorize. You cannot rock up in an old tracksuit to your first dance!"

"It's just a Year Nine dance, not a prom," I protest, although I can feel niggles of panic worm their way into my head. "Nobody is going to be making any effort."

"Ha!" Her laugh is sharp, like gunfire. "They might not *say* they're making an effort but believe me, they will be. It's the ultimate goal, isn't it – to look incredible while also appearing to have just rolled out of bed?"

Much as I want to now go and hide *under* my bed, her words do have a ring of truth to them. Maybe the school dance is going to be like every single status posted online – showing how utterly incredible your life is and how absolutely amazing you look without any reference to all hard work and faffing about that goes on behind the scenes.

"I'm not going," I tell her, pushing my plate away. My appetite has suddenly disappeared. "It sounds awful."

"But what about your friend?" she asks, and once again her eyes are flashing with something that looks suspiciously like excitement. "You told him you'd go along with him – you can't let him down now."

"He won't care," I snap. "It's not a big deal." But even as I say it, I know that I'm lying. Riley invited me to go to the dance and it'll be the first time we've hung out in real life. It's a big deal and it's going to mark the start of us being proper friends at school. I've decided to wait to join the track team until after the dance, once I've spent some time with them and figured out how the whole thing works.

It's a really, really big deal.

"We'll go shopping after school tomorrow," she says decisively. She knows I'm bluffing. "We'll find you some clothes and we'll get cake, and it will be great." She looks at me across the table. "What do you say, honey? Will you let me help you?"

I open my mouth to say no, and then I think about my cactus plants upstairs in my bedroom. About how they hurt anyone that touches them, even if that person doesn't mean them any harm.

"That'd be good," I tell her. "Thanks, Melissa."

She stiffens slightly but then smiles at me and stands up to clear the plates away. I still have work to do on retracting my prickles, but I want to.

I really do.

Look Like A Girl

"What about this one?"

"Nope."

"OK – how about this?" My mother's voice is slightly less perky than it was half an hour ago.

"Definitely not." I shake my head.

"Maybe this one, then?"

"That is disgusting! What is this – two-thousand-and-ten? Who even buys this stuff?"

"This rail says it has the bestselling products in their teen range," Melissa points out. "So presumably someone must be buying it."

I look at the offending item once again.

"I'll be arrested for indecent exposure if I go out in

public wearing that," I mutter. "That's if I don't die from hypothermia first."

"Eden!" My mother is attempting to sound serious, but she's trying not to smile. "OK – maybe that one is slightly lacking in fabric." She turns back to the rail. "Let's look for something a little less revealing."

I roll my eyes. I'm fairly sure there is not one single item in this shop that I would be seen dead in.

"How about this?" she says, rummaging through the clothes and then pulling out a white, long-sleeved T-shirt, holding it up for me.

"Are you serious?" I splutter. "Do I look like someone who would wear something with *Living the Dream* scrawled across the front of it?"

"Well, I'm certainly not," says my mother, wrinkling her nose up at me and then turning back to the rail. "How about this one? It says *Always Smiling* on the front. Would that be more your kind of thing?"

She turns to look at me and then starts laughing. I suspect that I am radiating quite clearly that this is not, in fact, more my kind of thing. "I think I would pay good money to see you wearing a top that says *Always Smiling*," she gasps, when she can finally catch her breath. "Oh, my goodness – we need to leave this shop before they throw us out."

The way to the exit is through teen boy-wear and I sigh

deeply as I see the rails of clothes designated for the male of the species.

"Where are the ridiculous slogans for boys?" I ask, picking up a perfectly normal-looking blue top, unadorned with inane phrases. "Why don't they have to be *Always Smiling* or *Living the Dream*?"

"It's a good point," agrees my mother. "But don't despair. This is only the first shop. We'll find you something that makes you feel fabulous."

"Only if it doesn't come with a hideous motto printed on the front," I mutter, following her out on to the pavement.

We spend the next forty-five minutes traipsing up and down the high street, going in shop after shop where my mother holds up potential items of clothing and I try not to swear. Eventually she gives in, and we retreat to a cafe, where we both finally agree on something for the first time all day.

"If only clothes shopping were as easy as cake shopping, then the world would be a happier place," she says, sinking into her seat and taking a sip of her coffee.

"I could just wear my tracksuit?" I venture, biting into my millionaire's shortbread and savouring the sweet, chocolate taste. "I'm not really a skirt or dress kind of a girl, you know?"

"I know," agrees Melissa. "But I have one more place to take you and I think you're going to like it."

I'm not convinced but a) I've got nowhere else to

be, b) she's paying and c) it's kind of nice hanging out with her.

"One more shop," I tell her. "And if we can't find anything there then we can go home. Deal?"

"It's a deal," she says, and we clink our coffee cups together and grin at each other.

The final shop isn't on the high street. We walk away from the regular shoppers and down the street and then she turns and leads us into an alleyway I haven't seen before. There are a few shops, all crammed together, and it smells incredible – like spices and smoke and danger.

"I used to come down here all the time before you were born," she tells me. "I just hope that the shop is still here. It's where I bought all my stuff – I thought I was a proper rebel!"

My heart sinks. I don't wish to be rude, but my mother is not exactly known for her up-to-date fashion sense and if she isn't wearing her scrubs then she's either in pyjamas or jeans and jumper. Any shop frequented by her is unlikely to yield a decent outfit.

We approach a tattoo parlour where a man is writing something on a display board outside.

"Melissa!" he says, turning around just as we reach him. "Long time no see!"

"Jonny!" My mother breaks into a huge smile and then

before I know what's happening, they're hugging each other in the middle of the alleyway. "How are you? I can't believe you've still got the shop! That's incredible!"

The man grins at her, revealing a row of golden teeth. "I've got a loyal customer base," he tells her. "They just keep on coming back." He jerks his head at her. "Most of them, anyway."

My mother laughs. "You know how it is, Jonny. Life goes on."

He looks at me and smiles again. "It certainly does."

"Well – seeing you has made my day, it really has." She steps away and puts her hand on my arm. "We're off to see if *Outside The Box* is still up and running – Eden needs an outfit."

Jonny nods his head. "It's still here," he tells us. "But don't be a stranger, Melissa – you hear me? I'd love to have you back in the studio again to finish that—"

"We'd better be off," she interrupts, shooting him another grin. "All the best, Jonny, and maybe I'll pop in before too long."

She turns and pulls me further down the alleyway.

"What was all *that* about?" I hiss, once we're out of earshot. "Who is he and how do you know him?"

"His name is Jonny, and he owns the tattoo studio," she tells me, looking left and right as if she's trying to find something. "We used to hang out together, back in the day."

"Have you got a *tattoo*?" I ask, my voice incredulous.

"I'm sure it's around here somewhere," she says, not answering my question. "Jonny definitely said that it was still open."

"Melissa? Have you got a tattoo?" I stop walking and stare at her back. There's no way she's got one. She's not exciting enough. And anyway, I'd know about it, wouldn't I?

"Melissa?"

She stops walking and points excitedly at a shop ahead of us. "He was right! It's still here!"

And then she's gone, pushing through the door, leaving me out in the alleyway with more questions than answers. I've always known that there are things I've kept from Melissa, convinced that she wouldn't understand me. I never thought that there might be stuff she hasn't shared with me too. Somehow it makes me look at her with fresh eyes, like perhaps we're not that different after all. I shake my head, wondering if maybe she has had a whole other life I don't know about. It's a disconcerting but interesting thought.

Although, when I catch sight of the bay window of *Outside The Box*, I find it hard to think about anything other than what is in front of me.

Slowly, quietly, I push through the door and step inside. When I was little, Melissa showed me a programme from her childhood called *Mr Benn*. It was about this bloke who went to a costume shop every day and tried on a different outfit. Then, when he stepped back through the changing room curtain, he was in a different adventure that was linked to the costume he had chosen. I'm not sure what kind of adventures I might be sent on if I was to wear any of the clothes that I can see in front of me, but I think they might be good ones.

"Eden!" My mother is waving from the other side of the shop. I walk towards her, looking around. All the clothes are arranged in their colour groups, and it feels like walking into a rainbow. I brush past skirts made of lilac net and trousers that look like lavender, running my hand over amethyst-coloured shirts and a dress that reminds me of a thistle.

"Look at this!" She is standing in the yellow section, holding a floaty dress that looks like a sunflower. "Can you imagine wearing this to the dance?"

"No." I pull a face at her. "But there might be something over here."

I turn and walk towards the back of the shop, pulled in by the depths of the colours that get darker in tone the further I go. The pretty pastel shades are at the front, followed by rich jewel-like materials and then burnt-orange hues than merge into earthy browns. And then finally, right at the back – black. But not just black. Walking in between the rails is like walking into midnight. Olive black with a green tint. Blackberry with shades of purple. Charcoal with a touch of grey. Raven with a hint of blue.

All of them glorious.

All of them perfect for a shadow dweller.

All of them exactly what I want to wear.

I pull out an oversized T-shirt with an elaborately drawn five-pointed star on the front and hold it up against myself.

"That would look great with these." My mother shoves a pair of black cut-off shorts at me and I wrinkle my nose. I don't usually tend to put my legs on show, unless I'm either in mandatory PE uniform or out on run and even then I'd rather wear tracksuit pants, even on the hottest of days.

"You can wear tights underneath," she assures me. "Just try it all on and see what you think."

I take the shorts and go into the changing room. Then, as quickly as I can, I put on the new clothes, tucking the T-shirt loosely into the shorts.

"Are you ready?" shouts my mother, and before I can answer she's peering inside. "Oh, yes! Eden – this is great!"

She pulls back the curtain and gestures me to come outside.

"Look at you." Her voice is quiet as she gently puts her hands on my shoulders and spins me to face the mirror. "What do you think?"

I stare at my reflection. What do I think?

I think the person who I am on the inside is actually showing on the outside, maybe for the first time ever.

I think I look like I feel.

I think that there might actually be other clothes out there that aren't tracksuits, school uniform or pyjamas.

I think I look amazing.

"You can wear this with my old pair of Doc Martens," she says. "We'll get you some make-up next and then maybe we can do something with your hair."

I've never been that bothered before about what I'm wearing or how I look, but maybe that's because I've spent so long camouflaging instead of showing.

I know now exactly how I want to dress and what I want to do for the dance tomorrow.

And that is to be brave enough to show Riley the real me.

Dream Like A Girl

17:54 **@just-eden**: So you're definitely coming here, right?

17:59 **@trackstar09**: Sorry, Eden 🙁 I have to get dropped off at school but I'll wait for you by the gates, OK?

18:03 **@just-eden**: I guess. But promise you'll be there or I'm not coming. No way am I walking into that hall on my own.

18:05 **@trackstar09**: I'll be there.

18:14 **@just-eden**: OK...

"You really do look great," my mother tells me for the hundredth time. She indicates and pulls out on to the main road. I protested when she told me that she would drive me to school but inside I was glad. While my new look feels completely right, I am painfully aware that the rest of Year Nine have never seen me looking anything other than nondescript and I'm quite happy to wait until I'm with Riley before anyone catches a glimpse of me.

I pull down the sun visor and examine myself in the mirror. My eyes are ringed with black eyeliner, and I've applied the deepest purple eyeshadow I could find. My hair is twisted into two dark plaits although most of my head is covered by the black beanie that I usually wear when I'm running in winter. Melissa has tried to persuade me to abandon the hat, convinced I'm going to pass out from heatstroke, but it makes me feel protected – I might be making myself a little more visible, but I have my limits.

"You can drop me off here," I tell her, as she takes the turning into the school road. She laughs and shakes her head, slowing her speed but continuing forward.

"No way," she says. "I'm taking you right to the gates. Besides, I want to see what this Riley looks like, don't I?"

She insisted I tell her about who I was going with.

"Melissa," I whine. "Please don't embarrass me."

We approach the gates, and she pulls up, turning to face me.

"I won't embarrass you," she says. "But he's not here so why don't I wait with you until he arrives?"

I shake my head. "Absolutely not." My hand pulls on the door handle, and I put one foot on to the pavement. "Thanks for lift," I tell her. "I'll give you a ring when I'm ready to be picked up if that's still OK?"

She smiles at me and reaches out one hand, giving my arm a squeeze.

"Of course," she says. "Have the best time and I can collect you whenever you want. I'm on chauffeur duty!"

"I'll see you later." I pull myself out of the car and then wave her off, checking she's really gone and isn't lurking somewhere to catch a glimpse of my new friend. I wouldn't put it past her – she's been almost more excited about tonight than I have.

Almost.

The road is empty, and I check my phone. It's two minutes past the time we arranged to meet and a prickle of unease fizzes at the base of my spine. I can hear faint sounds of music floating through the air from the direction of the school hall and for a moment my feet long to sprint after our car and go back home, safe and sound with my mother and a takeaway curry.

And then my phone pings with a message.

19:17 **@trackstar09**: Sorry, got dragged inside by the others! Come on in – we're in the hall.

19:18 **@just-eden**: Can't you come out & meet me?

19:20 **@trackstar09**: We're right inside the door! I'll watch out for you, OK?

19:21 **@just-eden**: Fine. But if I can't see you in the first 3 seconds then I'm leaving.

This was not the plan. I walk slowly into school, cursing Riley.

As I get closer and closer the music gets louder and louder. It's got a driving beat and a thumping bass and suddenly my feet are speeding up and I'm walking faster and faster. I can do this. I am a person who can walk into a packed hall and find her friend and have a good time.

I take a deep breath and push through the doors to the hall. Several things hit me at once. The first is that the place is crammed – it looks like the entirety of Year

Nine is here. The second is that Riley is nowhere near the door – I can see him and the rest of the track team on the other side of the hall by the buffet table. He's laughing at something Hope has just said and doesn't appear to be watching out for me.

Carefully, trying not to stand on anyone's toes, I push through the crowds of people and head to where they're standing, avoiding the part of the dance floor where I can see Mikki and Autumn throwing some shapes. I manage to manoeuvre myself into a space on the other side of Riley and wait for him to see me. We haven't spoken loads since Wednesday as he's been busy – but I did tell him I had new clothes and would be launching the "new Eden" tonight. It seemed funny at the time, but now I'm here and actually doing it, my stomach is flipping over like I'm on a rollercoaster.

He's deep in conversation with one of the boys from track now, and I'm getting too jittery to wait. I tap his arm and then, when he turns to look at me, strike a dramatic pose. I don't know why I do it, and it feels weird the second I throw my arms out, but there's nothing to do now but go with it.

"Ta-dah!" I sing. "What do you think?"

"Eden!" He blinks and stares at me. "Erm – hi?"

"Hi yourself." I lower my hands and jerk my chin

at him. "So, do you like my transformation? It made me think about what you said about Wednesday Addams."

He blinks again, looking confused. "You look … great," he says, glancing around at his friends. "But I don't think I said anything about Wednesday Addams?"

"Come on!" I punch him lightly on the arm. "We've spoken about it a couple of times and you said that if I leant into it more I could have a bit of a Wednesday look? You must remember – cos I asked if that made you Thing!"

Why are so many words coming out of my mouth?

"I never said that." He takes a step back.

My internal alarm signal is sounding off so loudly that I can barely hear the music, but I don't know what to do. So, I keep talking.

"OK," I say, rolling my eyes. "You didn't *say* it – but you messaged it. That's why I said that Wednesday is my day!"

Riley stares at me. "No, I didn't. I've never sent you a message."

And now I know that something is very, very wrong but all my adrenaline seems to be going to my mouth not my legs and I have no choice but to stand here and try to find the right words to make him start behaving the way that I was expecting, needing him to behave.

"Yes, you did." I look around at the track team, a couple of whom have stopped their own conversations and are listening to ours. "We chat every night… It was your idea for us to come to the dance together…"

"I've never messaged you in my life, Eden." Riley's face and voice has changed now. He's less confused and more careful, like he's talking to a small child. "Do you think that I invited you to come to the dance? Cos I didn't. I wouldn't."

I flinch and he sees, rushing to try and soften his words.

"I don't mean it like that," he tells me. "I mean – I'm sure you're great. But I don't know you – that's what I meant. I wouldn't invite you to the dance cos I don't know you."

The DJ changes the song and everyone around me cheers.

"It's our song!" yells one of the track team. "Come on – let's dance!"

Then they're gone, Riley giving me one last sympathetic look before leaving me standing on my own next to the breadsticks and sour cream dip. I will my feet to start moving, one step at a time towards the door, my only conscious thought being how to *get out of here*. I need to drag some air into my lungs, because it feels like I stopped breathing about two minutes ago.

It wasn't him.

I've been messaging someone for weeks and sharing

my deepest feelings with them and it wasn't him. The knowledge makes me want to throw up. *Who was it?*

I step outside into the night air, but it seems that I can't catch a break. Leaning against the wall with her foot propped up behind her and her arms folded, the perfect picture of an avenging demon, is Bea.

"I don't know why, but I thought better of you, Eden," she says darkly.

I ignore her and keep walking. I have bigger problems than Bea Miller right now.

"How could you do it?" she goes on. "How could you send that video of me to Autumn?"

"Please, leave it, Bea," I mutter. I need to focus on just trying to breathe.

"Well, I bet you regret it now," Bea calls out. There's an edge to her voice, a kind of bravado, but it wavers.

I stop walking. "What?"

"You told @trackstar09 that I had it coming. That I deserved it. So now you're getting what *you* deserve."

I turn to face her. Her jaw is set but there are tears in her eyes, and she nods at me. Just one nod, but it tells me what I need to know.

"It was you?" I gasp in air, trying to stop the ground from opening and swallowing me whole. "*Why?*" The word is only a whisper.

"It's done. It doesn't matter any more," she says flatly. "Everything's over."

"Of course it matters!" I swallow down the feeling of sickness and stare at her. "Why would you go to all that effort – for weeks – just to hurt me?"

She stares at me. Loose hoodie sleeves hang over her hands, and her eyes are bloodshot and hollow. She is almost unrecognizable as the former polished, well-put-together style queen of Year Nine. "It wasn't about hurting you."

"Then *why*?" I cry, my ears ringing.

"I was checking up on you, OK?" she snaps, then she looks away, staring distantly over my shoulder. When she speaks again her voice is so quiet that I have to strain to hear her. "I knew you wouldn't reply if you thought it was me, so I pretended to be someone else. I wanted to see if you were OK after the first test. I thought I could try to encourage you to complete the next one, so the girls would accept you into the group and you'd stop getting hurt. And then once it became obvious that you weren't going to do them, I just tried to be there for you." She gulps and looks at me. "To be a friend."

I stare at her. "Are you joking? I was getting hurt because of the tests that *you* set up!"

"I was trying to give you a way out! Mikki was ready to destroy you after sports day, remember?" she interrupts.

"I came up with an idea to protect you. I remember how much fun we used to have. I actually thought we could be friends again. I've missed you, Eden."

A snort of laughter erupts from deep inside me, even though none of this is entertaining.

"This is so messed up," I tell her, starting to walk towards the gates again.

"Maybe. But I was genuinely trying to help you. I thought you'd just do the test and it would be over, and things could be better between us. I know you're still mad at me for going to Jessie Perkins' party at the end of Year Six and I feel bad about that. I really do."

"Are you for real?" I mutter, not slowing down. "You think this is still about a stupid party when we were eleven years old?"

"Isn't it?"

I spin round. "No! It's not because of − of − chocolate fountains or tiny ponies or bouncy castles. Jessie Perkins' party was just the trigger. After that, I lost my best friend and had to start at Woodford High, miserable and alone. And that was one hundred per cent your fault."

I turn again and walk faster. I don't want to look at her. I don't want to see her. I don't want her in my head, full stop.

"That's not true!" she yells, keeping pace. "Some of this

is on you too, you know? I messed up, I know that – but I was a kid, Eden. I tried to talk to you after the party and you wouldn't have anything to do with me! That really hurt. So, I started hanging out that summer with people who wanted to spend time with me – and then you completely blanked me when we started in Year Seven and I didn't have a choice. I moved on." She catches my arm and we stop. She stares at me. "I can't be on my own, Eden. I'm not like you – I'm not brave."

Her words prickle at the base of my skull, reminding me of things I would prefer to forget. A text message sent on the last day of Year Six. A postcard through the letterbox when she went on holiday to France, which I put in the bin without reading.

It never dawned on me that she could think I was the one abandoning her.

"I'm not brave at all," Bea goes on. "And it's like I told you in that first letter. Reputations are fragile." She looks away. "I guess I clung on to it. Along the way, maybe I sometimes lost sight of what was OK and what wasn't—"

"Uh, you think?" I interrupt. "The things you've done to other people is not OK, Bea!"

Bea sighs. "Look, you know Mikki and Autumn. They're good at getting their own way. I *know* the test thing did go too far. I tried to back away from the whole thing when I realized that you weren't ever going to do them, which is why they started coming for me. And I was furious when they pinned you down and spat at you – that was never part of the plan, Eden. But they sensed weakness, said I'd gone soft. When @trooth-hurts posted that horrible stuff about me and it was made to sound like it came from you, I thought it was real at first. You have no idea how relieved I was when I messaged you and you assured me that it wasn't you."

My mouth drops open. "I wasn't assuring *you*. I was assuring *Riley*. Let's not forget that little detail, yeah?"

She carries on, as if I haven't spoken. "And then finding out @trooth-hurts was Mikki's alt-account? She completely backstabbed me. They both did. Don't you see? I've suffered here too, Eden. We've both been betrayed."

I glare at her. I'm properly shaking now. "I don't know how you're trying to get my sympathy when you're the one who *catfished* me! You lied to me every day, leading me to believe I had a friend and it was all fake. Before the karaoke video, how was this going to wind up? What was your end point, Bea?"

"It wasn't fake, Eden!" She looks at me earnestly and I feel my fists clench at my sides. "It was genuine. I started out just trying to make sure that you were OK, but then we started talking. We connected. All that stuff we spoke about, that was *real*. I was figuring out how to let you know that @trackstar09 was me. But then you betrayed me by sending that video to *Woodford Whispers*. And to make it worse, you bragged about how I had it coming. That hurt, Eden." She shakes her head, eyes shining with tears. "You had to find out the truth somehow, so here you go!" She gestures at the school hall, her words bitter now. "It's not exactly how I thought this would all finish, but I guess we're even."

I shake my head, trying to get rid of her ludicrous words. "You think that catfishing me for weeks on end is equal to some stupid video of you when we were eleven?" My voice is incredulous. "I feel bad about the video, is that what you want to hear? I do. But this is *not* the same. I wonder what everyone will say when they find out the levels you're prepared to stoop to?"

Bea gives a dark, humourless chuckle and it sounds like the laugh of a person who has run out of anything to care about it. "And what are you going to do? Tell them? How can you do that? Imagine how they'll react, Eden, finding out you were tricked into spilling your heart out to Riley! You know as well as I do that they'll eat it up just like they ate up that awful video of me, and it'll be humiliation all over again."

This throws me, and my heart races. She's right. It was

hard enough experiencing the shame of it just now in front of Riley and a couple of his confused track friends. Imagining the story spreading, growing, catching fire – how pathetic, tragic Eden got tricked by her worst enemy into thinking the captain of the track team would ever want to be friends with her and ask her to the dance… I can already feel the sting of it.

Panic rises in my chest. "So, what? This is it? You just get away with it like you always do?"

"Don't you think I'm suffering enough after what you did?" Bea counters. "I'm a laughing stock. The other two hate me. Woodford High is *ruthless*, Eden. That's how it works. Mikki and Autumn will go on to rule those halls with barely a scratch and find their next victims. That's that. We just suffer in silence."

"Don't compare yourself to me! We are *not* the same and you can't treat people like this, Bea."

Bea looks down at the ground, as if she's resigned to her fate. "Face it, Eden – it's over. There's nothing you can do about it. There's nothing either of us can do now. It is what it is."

Then she spins around and heads off in the direction of the gates, leaving me once again alone in the dark.

And there is only one person in the entire world who can help me now.

I pull out my phone and call her number and the tears are already falling before she's even picked up.

"Eden? Is everything OK?" I can hear the concern in her voice, and it just makes me cry even harder.

"Eden? Honey? What's going on?"

I take a deep breath and manage one word. "Mum."

And then the tears take over and all I can do is listen as she tells me not to move because she'll be there in just a few minutes.

And that it's going to be OK. She promises that it's going to be OK.

But she shouldn't make promises like that because nothing she can is going to make this better.

Rage Like A Girl

The weekend is long. I lie on my bed with Midnight beside me, only coming out when my mum insists.

"You can't stay there all day," she tells me, coaxing me downstairs with offers of chocolate and my favourite film. I give in because I need the distraction, although it is kind of nice snuggling up with her on the sofa. But as soon as the movie is over and I've returned to my room, it all crushes me again like a landslide of pain.

15:03 **@just-eden**: I feel sick.

15:05 **@TKOcactus**: You need to let it go, **@just-eden**. She's not worth it.

15:07 **@just-eden**: You don't get it. I've been going back through all the conversations I had with **@trackstar09** and I told him stuff. I mean, I told her stuff. Oh God…

15:07 **@aussiekid**: It's not as bad as you think. Honestly.

15:08 **@just-eden**. No. It's worse. I'm going to find that dark, dank cave and crawl inside and stay there for the rest of my life.

15:09 **@aussiekid**: Don't do that. Well, only if the cave has wifi…

15:12 **@just-eden**: And Colin's not OK either. I think he's got root rot and it's my fault for overwatering him.

15:13 **@TKOcactus**: OK, well, that's not good. Have you changed his soil?

15:14 **@just-eden**: Yes. But the rot looks like it's spreading.

15:15 **@aussiekid**: I had that with my moon cactus

and it died. That really sucks – sorry, Eden. But maybe there's a chance it'll pull through.

15:20 **@just-eden**: Yeah. Maybe.

@just-eden has left the chat.

I am not OK. The knowledge that I was opening myself up to Bea, of all people... I thought I was connecting with someone who really got me. Instead, I was sharing my deepest feelings with someone who was out to get me.

And I know it's stupid, but I'm sad that Riley was never my friend. It feels like I've lost someone – even though I clearly never had them in the first place.

But most of all I am angry. Angry with Bea and the Glossies for making me the focus of those awful tests. Angry with Hope for getting me noticed in the first place when I stood up for her. Angry with Riley for volunteering me for the race, and for not knowing me. Angry with myself for ever stepping out from the shadows.

"I'm popping to the shop before it closes," Mum tells me, poking her head around the door on Sunday afternoon. "We're out of milk. Are you feeling any better?"

I shake my head and she throws me a sympathetic smile. When she picked me up on Friday night it all came spilling out of my mouth in one long torrent of pain. First the catfishing and the tests but then everything else. What happened with Bea back in Year Six. How I've been on my own ever since. She held me and listened and then, only when I'd finally stopped crying did she ask why I hadn't told her any of this before.

Confessing that I didn't think she'd understand and that I didn't want to burden her with any of my stress, when she always seems to have so much of her own, was the hardest conversation of my life. There were more tears and they weren't all mine. But things between us have felt better since I got it all out — like it's finally stopped raining and even though the sun hasn't come out yet, there's the promise that it might.

"Oh, honey, I'm so sorry. But it will get better over time, it really will. And I'm cooking lasagne for supper!"

She's trying so hard to cheer me up. As if some minced beef and cheese sauce could solve the problem of my sad little life.

"Sound great," I say, staring at the ceiling. "See you in a bit."

"You could go for a run," she suggests. "That might help. Do you need anything from the shop?"

"No, thanks." I twist myself up so that I'm sitting on the edge of the mattress, ignoring Midnight's purr of protest.

"OK. Well, I won't be long. And if you do decide to go out just leave me a note on the fridge, OK?"

I nod, and she leaves. I wait until I hear the front door slam and then I get up, stretching my arms and easing out the knots in my spine. My entire body is tense and on edge. Maybe Melissa – Mum – is right. Maybe getting out will help.

My trainers are on the floor, next to the pile of discarded clothes from *Outside The Box* which were flung there on Friday night. It feels like a lifetime ago. I change into my tracksuit and a vest and pull my trainers on, before pushing Colin's ceramic pot into the warmest position on my window sill. Although he needs more than sunshine right now – he needs a miracle. Then I plod downstairs and leave Mum a message, telling her I'll be back in an hour or so.

Once I'm outside I start to run. Only again, something is wrong. My legs feel like they're made of lead and my heart is beating too fast and my lungs can't grab enough air. I only make it as far as the end of the road before my side is aching with a stitch. I slow to a walk and rub furiously at my abdomen, easing out the pain and gasping for breath.

I tried to be smarter than the Glossies and now I can't even run away any more. They've taken everything from me. I was naive enough to fall for Bea's catfishing and to think that Riley would ever want to be my friend, and that's all because I thought I could change who I am. I messed with the status quo, and this is my punishment.

I know it's pathetic, but this is *my* pity party and I can wallow if I want to.

How could I let myself be tricked into sharing my thoughts with Bea? How did she get away with it, without me finding out? I think back to the first time I almost spoke to Riley at school, when Bea dragged me away. I remember the conversation when @trackstar09 suggested that we didn't acknowledge each other in school, and wince. If I'd mentioned anything to Riley in person, the whole thing would have come tumbling down. Instead, she made sure that didn't happen.

The sun disappears behind a cloud, and I shiver, picking up the pace slightly while snippets of text conversations come back to me.

I told @trackstar09 about my relationship with Mum.

I confessed how it feels to be constantly alone.

I laid myself completely bare; I showed @trackstar09 *me,* and the whole time "he" was a complete lie.

And the Glossies are going to get away with it, like they always do. Sure, Bea is on the outside now and *Woodford Whispers* is buzzing with inside jokes about her terrible singing, her complete overreaction to the video – but I know Bea, she'll bide her time and then reincarnate herself in some new guise, with new loyal subjects to do her bidding. And there's been zero comeback on the other Glossies too. Mikki and Autumn might be keeping their side of the bargain, but that doesn't mean they're any more pleasant to be around. Every day feels like a ticking time bomb, waiting to see what they're going to do next.

That's if someone else doesn't do something first. If Riley or one of the track team tells people about what happened at the dance then I'll be forever known as the delusional girl who fabricated a friendship.

I stop and stand very still in the middle of the pavement. What if Bea was right? What if we *are* the same and both just have to suffer in silence? After all, I let Mikki and Autumn manipulate me into doing their dirty work and now they're adjusting their new crowns. What if this is just the natural order of things and there really is nothing that I can do about it?

I tip back my head and let out a huge, guttural roar, startling a nearby pigeon. Ahead, a man gives me a worried look and crosses the road to the other pavement.

They *should* be worried. Everyone should be worried.

There is a fire burning inside of me; it's not blood running through my veins but rage and if I don't figure it out what to do with it soon then it's going to erupt out of me and I won't be able to control what happens.

I keep walking, stomping my feet into the pavement in an attempt to remind myself that I am here; I am solid; I am not going to break or fragment into a million pieces. After a while I look up and see that my legs have brought me to the one place where I can think, which is helpful because I know that I have a decision to make.

I skirt around the edge of the school building and head for the side gate which leads to the track. The team trains here on a Sunday, but a quick glance at my phone reassures me that I have plenty of time before they arrive. The gate is open, and I slip inside.

The track is empty and when I walk across to the stands, climbing up to sit in my favoured spot at the back, there isn't a soul to be seen.

After all that has happened, nothing has changed. I'm still sitting here in the shadows, all on my own.

And I am not OK with that.

The thought surprises me. My legs start to jiggle, and I can feel my heart rate increasing, even though I'm just sitting still. The track is spread out below me and before I can question it too much, I'm walking down the steps of the stand and on to the rubbery surface.

And then I start to jog. Slowly at first, while I test out

my side for any more stitches and then, once I'm certain that it's gone, breaking into a proper run. My feet pound the ground and my arms find their rhythm and I feel the strength in my legs, pushing me further.

I am wind and fire, one fuelling the other.

And now I can think.

Option one: flight. Keep running, which is what I'm good at. Run away from the unkind comments and my embarrassment and the toxic environment of Woodford High. Refuse to go to school. There're only three days left of this term anyway. I could remove myself from the firing line, whatever it takes. They can't hurt me if they can't catch me.

Option two: freeze. Do nothing. Bury my head in the sand. Say nothing, take no action. Accept the miserable status quo, like Bea said.

Option three: fight. I could lash back at Bea, Mikki and Autumn even harder. Make them hurt the way I'm hurting.

Option four: fawn. Try to win favour with Mikki and Autumn. Accept that the Glossies run the world and that the only way to survive is to bow down to them.

One, two, three, four.

Flight, freeze, fight, fawn.

You'd have thought with so much choice there would be an obvious winner.

I slow slightly, enjoying the feeling of the wind on my face. Option one and two are both going to produce the same end result: me being right back where I started, and the remains of the Glossies back where they started too.

I pick up the pace again, rounding the corner by the stands and beginning my second lap. My breathing is steady and I'm in control of my body and my mind.

The problem with option three is that I already tried to fight back, and they still got the better of me. Not only did humiliating Bea backfire, it didn't feel good to sink to their level.

And option four is a definite no-go — I am never going to join the grovelling sycophants who do whatever it takes to stay on the good side of the Glossies.

I keep running, up the long straight and around the top curve, my thoughts bouncing with every leaping step that I take.

A movement by the stands catches my eye, and as I round the corner and head down the far side of the track, I see that the track team are arriving. Riley is there and so is Hope, chatting and stretching and starting to warm up for the session. I breathe in deeply, feeling the oxygen fill my lungs and my legs start to fizz as I break into a full-out sprint — and suddenly, even though it seems so counter-intuitive, I know exactly what I need to do.

I don't want to run off.

I don't want to hide away.

I don't want to lash out.

I don't want to give in.

Most of all, I don't want to stop feeling what I've started to experience and enjoy over the last few weeks – that feeling of being connected; a part of something.

I don't want to run away. So, I choose option five.

I run *towards*.

Sometimes, a person can be braver than they ever thought they could possibly be. If anyone had asked me, a couple of months ago, whether I would have the guts to walk up to a boy I don't know, a boy whose only real interaction with me has been mortifyingly embarrassing, and confess the truth and ask for his help, I would have told them the chance was zero.

I'm always the narrator, never the main character. But in the Netflix version of my life right now, the camera would start on a wide, tracking shot of a girl running. It would pan closer as she gets nearer and nearer to the group of kids who are warming up for their track session. And then, as she slows to a halt, right in front of Riley, captain of the track team, it would zoom in, capturing the way she is shifting awkwardly from one foot to the other.

The camera would swing to an over-her-shoulder angle, showing Riley looking intrigued but slightly nervous. Is she about to declare some kind of fantasy friendship again? Does he need backup from the rest of the team? Hope is standing next to him and he gives her a quick nod, glad to have a friend nearby.

And then the camera would move, framing the girl in the centre of the screen. The sun is shining but as she opens her mouth to speak, it suddenly starts to rain. The sky was completely clear just moments ago, but the audience appreciate the pathetic fallacy and go with it, holding their breath. This could go either way. Does the rain symbolize the washing away of all the hurt and pain – or is it a portent of doom?

"Hi."

The audience are cringing now. As openers go, it's not very strong.

"Hi."

The viewers relax. Riley is engaging – there's everything to play for.

"I need to tell you something and it's going to sound totally weird so I'm just going to say it, OK? So – you know I thought you'd invited me to the dance? And you know I said we'd been messaging each other online?" I pause momentarily for a quick intake of breath. It's a risk, but I've already humiliated myself in front of Riley – how much worse can the truth make it? "Well, here's the thing. Bea created a fake account pretending to be you and messaged me, being all supportive about what was happening at school. And I got totally suckered by the entire thing and believed that it *was* you. We became friends and I told you a ton of stuff, only it wasn't actually you – it was Bea all along."

Riley frowns slightly, probably trying to process. Hope lets out a long whistle of disbelief and behind them, Coach is finishing setting up some cones on the track. I know I don't have long.

"Are you saying she faked an account in my name?" Riley asks. "How come I haven't seen it?"

I grimace. I don't love this part. "Well, she was smart about that. She called herself @trackstar09 and all the photos on the account were of you and the rest of the team. But when I looked later, I realized she'd not tagged anybody in those pictures, and most of the followers were bots and random accounts, not people from school. You'd never have even known about it – she just let me believe that it was you."

"Whoa. That's screwed up," says Riley.

"She's really gone too far this time," adds Hope, sounding shocked.

"Right? And she shouldn't be able to just get away with doing something like that. I ... was wondering if you would help me?" I hold my breath.

He throws a quick glance towards Hope, then back to me. "What do you need us to do?"

I exhale in relief. "She impersonated you, so you're the only person who can report the account," I tell him. "You can get it shut down. That's a good start."

"Sure. That won't really change much now though, right?"

My mouth stretches into a smile. It is a nervous, unsure smile but a smile, nonetheless. "No. But I have a plan."

At that moment, the rain intensifies and Coach yells at everyone to break into two teams and line up at the start line.

"What are you going to do?" Hope looks at me, her face creased with concern. "Eden – you need to be careful. Those girls don't mess about."

I shrug. "I'm done letting them determine what happens next. Someone has to do something. If Riley reports her then Bea will get her main account shut down for a while, as well as the fake one, and that's a start. I'll deal with the rest myself."

I need to take some control of this whole situation.

I need to trust myself.

"Well, I'll report her for the fake account," says Riley, as Coach beckons him to join the teams lining up at the start. "And we won't tell anyone about this, Eden. You have our word."

"Why don't you stay?" asks Hope, putting one hand gently on my arm. "You could train with us."

I open my mouth to make an excuse and then I shut it again. If I want things to be different, then I have to do things differently. And that might as well start now.

"OK, yeah," I say. "Do you think Coach will be OK with it?"

Riley nods. "I'll tell him you're having a trial session. He'll be pleased."

He walks across to where Coach is standing and starts talking, gesturing a couple of times in my direction before turning to give me a thumbs up.

"You can join our group," says Hope, grinning at me. "We need someone to replace Mikki."

"Thank you," I tell her, as she leads me to where everyone is lining up. "You've been pretty good to me since this all started."

She shakes her head and looks at me. "No, I haven't," she says. "Not really. I let Bea and the others scare me, just like everyone else. Not you though." She gives me a shy smile. "You're really brave, Eden. And it's great to have you on the team."

I smile back and take my position in the line behind Hope. I let her words settle inside my head. *You're really brave.*

I'm going to need them if I'm going to be strong enough to carry out the last part of my plan.

Brave Like A Girl

I open *Woodford Whispers* once Mum has gone to bed. There's yet another meme about Bea's singing and someone has rehashed the photos of me being attacked with doughnuts because *"there will never be a time that this isn't funny"*. The most popular post comes from a new anonymous account with the profile name @notgonnalie, spreading a rumour about a girl in my PE class, which everyone else has piled on top of. What there isn't is anything about me or Riley – he's stuck to his word and neither he nor Hope have told anyone about what happened with @trackstar09.

It's late, but I know that most kids will be up. Taking a deep breath, I remind myself of all the things I've spent the last few hours churning through my brain.

311

Pushing everyone away is fine – if I always want to be on my own.

Hiding from the things that scare me is OK – if I want to stay afraid of them for ever.

Not taking risks might sound sensible – but occasionally taking a chance might end up with a better result.

I give Midnight a quick cuddle for good luck and then I send the first message.

I need Autumn to publish this one post. That's all. Once the first post is on there I can direct them to my own page – and the real story.

I clean my teeth and get into my pyjamas, before sitting on my bed with my phone. I swipe the screen. And there it is. She's bitten. Hook, line and sinker. I tap on the post and look at the comments, allowing myself a small smile as I see that there are already several people engaging. Now it's time to reel the rest of the year group in.

> **@just-eden**: Hi, everyone. I know you've all been posting on here about me. I think it's time you heard what's really been going on, and how one girl at our school made it her mission to make my life a living hell.

I deliberately made it sound like I was only coming for Bea. After our deal to end the tests, Mikki and Autumn have every reason to believe that they successfully manipulated me to focus all my hatred on Bea. I knew this would be the only way to convince Autumn to post something that I sent in. She still hates me, but she clearly hates Bea more.

@ethan-is-king: Hey! Sprinkles is coming out to play!

@kacey789: I think I know who this is about...

@just-eden: Do you? Are you sure? I'm not posting anything else here but the whole truth is on my page. If anyone is interested.

I exhale and remind myself that I can stop here. I don't have to go any further. I will still be on the track team and the Glossies will move on. I can go to school and hang out with a few kids and do my running and it'll all be fine. And then I'll come home and spend time with Mum and Year Nine will pass into Year Ten.

But I'd be letting them have the final word. Accepting that what happened was OK. I swallow hard and then let my fingers swipe across to my own page, where my words are already waiting. I know that the instant they hit the screen I'll be exposed, just like Bea warned me. I'll make myself even more of a target, but I'm not going to sit here and take it any longer.

I hit the *post* button.

@just-eden: What I'm going to say is embarrassing but you all need to know what's been going on. For the past few weeks, I thought I had been talking to Riley online, and he invited me to the dance. But when I got there, he didn't know me. Bea had been catfishing me the whole time by faking an account.

@virtuallyviolet: What? That's – weird...

@ethan-is-king: Ha! That's pretty funny. Can't believe you fell for it!!! When do the screenshots of these chats drop?

@just-eden: Bea could share them if she wants. I can't stop her. I told "Riley" a ton of stuff. But even if it's embarrassing, I'm not going to keep quiet and pretend it didn't happen. That's what she's counting on. I'm not going to let her win this time. It was a terrible thing to do, and I shouldn't have to pretend it never happened.

@kacey789: Shut the hell up, Ethan. There's nothing

funny about catfishing. It's creepy.

@silverbullet: Super creepy.

@hopeishere: This was a truly awful thing for her to do, Eden. It wasn't your fault and you're amazing for being open about it. We should all report that account and get it shut down.

@therealriley: Already done it. This whole thing was totally not cool.

I pause for a second. My plan has mostly been achieved – everyone knows now what Bea has done. I've taken away her power with my honesty. I could leave it here.

@silverbullet: Yeah, totally not cool. Bea's pathetic. Can't believe she was such a cow to poor Eden. We should totally cancel her, right?

Mikki's sly hypocrisy makes my stomach churn.
I cannot leave it here.

@just-eden: This isn't the whole story. Over the last three weeks Bea, Mikki & Autumn have been trying to force me to complete a series of tests.

@kacey789: What are you talking about? Is this about the pranks they asked some of us to play on you? You kind of asked for it, posting that stuff about everyone as **@trooth-hurts**.

My heart is racing. Exposing Mikki and Autumn alongside Bea is either the bravest or most reckless thing that I have ever done. Pausing for a second, I wander across to the window sill where Colin is slowly dying.

"Get it together, McCoy," I whisper to myself. And then I turn back to my phone.

@just-eden: That account isn't mine. Bea wasn't lying when she said that Mikki is **@trooth-hurts** and just for the record, the so-called "pranks" started way before that foul **@trooth-hurts** post. You know the horrible stuff that's been happening to me? It was supposed to happen to all of you. Bea, Mikki and Autumn wanted me to humiliate YOU.

@silverbullet: Ignore her. She's just trying to cause trouble and wriggle out of everything she's done.

@kacey789: What the hell?

@daisychain: I hope you can back it up otherwise it just looks like you're trying to stir something up.

@bonbon01: Yeah. Proof or it never happened.

@footballrules: Getting bored now. What's Sprinkles wittering on about?

@alwaysautumn: Did everyone see the post that just dropped on Woodford Whispers?! OMG – I would not want to be that girl right now. Lol.

And then they're all gone, like a shoal of fish suddenly swimming in a new direction.

I lie back on my bed and stare at the ceiling. Midnight immediately flops herself on top of me and her warmth seeps into my legs as she purrs contentedly.

They don't believe me. And even if a few of them do, without any hard evidence it's just my word against the Glossies. Mikki and Autumn are probably congratulating themselves right now for allowing me to expose Bea while shutting me down before I could properly reveal their part.

They think it's all over. They think they have won.

But I am Eden McCoy and I run towards my problems.

I deserve to be seen and heard.

And I decide how this whole thing ends.

Fierce Like A Girl

I'm awake well before my alarm on Monday morning. Mostly with nerves, it's true – but there's a tiny bit of excitement mixed in with the fear. I know what I need to do. What I can't predict is how it's going to land with the rest of Woodford High.

I eat my breakfast quickly, forcing down a piece of toast. Mum asks me several times if I'm OK and it's obvious she doesn't believe me when I tell her I'm fine. Eventually she gets the hint and stops asking, instead restricting herself to adding a bar of chocolate to my packed lunch when she thinks I'm not looking and giving me an extra hug when she heads off to work.

I'm the first person to arrive at school, slipping in through a side door the minute I see one of the site staff unlock it. There's a tense moment when I almost walk into a group of teachers walking in the direction of the staffroom for an early-morning meeting, but I manage to dart into an empty classroom before they round the corner, where I stand with my back against the wall and my heart pounding in my chest.

I am clearly not cut out for a life of subterfuge.

Once they've passed, I creep back out and tiptoe through the corridors until I get to the library. The photocopier is right at the back of the room and, once I'm safely hidden behind a bookshelf, I open my rucksack and pull out all the notes from the tests. They still look a bit crumpled, from being screwed up in the bottom of my sock drawer, but they're flat enough to be readable. And that's all that matters.

It only takes a few minutes to make enough copies. Then, after making sure that the coast is still clear, I retreat to the girls' toilets, checking my phone every thirty seconds until it's time for the main entrance to be unlocked and the school day to officially start. Phase one of my plan has been achieved.

"Now don't forget that the Key Stage Three End-of-Year Assembly is today at eleven o'clock." Mr Danes closes his laptop and looks around the class. "Go straight to the hall after break, please. Period three is cancelled."

There is an enthusiastic cheer from the football lads, and a groan from the kids who would rather do maths than be forced to sit in a hot hall, listening to the head teacher bang on about "progress" and "resilience" and "fresh starts in September" before having to endure the annual celebration awards where the same kids as last year get invited on to the stage to be given a certificate for outstanding achievement or excellent attendance or something else that seems to be a big deal to the staff and is utterly meaningless to the rest of us.

I try to stay calm throughout period one but my head is pounding with tension. By the time I walk into the science lab at ten o'clock, my heart is racing so hard I'm surprised the rest of the class can't hear it.

"I'm not feeling well," I tell Mrs Lipscott, approaching her desk.

She holds up her hand, keeping me at bay. "You do look very clammy," she confirms. "Go straight to the nurse's office, please, Eden. The last thing I need this close to the holidays is to catch whatever germs you're harbouring, thank you very much."

I make my escape before she decides to ask someone to assist me. I don't need any help and I don't need the nurse. What I need is the next hour without anyone paying attention to where I am and what I'm doing. I've already managed to pilfer some scissors and a roll of Sellotape from Mr Danes' desk and, unless I get really unlucky, nobody is going to miss me until eleven o'clock.

I have one whole hour to implement phase two.

The bell rings, signalling the start of period three and it's easy enough to sidle into the crowd of kids making their way into the hall. I head towards the Year Nine section, slipping into an empty seat beside Hope and Riley. I haven't told them what I'm doing but I'll need their help if I'm going to pull this off.

"Mobile phones should all be on silent and in bags!" reminds Miss Robinson, stalking in between the rows of kids. She's wasting her breath. They'll be on silent already – nobody wants to risk having their main source of communication confiscated, but there's no way a single phone in this room isn't either in a pocket or tucked surreptitiously into a hand.

"Welcome, Years Seven, Eight and Nine, to our final assembly of the year!" intones the Head, striding on to the stage. "And everybody listening, please!"

He claps his hands, and the hall falls silent.

"Now, then, it has been a year of terrific progress," he begins. "Some of you have shown magnificent resilience in your attitudes to learning and…"

I zone out, along with everyone else, my eyes on the clock above his head. This speech usually goes on for about ten minutes and then the awards ceremony will start. I need to be ready – and that means prepping my allies for their roles. Keeping my phone low down by my knees, I tap out a quick message into the group chat Hope set up after track training yesterday.

11:51 **@just-eden**: Will you both do me favour?

Their phones vibrate and I watch as they covertly read my request. Hope turns to me, a questioning look on her face. I give her a small smile and she nods. On the far side of her, Riley peers around her and gives me a thumbs up. I tap out my next message and, although they both look confused, they again give me a nod.

So now the only thing to do is to wait. The Head keeps talking and then finally, once he's managed to say the same thing in fifty-five different ways (basically that we all need to pull our fingers out if we want to have any hope of ever being gainfully employed), he announces that the awards ceremony will begin.

"Our first award is for voluntary work in the community," he drones, and some poor Year Seven kid who was chosen to deliver Christmas cards to the old people's home is forced to stand and plod up the steps to be given a laminated certificate and a half-hearted round of applause.

"Our second award is for resilience in the face of adversity."

"Our third award is for representing the school in a sporting capacity."

And on and on and on, until he's almost at the very end.

"When do you want us to do it?" hisses Hope, under the cover of whistles and jeers as the school choir attempt to howl their way through what, the Head has assured us, is an inspirational song of aspirations and dreams.

"Soon," I whisper back.

And then the choir are sitting down, and the Head is back onstage.

"Our last award is the ever-popular Students' Choice," he says, projecting his voice to the back of the hall in order to regain the attention that was lost during the musical interlude. "As you know, this award was voted for by all of you several weeks ago – and will now be given to the student, or students, who you feel have given the most to life at Woodford High."

"He should call out your name," murmurs Hope. "You've done the most good out of everyone here."

I shudder. I might not want to live in the shadows any more but there's a long way to go before I'll be happy with getting that kind of attention. As in, never.

"So, without further ado, I am pleased to announce that, for the second year running, the Woodford High Students' Choice Award for Significant Contribution goes to … drum roll, please … three of our Year Nine students, Bea Miller, Mikki Potts and Autumn Addiman." He stares out across the hall. "Come on up, girls and let's give them a huge, Woodford High round of applause!"

"Oof," murmurs Hope. "Bea's not going to be loving this."

The half-hearted clapping starts, and I turn to Hope and Riley.

"Now," I mouth.

Their thumbs skim across their phone screens and then it's done.

And I wait. I wonder if anyone will notice their phones vibrating with a notification over the applause. This whole thing will be completely wasted if people don't see the message until later.

When it starts, it's almost like a spark. A flickering at first and then a flash of flame, until the air all around is shimmering with heat. This is why I needed Riley and Hope to send the message. Unlike me they're both part of Year Nine group chats and they can reach far more people than I can.

Four simple words. That's all it needs to start an inferno.

Look under your seat.

"What's this about?" mutters a kid from the row in front of us. He leans forward and I see him reach underneath his chair – and the relief I feel when he sits back up, holding a piece of paper in his hand, is immeasurable. I knew that the chances of anyone finding out what I'd done and removing the evidence was almost non-existent, but still – the reality of this insane idea working is making it hard to take a proper breath.

And now the awkward clapping in honour of the three girls who are making their way to the stage is consigned to the first two thirds of the hall, as more and more Year Nine students reach under their chairs and pull out the pieces of paper that I taped underneath. And the murmurs and whispers are getting louder, as all around me kids read the words that were written for me, about them.

"What the hell?" calls Kacey.

"Settle down at the back!" calls the Head, but this fire is burning too fiercely for him to stop it.

"I've got one too!" shouts Violet, from further down the row.

"And me!" yells someone else, and someone else, and someone else. Which makes me want to laugh because they've all got them. They're really not that special.

"Mine is a note telling Eden to hide Kacey's clothes," shouts Kieran, turning his head to locate me on the back row. "What is this, Eden? Is it a game?"

I wasn't expecting to have to say anything. I thought the notes would make it perfectly obvious what has been happening. I've kind of used up all my recklessness and bravery for one lifetime – I can't explain the whole thing all over again, in front of everyone.

"It's not a game." Hope's voice rings out and I turn to stare at her, my mouth gaping open as she stands up and glares around at the surrounding Year Nines. "These are the tests *they* gave to Eden. It's not a game – it's your proof. They wanted her to hurt you – and because she refused, you were given the test to do right back at her."

She points up at the three girls who are frozen in place onstage, and then sits down again. And the back of the hall erupts.

"They told her to trash my lunch!" shouts Violet. "What have I ever done to them?"

"Year Nine! Settle down NOW!" shouts the Head, from up on the stage.

The kids in Year Seven and Year Eight have utterly no clue what is going on, but they take this God-sent opportunity to start screeching and pushing each other off their chairs. Teachers stalk the hall, issuing threats of detention to random people in a pathetic attempt to regain control, and it's obvious that none of them are aware of the reasons for the chaos.

"She was supposed to spread a false rumour about me!" yells Britt from the back of the hall.

"And me!" whines Daisy.

"And me!"

"And me!"

"They wanted her to destroy *my* science project!" calls Bonnie. "What exactly is their problem?"

"They told her to put my name on that list of grossest Year Nine girls," howls someone else.

"And mine," calls a voice, and then another and another.

The air is filled with the indignant cries of angry kids, all waving my photocopied notes in the air.

"I said, THAT'S ENOUGH!" The Head crashes his fist down on to the podium in front of him and finally, everyone stops shouting and sinks back into their seats. "Right – I don't know what is going on here, Year Nine, but I'll get to the bottom of it later." He pauses to compose himself and then attempts to return to the jovial, end-of-year persona he likes to assume for these events. "Let's remind ourselves of why we're here – which is to celebrate these three wonderful students." He looks at the girls on the stage, and the smile he gives them makes it clear that he hasn't understood a single thing that just happened. The Glossies, however, are standing stock-still as if they've been bewitched; like they would rather be anywhere but here. Held to account in a public forum. No screens to hide behind. No anonymous accounts to keep them safe.

Just them.

In real life.

"Let's put our hands together for your Students' Choice winners! Very well done, girls!"

He starts to clap, joined by the teachers who are now spread out around the room, and a few of the less delinquent Year Sevens and Eights. It's almost embarrassing, a random selection of people clapping in a packed hall of otherwise silent witnesses.

Silent until the hissing begins, that is. I don't know who starts it, and the sound makes the hairs on the back of my neck stand on end. I slump down in my seat. It feels like a step too far, even after everything they've done. Up onstage, Bea's face crumples and I will her not to cry – not in front of everyone. Not because of something that I've done.

"Right – this assembly is over!" calls the Head. "I will be investigating this, so if you have anything to tell me, please stay behind now. Otherwise, back to class immediately."

The spell is broken. Bea, Mikki and Autumn dash off the stage and out of the hall, together but not together. Around me, kids move away, voices loud with the excitement of what just happened. I join the throng of people making their way out of the hall and through the corridors until I reach the relative sanctuary of my locker with Hope beside me, which feels quietly reassuring.

"Why did they send these to you?" Violet approaches me with a group of girls close behind her, a handful of the photocopied notes in her fist. I step backwards but there's nowhere for me to hide.

And I don't run away any more.

I shrug. "Because they can."

"So why didn't you do it?"

Kacey walks across to join us. "Yeah, Eden." She looks at me with confusion etched across her face. "Why didn't you just do the tests? They'd have left you alone if you'd gone along with it. Why would you take it on yourself, instead of dishing it out?"

I shrug again. "Because I didn't want to be the kind of person who would do something like that, just because they were told to."

There is silence for a moment and Violet's face flushes a deep pink.

"I'm really sorry," she mutters.

"Me too," says Kacey. "It all got way out of hand."

I stare at my feet. I think I probably needed to hear this, but it doesn't make it any less awkward. Thankfully, Kieran inadvertently breaks the tension by pushing through the throng of people.

"Are you saying Bea and the others gave Sprinkles a prank to play on the rest of you, and if she didn't do it they made you do it to her?" He throws a look at Ethan and the other football lads. "Is that what was going on with her wet clothes and trashed lunch and that whole doughnut attack? Girls are *wild*, man."

"And you think you're any better?" Hope asks. "It wasn't you who joined in with spreading nasty rumours or making people feel humiliated, just because you could?"

Kieran blinks and then retreats to the safety of the rest of the football team.

"He's not wrong though." Kacey scowls, the piece of paper with the photocopied note fluttering from her fingers. "It *is* wild, what they did."

"What *we* did," corrects Violet, and a few other girls murmur their agreement. "If we'd all said *no*, like Eden, there wouldn't have been any tests."

And then the bell rings. I stand still, letting the flood of people flow through the corridor until it's just me and Hope.

"Thanks," I tell her. "You know, for speaking up for me. I wanted them to hear me but I lost my voice for a moment back there."

Hope laughs. "Your voice is plenty loud enough," she says. "And I was just following your lead. You're kind of a hero, Eden."

A snort of laughter erupts from my throat.

"I am *not* the hero of this story," I tell her, turning to my locker and opening the door. "Nothing like."

And then I freeze, unable to do anything except stare at the item lying neatly on top of my maths book.

She nudges me with her elbow, sensing my distraction. "Whatever you say. You coming to class?"

"You go ahead," I tell her, holding the locker door open so that she can't see what's inside. "Just give me a minute, yeah?"

I sense Hope giving me a strange look, but I can't tear my eyes from the white envelope and after a moment's hesitation she turns and walks off down the corridor. I wait until she's definitely gone and then reach inside and pick it up, turning it over in my hands for any clues about what might be waiting for me inside.

But other than my name, written in fancy handwriting on the front, there is nothing.

My hands are shaking slightly as I rip open the top

of the envelope and pull out the piece of paper inside, unfolding it and taking a big breath in before allowing my eyes to skim over the words.

They are not what I was expecting.

Monday 16th July

Dear Eden,

I'm sorry. I know that those words probably don't mean anything but they are true. I am really, truly sorry for the way I've treated you. And I know that you probably can't ever forgive me so I'm not going to ask you if you could ever do that. I wish things had been different. I wish I'd been different.

Bea

P.S. I lied. I prefer custard doughnuts. Sorry ☹

I put the note in my rucksack and slam my locker closed. A white envelope. A white flag.

I lied too. I've always secretly preferred custard.

Think Like A Girl

"And then what happened?" Jimmy is perched on the edge of his stool, his eyes wide as I regale him with the whole story.

It's a good job the shopping centre is quiet because neither of us is really in the zone to promote the latest flavour of Delicious Doughnuts, which is a combination of orange peel and lemon and is aptly named Bitter Offerings. I don't see it being a bestseller.

"Then I cleaned off my sword, put it back in its sheath and walked away," I tell him. "Leaving everyone else to clear up the mess. And now it's the summer holidays." He narrows his eyes, and I relent. "Fine. I went to my next lesson and a few kids told me that it was cool, the way I'd single-handedly brought down the school bullies. And at lunchtime I got dragged in front of the Head and forced to tell him what had been going on. And by the end of the day, I heard that all the Glossies' parents had been informed they had been using social media as a form of bullying and intimidation and they'd all had their accounts deleted."

"Blimey." Jimmy whistles. "I mean, you know they'll just get new profiles, right?"

I nod. "Of course. But that's not the point. The important thing is that everyone knows now how dirty they play. And not just through rumour and whispers that people can pretend isn't happening, but out in the open, where it can't just be ignored or accepted any more."

"And what about you?" asks Jimmy. "How are you doing?"

I think for a moment and then smile. "I'm OK."

It's not even a lie. I am OK. The last couple of days of term, without constant fear of another test or an encounter with the Glossies, were pretty acceptable. I might go so far as to say that I'm not completely dreading the new school year.

Unlike the Glossies. As well as having their accounts shut down, they all got suspended for the last few days of school. The Head phoned my mum (he was probably trying to get her off his back as she'd apparently been emailing him about five times a day since the school dance, demanding to know exactly what was being done about the *toxic bullying culture* at Woodford High) and told her that Bea had backed up everything that I had said, which was a surprising but welcome discovery. Mikki and Autumn turned on each other as soon as they came off the stage, each trying to blame the other for everything going wrong. Mikki outed Autumn as the admin for *Woodford Whispers* and Autumn's parents had a complete meltdown, blaming Mikki and Bea for being bad influences. Autumn will be starting at yet another new school for Year Ten.

One of the best things to happen is the taking down of the *Woodford Whispers* page. I mean, the Year Eight kids have already replaced it with *Woodford Words*, and I realize I can't change a whole system all at once by myself. What matters is I've done my bit. Maybe I'll keep an eye on what gets posted over there and chime in if it all starts to go downhill again. Plus, everyone knows now that Mikki really was @trooth-hurts and she was whipping up all the drama, just to keep herself in the spotlight.

So, things are good.

But there is something missing.

There is someone missing.

I can't sleep. The temperature has been getting hotter and hotter over the last few days and even with my window open, the night air is heavy and warm. I lie on my bed, hoping that if I close my eyes and lie still enough then I'll finally be able to drift off, but it isn't working. My head is too loud, and the things it is saying are making it impossible for me to relax.

I miss @trackstar09.

I know, I know — it's ridiculous. I shouldn't be able to miss something that I never had, but I do. Hope and the real Riley and the rest of the team are great, and I'm enjoying running with them most days at track now it's the summer holidays, but it's not the same. I can't talk to them quite the way that I could talk to @trackstar09. About the mundane stuff. The important stuff.

There's something else too. The other day, Riley started messing about at track, singing a song in a daft voice, and everyone was laughing, including me. And then someone said that he still sounded better than Bea in that karaoke video, and everyone laughed even harder.

Not including me.

Because I did that.

I took something fun and good and lovely, and I used it against her. I showed her being vulnerable and let everyone shoot her down — exactly the same thing that happened to me. Nobody deserves that.

I'm not suggesting for an instant that she isn't guilty, or

that I'm ever going to forget what she's done. She made some truly terrible choices. But I also made some mistakes in my strategies to survive at Woodford High. It's true that she has suffered too, and a big part of that was down to me.

I can't stop thinking about what she said outside the school dance, about her side of the story, back when we started Year Seven. Because maybe, just maybe, there is a nugget of truth in her words. I was waiting for her to make the first move and come to find me — but maybe she was waiting for me to do the same? Maybe we both waited too long, and the space between us just became too much to fill?

I give up on sleep and get out of bed, padding across the carpet to the window. My cacti are lit up in the light of the moon and I gently touch Colin's spiky tips with my finger. Against all the odds, he seems to be recovering. He won't live for ever, I know that. But he's here now and I'm grateful.

I feel bad about the video. And it's hard to enjoy hanging out with the others when, in the back of my head, I know that Bea is all on her own.

And what's the point of all of this, really, if it doesn't make me feel better than I felt before?

Just Like A Girl

14:18 **@aussiekid**: You can't be serious. After everything she's done?

14:19 **@TKOcactus**: Right? How can you even consider being friends with her?

14:22 **@just-eden**: I'm not saying I'm going to be friends with her.

14:23 **@TKOcactus**: Good. For a mad minute there I thought you were suggesting something else.

14:26 **@just-eden**: Maybe she wasn't brave enough to walk away from the other Glossies or stand up to them, but a person shouldn't be punished for ever for being afraid.

14:30 **@aussiekid**: I disagree. You can't trust her, you know that.

14:33 **@just-eden**: I'm not saying I can. But maybe I trust myself a little bit more. Life is tricky enough without holding grudges.

14:34 **@TKOcactus**: She's a lost cause, **@aussiekid**. There's nothing we can do to help her.

14:35 **@just-eden**: You can keep on being my ridiculous, prickly friends. I'll be careful, I promise.

13:41 **@TKOcactus**: Fine. We'll be right here when it all goes wrong.

14:42 **@aussiekid**: And we'll be right here if it goes right too.

14:44 **@just-eden**: For a group chat with a lot of pricks, you all are the best… 🌵

I might sound confident on screen, but the reality is that I'm conflicted too. Although what I said to them was true. I do trust myself a tiny bit more than I used to, and I don't want to keep doing things the same way I've always done them. Which means pushing myself out of my comfort zone and taking a risk – and maybe even giving other people a chance.

Midnight is lying on my bed, and I decide to give myself one final opportunity to get out of this.

"Shall I do it?" I ask her. "Say *no* if this is the worst idea that womankind has ever had."

The absence of my cat suddenly developing the art of speech is the deciding vote. I quickly change into my tracksuit and running vest and then send the message before I can talk myself out of it.

15:14 Do you still own a pair of running trainers?

The response is almost instant.

15:15 Why?

I might well end up kicking myself for this decision. But one thing I've learnt recently is that I can't always put up spiky defences; sometimes it pays to be open and real. And it's not like there's a finite amount of happiness around – I'm not going to lose out by offering to share.

15:19 You used to be fast. Maybe you should consider joining the track team next year.

Three little dots.

She's thinking about it. She's wondering if it's a trick. Maybe she's going to say *no* – I think I would say no if I were her. And that's OK because fearing rejection isn't a reason not to try. I've been rejected a ton of times and the earth didn't stop turning. The sun kept shining and my legs kept moving and I ran out of the shadows. Now I'm giving Bea a chance to do the same thing – it's up to her whether she takes it or not.

People have to choose for themselves.

Three little dots, flickering on the screen.

Three little dots…

And then the dots turn into words and the words turn into something else. I'm not entirely sure what. Maybe opportunity. Maybe disaster. Whatever it is, it's the possibility of something unknown and I'm ready to take the chance.

Bending down, I lace up my trainers and move across to the small wooden box on my desk which houses the few bits of jewellery I've accumulated over the years and never wear. I open it and rummage around, pushing aside the mood ring I got given one birthday and a few colourful bangles that used to belong to Mum. And then I find it, hidden right in the corner. Pulling it out, I hold the necklace up in the air, watching the sunlight glint off the tiny star charm. Nothing is ever as simple as it first appears. I might be the narrator, but Bea has a whole other version going on and it would be wrong to think that I know the whole story.

Carefully, I tuck the necklace back inside the box, and give Midnight a quick stroke before bounding down the stairs, popping my head into the kitchen to let Mum know I'll be back in an hour. Then I slam the front door behind me and jog down the road to warm up my legs.

I let my feet fly, soaring across the pavement towards the school track and my new friends, any worries and doubts floating away. If the whole butterfly effect is true, this tiny action might grow into something bigger.

My story starts with me running and I'm pretty sure that it ends that way.

But that end is not today.

Acknowledgements

I need to start by saying a huge thank you to all the children and young people who participated in the 'Say It Like It Is' survey, and the teachers and librarians who worked with me to facilitate this. Without their voices, this would have been yet another book written by an adult pretending to know what it's like to be a teenager in the twenty-first century. While some aspects of being a teenage girl are universal, others are definitely unique to the times we live in: teenagers today may struggle to comprehend a world in which we adults roamed around, without anyone ever being able to contact us nor track our location, and in the same way I cannot possibly fully understand what it is like to be constantly under the spotlight of attention nor how it feels to be targeted online by kids who sit behind you in maths class. The young people who offered their thoughts and opinions on social media showed me that, for the majority, the positives of connectivity, friendship, entertainment and learning opportunities outweigh the negatives of abuse, bullying and unwanted exposure to inappropriate content. The kids are doing pretty great in a world in which the adults are often the ones posing the problems...

I need to thank the amazing team at Scholastic, who as always have been a wonderful support, particularly Fiz Osborne, Julia Sanderson and Wendy Shakespeare. Also the fabulous Julia Churchill – I am forever grateful that you are my agent!

A massive thank you to my incredible family, Adam, Zachary, Georgia and Reuben. Ten years of dealing with me disappearing into a book project and you are as enthusiastic as ever. (Although don't think I'm unaware that you all kind of like it when I'm distracted and you can crack on with doing whatever you want without me having an opinion...!)

Lastly, thank you so much to my fabulous readers. Writing books is a whole lot of good times, but it wouldn't be anywhere near as fun if you weren't reading them. I really hope you've enjoyed this one.

Say It Like It Is Survey (2022)

Who? 1,024 participants aged between 10–15 years from across the United Kingdom.

How? 83% access social media on their phones.

When? 28% spend 3–4 hours a day on social media and 17% spend 6 hours or more daily on social media. The majority are happy with how much time they spend on social media although 26% would like to reduce their usage.

Why? 78% have experienced feeling happy and accepted because of social media. 68% say that they have never personally had a particularly negative experience on social media, although 65% have witnessed someone being racist, homophobic, sexist, or bullying another because of their religion. 94% said that the adults in their life use social media.

Rebecca Westcott is an author and deputy headteacher, working with children and teenagers with autism and SEMH (social, emotional and mental health) needs. She co-authored the bestselling novels *Can You See Me?*, *Ways to Be Me*, *Do You Know Me?* and *All the Pieces of Me* with Libby Scott, as well as writing her own novels: *Dandelion Clocks*, *Violet Ink* and *Five Things They Never Told Me*.